IT WAS SO
DREADFULLY WARM . . .

Eliza unfastened the top four buttons of her white, high-necked blouse and folded the collar back, then unbuttoned the cuffs and rolled the sleeves to just below her elbows. Removing a fan from her handbag, she began to cool herself. "Ah, that's better."

Case's gaze moved down the ivory skin of her exposed throat, instantly imagining what delights awaited farther down. The summery white material outlined her breasts and trim waist, giving rise to all sorts of thoughts, none of which were virtuous.

Eliza gave Case a questioning look. "You don't mind, do you?"

Mind? Hell, yes. He felt a tightening sensation in his groin and knew he was in trouble. If she removed that hat and let down those long black curls, she'd really seal her doom.

LINDA O'BRIEN

Beloved Protector

AVON BOOKS
An Imprint of HarperCollinsPublishers

This is a work of fiction. Names, characters, places, and incidents are products of the author's imagination or are used fictitiously and are not to be construed as real. Any resemblance to actual events, locales, organizations, or persons, living or dead, is entirely coincidental.

AVON BOOKS
An Imprint of HarperCollins*Publishers*
10 East 53rd Street
New York, New York 10022-5299

Copyright © 2001 by Linda Tsoutsouris
ISBN: 0-380-81344-0
www.avonromance.com

First Avon Books paperback printing: November 2001

Avon Trademark Reg. U.S. Pat. Off. and in Other Countries, Marca Registrada, Hecho en U.S.A.
HarperCollins ® is a trademark of HarperCollins Publishers Inc.

Printed in the U.S.A.

10 9 8 7 6 5 4 3 2 1

To my mother,
the woman who inspired me
to be whatever I wanted to be,
to reach for the stars,
to stay true to myself,
to love my family, and
to let the Golden Rule be my guide.
I love you, Mom.

To Natasha,
my inspiration for Eliza.
And, as always,
to my husband
and children
for their understanding
and support.

Prologue

Cheyenne, Wyoming
September 3, 1898

My Dearest Friend,

You must help me! Francis is shortly to be arrested for a crime he did not commit and for which he will surely be imprisoned. Oh, Eliza, what shall I do without my husband, when I am even now carrying our child? If you were here I would not be so frightened.

Francis says our only chance is to flee the country until he can find a way to clear his name. If you could see your way to lending us one thousand dollars, we would be forever in your debt.

I beg you, Eliza, if you love me, please come at once. I shall check at the telegraph office every day for your answer.

Your true friend,
Eileen Caroni

WESTERN UNION

DATE: SEPTEMBER 10, 1898

SEND TO:
EILEEN CARONI
CHEYENNE, WYOMING

PLEASE REST ASSURED I SHALL HELP YOU. STOP. YOU ARE AS CLOSE TO ME AS MY OWN SISTER. STOP. SEND ME A WIRE WITH INSTRUCTIONS ON WHERE TO MEET YOU AND I WILL BE THERE. STOP.

SINCERELY, ELIZA

Chapter 1

The doorbell buzzed, causing both women to pause in mid-argument. Eliza Lowe glanced up the wide, black marble hallway, to where the outline of a man was visible through the door's frosted glass. She glowered at her aunt. "That's him, isn't it?"

"Eliza, please listen to reason. A young lady of your class cannot travel West alone. It's unseemly, not to mention that traveling with such an enormous amount of money is dangerous. And Mr. Brogan will make a perfectly wonderful escort for you."

3

"Mr. Brogan is a *Pinkerton*, Auntie Vi, not an escort."

Short, plump, and white-haired, Violet Lowe wrung her hands, her soft features puckering in distress. "Yes, but he's the best Pinkerton the agency has. Mr. Riley, the assistant chief of the agency, assured me that Mr. Brogan was just the man for your purposes."

The bell sounded again, more insistent this time. Violet's gaze darted nervously toward the door. "We should answer that, Eliza."

"Please, Auntie Vi," Eliza continued, ignoring the buzz, "let me do this myself."

"Eliza, child," her aunt said in exasperation, "why must you be so headstrong? Your sister Mariah wouldn't go traipsing off alone."

"I won't be traipsing, I'm not a child, and I'm most definitely *not* Mariah: she's much too serious-minded. But I *am* nearly as smart as she is, though no one believes it."

"Eliza, if you persist on seeing this plan through—"

"You know I must."

"—then, as your legal guardian, I insist you have a proper escort."

Eliza was growing desperate. "Proper? Auntie Vi, I've seen these Pinkerton men skulking around town—burly, aging bullies with thick mustaches, scraggly sideburns, dusty clothing, and wads of tobacco in their cheeks. Hardly proper escorts."

"Meet Mr. Brogan, Eliza. That's all I ask."

The doorbell buzzed three times in succession.

Eliza huffed in annoyance. "Very well. I'll meet him. But that's all I'm agreeing to do." She marched up the hallway, muttering under her breath. A Pinkerton! She threw a quick glance at the tall case clock against one wall. "It's two o'clock, Auntie Vi. I have exactly one half hour to talk to this *Pinkerton*."

She flung open the door and stared straight into the lapels of a man's dusty brown suit coat.

A deep voice above her said, "One half hour will be sufficient."

Eliza tilted her head up, her mouth falling open in surprise. Ye gods! He was *handsome*.

His shrewd, sage-green gaze assessed her, moving slowly from the hem of her blue silk dress to her upswept black curls. "Case Brogan," he said, adding with a note of sarcasm, "the Pinkerton."

Eliza's stunned gaze traveled the length of him. His clothes certainly fit the image, as did his stiff, expressionless features. But nothing else about him did—not his age, or his proud bearing, or his wide, straight shoulders, or his neatly shaved face that smelled of bay rum, or the thick sandy-brown hair that was so clean it gleamed. Even his voice—deep and resonant—was a surprise. Unable to stop gaping, Eliza took a step back.

"Do come in, Mr. Brogan," Violet chirped happily, sweeping toward the door.

As Case moved into the spacious hall, Eliza backed up further and nearly tripped over one of her aunt's three Siamese cats, who'd come to investigate their guest. The cat let out an indignant howl and fled, drawing the hired detective's attention straight back to Eliza.

Her cheeks burned as she gave him a brief smile, smoothed her skirts, and tucked an escaped curl behind her ear.

"This is my niece, Eliza Lowe," Violet went on smoothly, pretending not to have noticed the near collision.

Eliza held out her hand and said coolly, "How do you do, Mr. Brogan?"

Case took her hand in his large, rough one. For such a stern-looking man, the warmth of his hand astonished her. "Miss Lowe."

His penetrating gaze held hers for a long moment, sending tingles of electricity all the way down to her toes. Was there a glimmer of interest in his eyes?

He turned to her aunt, took the woman's plump little hand, and pressed her knuckles to his lips. He certainly did not lack manners. "How are you today, Mrs. Lowe?"

"Wonderful, Mr. Brogan," Violet gushed. "Thank you for asking. I was just telling my niece about you . . ." She trailed off, no doubt figuring that Case had overheard their conversation through the door. "Why don't you come into the parlor? Mary has set out tea and cakes for us."

He glanced down at his clothing. "I don't want to soil your furniture. I walked quite a distance along the lake this morning."

Eliza gazed at him speculatively. "For exercise?"

One corner of his mouth twitched slightly, as if the thought amused him. "For my job."

"Land sakes, don't give it a thought," Violet said. "I've never seen such a dry, windy September."

As they chatted about the weather, Eliza briefly considered slipping out with what was left of her dignity, but Case swung back around and fixed her with his devastating gaze.

"After you, Miss Lowe."

Eliza drew herself up to queenly heights and swept regally past him. Seating herself on one of the twin rose damask sofas in front of the hearth, she daintily plucked a bite-sized, sugared rum cake from the tray and placed it on a dessert plate. Case took a seat on the opposite sofa.

"Tea, Mr. Brogan?" her aunt asked, hovering over the silver tray on the mahogany butler's table between the sofas.

He accepted a cup with thanks and sipped the brew without sugar. Eliza shuddered at the thought and dropped three cubes into her cup. Was there any way she could get rid of him? Her aunt was genuinely concerned about her, and, just as importantly, controlled the purse strings.

But perhaps she could wiggle out of it yet.

While Violet made polite small talk, Eliza munched on her cake and studied him. How sad that he had chosen such an inglorious occupation when he could easily have been a theater actor. He had such a commanding voice, such a virile presence, and those eyes . . . were staring straight at her. Eliza froze. Had he asked her something?

She hastily applied her napkin to the sugar crumbs on her lips. "I beg your pardon?"

"I said I'd like to hear more about your trip."

Eliza heaved an exaggerated sigh as she set her dessert plate aside. "It's nothing, really. My closest friend has asked me to lend her some money, and I simply want to take it to her. Actually, Mr. Brogan, I would imagine this venture to be a waste of time for someone of your . . ." She paused to search for a flattering word. ". . . caliber. And it will almost certainly tie you up for weeks. I would understand completely if you didn't wish to take on such a boring job."

Case's eyes narrowed in an unmistakable

show of distrust. Did he actually doubt her word?

"Many of my assignments are boring, Miss Lowe, but I was hired to escort you, not to be entertained."

Eliza sipped her tea and regarded him coolly over the rim. He was much too rigid and cold for her liking; she couldn't imagine having to travel with him. But her plan to discourage him didn't seem to be working.

"When are you supposed to deliver the money to your friend?" he asked.

"As soon as I can get there."

"Where is that?"

"In Wyoming. I'm waiting for directions as to where to meet them, which I should receive by wire this afternoon. Mr. Brogan, to be honest, I simply don't need you to accompany me. I can do this alone."

"Eliza, we've already had this conversation," her aunt said firmly. "Mr. Brogan has been hired, and that's the end of it."

"Why don't you tell me what circumstances caused your friend to need the money?" Case suggested, clearly impatient to get down to business.

Eliza gave him a doubtful glance as she balanced her cup and saucer on her knee. "All I know is what Eileen wrote—that her husband is in trouble and must clear his name or face serious consequences."

"Imprisonment is the word Eileen used," Violet interjected vociferously. "Francis Caroni faces *imprisonment*! To be accused of a crime warranting such a punishment surely means the man did *something* wrong. You know what I always say, Eliza: where there's smoke, there's fire. And *this* smoke could put you in danger—which is why I'm insisting upon an escort!"

Eliza jumped up to protest, knocking her cup and saucer onto the Persian rug. Case scowled with impatience as both women hurried to mop up the spill, arguing like magpies.

If not for Francis Caroni, he would have refused this assignment.

That morning his boss, Assistant Chief Malcomb C. Riley, had told him:

"Brogan, an old friend of mine, Violet Lowe, came to see me yesterday afternoon, and after listening to her request, I've decided to turn the matter over to you. Normally I wouldn't assign you this type of job, but when you hear the details, you'll understand why."

Case had watched him curiously. "Go on."

"Mrs. Lowe's niece has a friend living out West who's asked for her help—to the tune of a one-thousand-dollar loan, which Mrs. Lowe has generously offered to provide. The niece is determined to take it to her personally and believes her friend's husband has

been falsely accused of a crime. They need the money to flee to Mexico, supposedly to give him time to clear his name."

"How is this important to me?"

"The man's name, Brogan, is Francis Caroni."

For a moment Case had been too paralyzed to speak, overcome by a heavy, smothering fog of rage. Frank Caroni—the man who had murdered his father—had surfaced at last.

"Here's the warrant," Riley had said, handing him an envelope.

Case had taken the envelope without opening it, his teeth clenched so tightly together that he'd barely squeezed out his next words. "Where is he?"

"As of the last letter, somewhere in eastern Wyoming. Apparently the niece has wired them for a meeting place. She's intent on helping them escape."

Case had squeezed the armrests until his knuckles had blanched. Escape? There wasn't a chance in hell he'd let Caroni escape again. This time he'd have his revenge.

"Your assignment, Brogan, is to deliver the niece safely to her friend with the money and return her back home again. As for Caroni—he's wanted dead or alive. I'm not telling you what to do with him—we'll get our fee in either case—but let me give you this piece of advice: don't let your hatred make decisions for you. I trust that you'll make the right choice when the time comes."

Trust. Case didn't believe in it.

He'd reminded his boss that he hadn't failed an assignment yet and had no intention of failing this one. However, Case always worked alone. The last thing he wanted was a traveling partner—a chattering, eyelash-fluttering one, at that.

And now that he'd met Eliza, he'd have to add willful and alluring to the list. Willful he could ignore. He wasn't so sure he could so easily disregard her allure. It was disarmingly intense.

"Just remember two things, Case, and you'll do fine," Riley had cautioned. *"First, you need this young woman to lure Caroni out of hiding. Second, her aunt is an old friend of mine who's entrusting me with the safety of her niece. So stay on good terms with her, but not too good. I know how the ladies take to you."*

"It won't be a problem."

Or would it? Case turned his attention back to the women. Violet was still arguing her point, while Eliza was on her knees reaching beneath the sofa to retrieve her cup, offering him a very tantalizing posterior view.

Then she rose, put the cup and saucer back on the table, and gracefully settled once again on the sofa. There was definitely no denying her attractiveness. Eliza had a magnetic presence about her that drew the eye. He couldn't imagine her as anything but a chaste miss, yet those demure glances and that sultry voice seemed more in keeping with a temptress.

For some reason, a picture of Eliza reclining seductively on that fancy pink sofa slipped into his mind. One hip up, one arm languidly behind her head, her legs slightly bent at the knees to expose a bit of ankle . . . Maybe she'd pull that stray black curl down over one blue eye and wind it around a finger. Or maybe she'd brush the tip of her index finger across her lips where a few sugar crystals lingered.

He had a sudden image of licking the crystals off those luscious lips himself.

Feeling the onset of a bad case of arousal, Case took a gulp of hot tea, wincing as the heat seared his tongue. But at least it served to cool his ardor.

"Is your friend from a wealthy family?" he asked Eliza.

"Yes. Why do you ask?"

"What do you know about her husband?"

"Francis came into my hometown in southern Indiana as a traveling salesman. He met Eileen, fell madly in love with her, and swept her off her feet. They eloped four days later." Eliza sighed wistfully. "It was so romantic! Poor Eileen had been certain she'd end up an old maid."

"Why was that?"

"Homely," Violet whispered.

"Plain," Eliza corrected, "but as sweet-natured as honey. No man could help but fall in love with her."

"No man ever did," Violet added in an under-tone.

"It just took the right man to appreciate her," Eliza said, with a scowl directed toward her aunt. "Mr. Brogan, Eileen has been my best friend since we were five years old. She's come to my aid more times than I can count. Now she's in trouble and she's asked for my help. I don't care how much of a bother it is or how long it takes, I'm going to give it to her."

"But only with your assistance, Mr. Brogan," Violet added.

Case glanced at Violet, perched on the edge of a chair, watching him hopefully, whereas Eliza seemed exceptionally eager for him to back out. He sorely wished he could go after Caroni alone, but, however vexing, he did need her.

"We'll leave at first light tomorrow."

Chapter 2

Eliza's aunt jumped up and clapped her hands together in glee. "It's all settled, then. Thank you, Mr. Brogan. I knew we could depend on you. Well begun is half done, as the saying goes."

Eliza looked far less grateful. "Until tomorrow morning, then, Mr. Brogan. Auntie Vi, I'll talk to you later." She threw her aunt a meaningful glance and swept out of the room.

Case followed the women into the hall. "Miss Lowe, we need to go over a few details."

"I really haven't time right now," Eliza said as she fitted a ridiculously ornate hat on her head.

Irritated, Case watched Eliza sail down the front porch steps of the impressive brick home, then he turned back to her aunt. "Thanks for the refreshments, Mrs. Lowe."

"Goodbye, Mr. Brogan," Violet called as he started down the flagstone path after Eliza. "We'll see you in the morning."

"Where are you headed in such a hurry?" Case asked, falling into step beside Eliza.

"The opera house."

"Shouldn't you be packing rather than watching a matinee?"

"I'm going to a rehearsal, Mr. Brogan. My last rehearsal, since I'm leaving tomorrow. I'm an opera singer."

Case grimaced. "An opera singer."

"You don't like opera?"

"That would be putting it kindly."

Eliza didn't act surprised, as though she'd expected such an answer from someone of his ilk. Casting him a coy glance, she said smoothly, "I would imagine there's little opportunity to cultivate artistic taste in your line of work."

Case let her remark go, although he was tempted to bring up taste in regard to her hat. They halted at the bustling corner of State Street and Monroe.

"What time will you be done?" he asked her.

"I'll be free at five o'clock. I'll meet you in front of the opera house."

Case couldn't help watching the enticing sway of her hips as she walked away. With a frown, he turned away and headed up State Street. He would be saddled with not only an alluring, willful chatterbox, but an opera singer to boot.

Eliza stood behind a curtain in the wings, waiting for her cue. She was to glide gracefully across the stage, hand a letter to Madame La-Toux, the company's temperamental diva, then curtsy and retreat. It was an insignificant part, but at least she got to wear a beautiful costume. And someday *she'd* be the one receiving that letter on stage. Until her voice was properly trained, however, this was the only kind of part for which she could hope.

She'd had only a year of voice lessons, so she really shouldn't be so impatient. Her teacher had enormous faith in her talent. He'd encouraged her to take acting lessons as well, but Eliza didn't want to act in common theater. She wanted to wear grand costumes, stand before magnificent scenery, and receive large bouquets of flowers and standing ovations from tuxedoed men and bejeweled women.

But Eileen was her main concern right now. After rehearsal, she'd have to tell the director she wouldn't be able to finish out her contract.

As she listened for her cue, a tall figure at the back of the auditorium caught her eye. Ye gods! It was Case Brogan, and he was *early*. Eliza's stomach knotted. He wasn't supposed to come inside. Now he would see that she wasn't an opera singer at all.

Her cue came, but she stood rooted to her spot. The stage director cleared his throat loudly, and when that didn't work he glared at her. Tilting her costume hat to hide her face, Eliza dashed out from behind the curtain, nearly tripped on a prop, and dropped the letter. With a gasp, she snatched it up, shoved it at Madame LaToux, and fled, forgetting to curtsy.

The wardrobe mistress was standing in the wings shaking her head in dismay. "You're in trouble now, Liza. You know how LaToot hates slipups. You'd better leave quickly."

Eliza took off the hat and handed it to her. "LaToot? You'd better hope Madame never hears you call her that, Suzanne. Besides, she likes me. And I can't leave until I talk to Mr. Dooney."

"About what?" a male voice asked.

Eliza swung to see the director standing behind her, his thin arms crossed over his chest, displeasure on his narrow, angular face.

"I hate to have to tell you this so close to opening night, Mr. Dooney, but I won't be able to finish the engagement."

"Really?" he said sarcastically. "And why is that?"

"I have to attend to a personal matter of grave importance."

"Is that so? Let's see. Last week you missed a rehearsal because you had to help your—aunt, was it?—find a missing cat. Three days ago you were an hour late because you had to carry groceries for a blind person you spotted on the street. Yesterday you were late because your watch had stopped; you'd forgotten to wind it. Now you're canceling out on me just before dress rehearsal for a personal matter."

"Of grave importance," Eliza reminded him.

"Well, that makes this so much easier, Miss Lowe. You're *fired*." He made an eloquent pivot and marched back onto the stage, where Madame LaToux waited, a satisfied look on her face.

"I told you," Suzanne whispered.

"I'm sure he didn't mean it in a bad way," Eliza said as she pinned on her own hat. "He's under such pressure now. I'm just sorry I had to back out on him."

"You're such an innocent, Eliza," Suzanne said as she gave her a hug. "Good luck on your important matter."

Case left the theater laughing, something he hadn't done in years. He doubted that the opera was supposed to be a comedy, but Eliza had certainly made it one. And although she'd been on stage only a few moments, she'd completely outshone the star. He didn't imagine the director was too happy about either of those outcomes.

For some reason Case had enjoyed Eliza's little blunder. It would certainly help diminish her haughtiness. Yet the moment she stepped out the back door of the theater, her expression downcast, he suddenly found himself feeling sorry for her—another forgotten emotion.

He stood at the mouth of the alley, and as she approached, he raised an eyebrow. "Is everything all right?"

Eliza sighed. "Not really. At least not for poor Mr. Dooney, our director."

Case gazed at her in disbelief as they crossed the street, dodging wagons and buggies. "*Poor* Mr. Dooney? He just *fired* you."

"And I know he feels terrible about it. Where are we going?"

"The Palmer House."

Eliza caught Case's cautious glance, as if he were expecting her to protest, so she figured she should put his mind at rest. "I'm familiar with the Palmer House. It's a beautiful hotel."

"You're not wondering why I'm taking you there?"

"I trust we're going for coffee to discuss the trip."

"You shouldn't trust so easily. No one is completely trustworthy. Not even me."

"But I have no reason not to trust you. Indeed, according to my aunt, I have every reason *to* trust you."

"Because Malcomb Riley said so?" Case answered with a scoff. "Why should you believe him?"

"Well, because," Eliza sputtered, nonplussed, "my aunt—"

"Trust no one, Miss Lowe. You'll be much better off."

"You're saying I shouldn't trust my aunt or—or my voice teacher, or Mr. Dooney?"

"He's a perfect example. You trusted Mr. Dooney, and what did he do? He fired you."

"Of course he fired me. That's his job. Who else would have done it?"

Eliza could see by the deepening scowl on Case's face that she wasn't getting through to him. Didn't he trust *anyone*? She imagined him going through life fearing that everyone was out to hurt him. What a sad way to live.

She'd have to change that.

They made their way down Monroe Street as an elevated train screeched to a stop on the tracks just above their heads. As Eliza paused under the hotel's wide canopy to watch a red-coated doorman help a well-dressed lady from her carriage, a man brushed rudely past Eliza, jostling her elbow. She saw him dart over to the open carriage, snatch the woman's handbag from the seat of the vehicle, and flee straight back in her direction.

Without hesitation Eliza grabbed the villain's arm as he passed and yanked him around. "You give that bag back!" she ordered, trying to tug the object from his hands.

Before the felon could react, Case knocked him to the ground and pulled his arms behind his back, holding him down while the doorman blew his whistle to summon a nearby policeman.

As curious onlookers crowded around them, the lady from the carriage swept past Case and embraced Eliza. "Oh, you sweet, brave girl! How can I thank you?"

"There's no need," Eliza told her. "I was glad to help."

"I insist. I'll speak to the manager at once. You and your husband shall have dinner in the hotel at my expense."

"My husband?" Eliza said, glancing around at Case, who looked ready to explode. She turned to politely decline, but the lady was already on her way into the hotel.

"If you *ever* pull a stunt like that again," Case said through gritted teeth, glaring at Eliza across the linen-covered table in the expensive hotel restaurant, "I'll turn you over my knee."

Defiance glimmered in her blue eyes. "*Someone* had to stop that man. As my aunt is fond of saying, nothing ventured, nothing gained."

"I was going to take care of it. You went charging after a man who might have been carrying a weapon, a man who might have *hurt* you, Miss Lowe."

"He wouldn't have hurt me—not in front of so many witnesses, anyway. Have faith in me, Mr. Brogan. I knew what I was doing."

Case drummed his fingers on the table as he contemplated Eliza, who was studying the menu. She had to be the most naive, blindly trusting woman he'd ever come across.

He'd have to change that.

Before he could begin his campaign, a waiter approached their table, a bottle in hand. "For you and your husband, madam," he said, showing Eliza the bottle.

She read the label and smiled in joyful surprise. "Why, it's champagne!"

"From Mrs. Winston Barton the Second," the waiter explained, showing it next to Case, "with her grateful appreciation."

"Oh, thank you. And please thank Mrs. Barton for me, and for my hus— For us."

The waiter gave a regal nod as he opened the

bottle. Eliza jumped when the cork popped, then laughed at herself. She leaned toward Case and held one hand to the side of her mouth to whisper, "Mrs. Barton must be the lady who owned the handbag."

"Mrs. Barton is also one of the most influential women in Chicago society," Case told her quietly.

"You see! I told you to trust me."

The waiter handed Case a tall, thin, long-stemmed glass filled only one-fourth full, then stood patiently at his side. Case took a sip, then gave the waiter a nod.

As the man filled both of their glasses, Case held up his to show Eliza, tapping one side. "See all these tiny bubbles? That indicates a fresh wine. The bottle should also be well chilled. Always feel it before it's opened. Champagne must be stored properly or it'll turn to vinegar."

He seemed so proud of his knowledge that Eliza couldn't bring herself to tell him she already knew about champagne. Her uncle had collected fine wines. "How do you know so much about wine?" she asked curiously, taking a soft roll from the bread basket on the table.

"I studied it."

"Must all Pinkerton men be knowledgeable about wine?"

"No, I studied it on my own."

"Interesting," she commented, regarding him

more closely. "You're nothing like what I expected."

Case paused, as though considering her remark, then asked in a low, almost provocative voice, "Is that good or bad?"

Eliza felt those electric tingles zip down to her toes again. "I haven't decided," she replied, giving him a sidelong glance.

Perhaps this journey wouldn't be so terrible after all.

After the waiter had taken their orders, Eliza picked up her champagne and said, "Let's toast to a successful trip."

Case couldn't argue with that. He touched the rim of his glass to hers, then took a sip, savoring the pleasantly tart fizz on his tongue.

"It's wonderful," Eliza remarked, then wiggled her nose. "It tickles."

"Haven't you ever had champagne before?"

"Only mulberry wine, Auntie Vi's favorite. After my uncle died, she refused to open any of his private collection. And my father didn't allow liquor in our house. As a doctor, he saw too often the damage it did."

A look of sorrow flickered in Eliza's eyes. She took another sip of champagne, then set it aside, as though it brought a painful memory to mind.

Case didn't want to know what it was; he never allowed himself to become personally involved with a client.

"In light of what happened in front of the hotel," he told her, "I want to make one thing perfectly clear: your aunt hired me to take care of you. From now on you'll do exactly as I say. Understand?"

Eliza put down the fluted glass, folded her hands in her lap, and calmly gazed at him.

He eyed her warily for a long moment, and finally asked, "What are you doing?"

"Waiting for you to tell me what to do. Should I drink my champagne or my water, or have a bite of roll instead?"

Case counted to ten, which was nine numerals higher than he usually counted. "I've been hired to take you to your friend," he explained slowly, trying to maintain an even tone, "but we're not going to get very far without some cooperation."

"You're absolutely right. All you have to do is treat me as a partner and not as a child. That means ask, don't tell." She picked up her water glass and took a drink.

Case shook his head in frustration. This was one of the prime reasons he preferred working alone.

"What a beautiful restaurant," Eliza said wistfully as the waiter brought their plates of food.

Case watched as she glanced around the sumptuously appointed room, with its crystal chandeliers, molded ceilings, and richly colored carpet. She picked up her fork to examine the exquisitely detailed silver handle. "It certainly was generous of Mrs. Barton to pay for our meal. This food is delicious beyond belief." She took another bite of chicken.

Case found himself staring hungrily at her lips as the tip of her tongue darted out to make a quick swipe, capturing a drop of juice that had escaped. As if suddenly remembering where she was, she pressed her napkin to her mouth, sheepishly glancing up at him from under a sweep of black lashes to see if she'd been caught in the act.

Case tried not to notice, yet his groin tightened as he next watched her lips close over a bite of potatoes. She drew the fork out slowly, a look of sublime bliss on her face.

"They use real cream," she said, heaving a sigh.

Case dragged his lustful gaze away from her mouth and focused on his own food.

Damn! He'd have to make quick work of the meal, or he'd risk shocking all the women in the room when he rose.

As soon as she'd taken her last bite, Case pushed back his chair. "It's getting late. I'm sure you need to pack."

"But you haven't finished eating."

"I've had plenty." He ushered her out of the restaurant and through the hotel lobby, out into the cool evening air, where he started to feel in control once more. A good walk home would help, too.

He flagged a hansom cab and put her inside. "I'll come for you at six o'clock in the morning— if that's all right with you," he added with exaggerated courtesy.

Eliza gave him a big smile. "Let's make it five-thirty."

As the clock struck the half hour, Eliza dragged the last of her trunks down the wide, curving staircase. Five-thirty in the morning. What had she been thinking?

"He's here, Eliza," her aunt said, peering out the parlor window into the darkness of the early autumn morning. "Are you sure you've packed everything?"

Bleary-eyed, Eliza sat down on one of the trunks and propped her chin up with her fist. "I hope so."

Violet admitted Case with a cheery "Good morning, Mr. Brogan. I trust everything is set for your journey?"

"All set."

Eliza gave him a fleeting glance. He had on another brown suit, undoubtedly the only color he owned.

"Here's the one thousand dollars, Mr. Brogan," her aunt said, handing him a thick leather wallet. "I want you to carry it."

"Of course."

Eliza watched as Case put the wallet in his inside coat pocket, then turned to eye her four big Saratoga trunks.

"Did you receive the wire?" he asked her.

Hiding a yawn, she pulled the telegram from her pocket and handed it to him.

He held it up to a lighted sconce on the wall. "This only says to go to Moline and wait for another wire."

"I would imagine they're trying to stay a few steps ahead of the law."

Eliza saw Case's gaze sweep up her full, coffee-colored moire skirt to the matching jacket with its large leg-o'-mutton sleeves and wide aqua sailor collar.

He scratched the back of his neck. "*That's* what you're going to wear on the trip?"

Eliza frowned at him. "It's a traveling outfit, perfectly acceptable for train or carriage. What could be wrong with that?"

"Nothing—if we were traveling by train or carriage." Case opened the door wide and gestured to the vehicle sitting in front of the house. "Your traveling conveyance."

Curious, both women moved to the door. Violet gasped and fanned her face, while Eliza simply gaped. She turned, sputtering, "But that's a dusty, dilapidated, covered wagon!"

"It's a rather . . . rough . . . form of transportation, wouldn't you say, Mr. Brogan?" Violet asked tactfully.

"Not for traveling across the prairie. Now, which two of these trunks can you do without, Miss Lowe?"

Eliza pulled her silk shawl closer around her shoulders and stared off to the right, none too pleased with the man seated next to her. It wasn't enough that she had to leave behind some of her best clothing. No, she also had to travel in a filthy old covered wagon that jostled her spine, and sit on a wooden bench that hurt her backside.

She glanced at Case with envy, sitting so comfortably at ease on that hard bench, in his dusty brown boots, dark brown pants, and white shirt, open at the neck and rolled up at the sleeves. He'd discarded his suit coat before they'd even started out.

Eliza could understand why taking a train was impractical, since they didn't know where they'd end up. But he could have hired a carriage; she'd have even settled for a buggy.

She'd had to rearrange her belongings so quickly that she feared she'd left out some of her necessary items. If that wasn't bad enough, they'd traveled for over three hours, with two stops to water the horses, and Case hadn't said more than ten words to her.

There's a gift in everything, she reminded herself. Somewhere there had to be a gift in this, too.

Annie, the woman who had raised her after her mother had died, always believed that you could find a gift in each of life's adversities if you looked hard enough. Having been blessed with an optimistic nature anyway, Eliza had taken Annie's words to heart and found that they truly worked. They had seen her through many difficult times during her childhood, including her brother's tragic death and, more recently, her father's.

Auntie Vi had another way of saying it: every cloud has a silver lining.

Eliza glanced up at the sky from beneath her hat brim. Not a cloud to be found, but at least the scenery was pleasant. It wasn't as breathtaking as a mountain or as awe-inspiring as an ocean, but there was something majestic about a forest, with row upon row of sturdy brown trunks lined up like soldiers standing at attention, and the endless variety of leaves that formed a canopy to shield them from the sun. Directly overhead was a slender streak of dazzlingly blue sky that nearly took her breath away.

Eliza sighed in contentment. "Isn't this heavenly? It reminds me so of my home in Indiana. Just look at all these trees—did you ever wonder why there were so many varieties? Surely there's a reason. Perhaps it's to keep God from being bored."

Case glanced at her, then away.

"Where did you grow up, Mr. Brogan? I'll wager it wasn't in the country."

"Chicago."

"Just as I thought: you're a city boy. You've never learned to appreciate nature's bounty. But I suppose the city has its advantages, too."

No response. Eliza tried again. "You must have been there during the great Chicago fire. Do you remember it?"

He gave her a disgruntled look. "How old do you think I am, Miss Lowe?"

"I don't know. Thirty-five, perhaps?"

"Twenty-seven, almost."

"Oh!" She studied him appraisingly. He was only six years older than she, yet he seemed ancient. Perhaps it was because he never smiled. "When is your birthday?"

"September twentieth."

"Why, that's in nine days."

He shrugged. "Birthdays don't mean anything."

"But they're such fun. Surely your mother makes a special dinner for you."

"My mother is dead."

"Oh, I'm sorry. Mine is, too. My mother died when I was five, and my father died just this past spring. How old were you?"

He sighed sharply, as though her questions were taxing his patience. "My mother passed on four years ago."

"I barely remember my mother, but I know she was beautiful. In fact, she won a beauty contest before she married my father. She was eighteen years old when she was voted the May Queen of Monroe County. Imagine that! I suppose that makes me a descendant of royalty." Eliza paused to see if Case would smile, but his expression never changed.

"Do you ever laugh?" she asked in exasperation.

"At what?"

"At anything!"

"What for?"

"What for?" she repeated incredulously. "To feel good. To stretch your mouth. To improve your lung capacity. Do you really need a reason?"

"My lungs are fine."

Eliza sighed. She might as well be talking to herself. Or singing. That was it! She could practice her voice exercises.

When Eliza suddenly began to sing, Case cringed. It was bad enough that she felt compelled to tell him her life story; now she was going to drive him insane with her warbling. He hunched over, his shoulders as close to his eardrums as he could get them. She ran up and down the scales so many times he was ready to chew through his tongue. Finally he pulled up on the reins and stopped the wagon.

"Enough!"

Eliza stared at him openmouthed.

Case glowered at her a long moment, not trusting himself to speak. Then he ground out, "I like silence."

She closed her mouth, folded her arms, and swiveled her body away.

Case flicked the reins, and the horses started off. Any moment now, he thought, she's going to start arguing. Ha! Let her try. He wasn't budging. He liked silence. Period.

And that's what he got: complete, utter silence. Just as he'd wanted. She wouldn't even *look* his way.

After more than an hour of it, he started to regret being so harsh with her. It wasn't Eliza's fault he liked quiet. He glanced over. She still had her back turned to him, sitting so rigid in her fancy traveling suit, and hat adorned with large aqua flowers and hovering butterflies. The only good thing he could say about the hat was that she didn't look the least bit alluring in it.

"All right, you can sing, but only one song— and no scales!"

"I'm not in a singing mood anymore."

"I'm not used to traveling with anyone," he

said after a moment, by way of an apology. "I'm used to working independently."

"That doesn't mean we can't be pleasant to each other. Haven't you ever heard of the Golden Rule?"

"Do unto others as you would have them do unto you? Nope. Never heard of it."

Eliza's jaw dropped. "But you just—" She saw the tiniest twitch of laughter tugging at one corner of his mouth. How about that! He'd made a joke. At least he'd proven he had a sense of humor.

"Tell me about your job," she asked, deciding to forgive his earlier outburst. "What do you do, exactly?"

"Other than escorting young ladies on fanciful missions?" he answered wryly.

"It's not fanciful, but go ahead."

"I track down criminals, hunt for missing persons and stolen goods—a variety of things; whatever I'm hired to do."

"Does it ever get dangerous?"

"Sometimes." Case shrugged as if danger meant nothing to him.

"Have you ever had to use a weapon?"

"Yep."

"A gun?"

"A gag."

"A gag?" she asked in surprise. "What for?"

"Silencing a talkative female."

Instead of taking offense, Eliza burst out laughing. "You really *do* have a sense of humor!"

Case was as amazed as she was. He'd almost forgotten how to jest. Of course, it helped to have an appreciative audience. He cast Eliza a swift glance. She might not be alluring in that ridiculous hat, but she *was* quite appealing when she laughed at his jokes.

An hour later, Eliza's stomach began to growl. She checked the watch pinned to her jacket. Luckily, she'd thought to wind it. "Are we getting near a town? I'm hungry."

"We're traveling straight through to Moline."

"How long will that take?"

"Should reach it in two days."

"But what about dinner tonight?"

"There's some bread and jerky in the back."

"Jerky? Surely you don't expect me to live on jerky."

"There's cheese, too. At dusk I'll stop and make a campfire. We can cook something then."

Eliza sighed. If she'd come alone, she could have stopped whenever she wanted and eaten real food at a restaurant. They'd traveled through a number of tiny burgs; one of them would have had a restaurant of some kind.

She pulled out her handkerchief and dabbed

her forehead. All morning she'd felt chill and damp in the gloom of the forest, but now the sun was directly overhead and her clothing was stifling.

She removed her jacket and placed it behind her in the wagon, unfastened the top four buttons of her white blouse and folded the collar away from her neck, then unbuttoned the cuffs and rolled them to just below her elbows. Removing a fan from her handbag, she began to cool herself. "That's better."

Case glanced over at her, his gaze moving down the ivory skin of her exposed throat to the last open button, instantly imagining what delights awaited further down. The summery white material outlined her breasts and trim waist, bringing all sorts of thoughts to mind, none of which were virtuous.

She gave him a questioning look. "You don't mind, do you?"

Mind? Hell, yes. He felt a tightening sensation in his groin and knew he was in trouble. If she removed that hat and let down those long black curls, she'd really seal her doom.

With his attention diverted, Case didn't see the muddy hole in the road until the wagon wheel hit it. The wagon bounced hard and so did they. Eliza grabbed for the nearest object and got Case. Or rather he got her—on his lap—and he suddenly found himself holding a bundle of squirming female with a soft, round bottom that nestled firmly against his hardening manhood.

The urge to jump out of that wagon and lay her down in a bed of leaves hit him hard. His arms tightened around her as his lust soared. He wanted her badly. He wanted her now.

Chapter 3

Case pulled the wagon to a halt with one thought on his mind. But then he felt a slight tremor run through the voluptuous form on his lap, and suddenly the form became a young woman, and the young woman became Eliza—the person he was supposed to be protecting.

"Are you all right?" he asked guiltily. Realizing his arms were still wound tightly around her, he released her.

"I think so." Eliza scooted off his lap and moved to the far end of the bench, keeping her gaze averted.

"I'd better have a look at the wheels." Case jumped down, glad for an excuse to move. It'd be a long time before he forgot the feel of her bottom against his privates.

The shock of finding herself on Case's lap wasn't nearly as great as the one of feeling his arms around her. At first Eliza had supposed he only intended to keep her from flying off the bench when the second wheel hit the hole, but when she suddenly felt something swelling beneath her, pressing upward against her derriere, she revised her opinion. The rake!

Wouldn't Auntie Vi be appalled? Eliza figured she should be appalled, too, yet deep inside, a part of her was also . . . Stimulated? Invigorated? Curious? She'd seen animals in heat many times during her childhood, but she'd never seen a man—*felt* a man—when he was aroused. What would he look like?

Shocked by her wayward thoughts, Eliza fanned her flushed face. She couldn't imagine what had gotten into her.

After inspecting the wheels and making sure the horses were fine, Case climbed into the back to check his supplies. "As long as I'm here, do you want some food?"

"Yes, please. I'd appreciate it."

He pulled out the jerky, cheese, and bread, his water canteen, and two tin cups. When he jumped down, he saw that Eliza had trampled through the tall brush some distance away from the wagon.

"Where are you going?" he called.

"I'm looking for a picnic spot. Here's a nice, dry place." She stopped in a small, grassy clearing and looked back at him. "Bring a tablecloth."

Case stared at her in amazement. A tablecloth? A picnic? She was treating this like a Sunday outing.

He could hear her singing as he rooted among his things. He found an extra horse blanket, then strode through the weeds to where she was waiting. Trying to ignore the fact that she'd removed her hat and was running her fingers through her curls, he spread the blanket.

"This is the only *tablecloth* I have."

"It'll do," she said amiably, kneeling on the coarse wool.

He set out the food, settled down cross-legged, and handed her the bread. "You shouldn't go charging willy-nilly into the woods; you don't know what might be out there."

"Yes, I do. I grew up surrounded by woods."

"Then you should be aware of the dangers."

"That's why I was singing: wild animals don't like surprises. I was giving them fair warning."

Case watched in grudging admiration as she nibbled the cheese. Eliza seemed to take everything in stride. She wasn't even complaining about the tough jerky.

"So you lived in the woods?" he asked, swallowing a bite of jerky.

She giggled. "Not *in* the woods. There were woods surrounding the town."

"I'll bet you had a lot of beaus back in Indiana."

Eliza gave him a coquettish glance. "What makes you think so?"

"You seem very comfortable around men."

Her mouth curved up impishly. "Perhaps I'm just comfortable around you."

"And you know how to flirt."

"That's just my gregarious nature."

Gregarious, hell. She had to be aware of what she did to a man when she batted those baby blues.

"If I were really comfortable around you," she explained, "I would take off my shoes and stockings."

Instantly an image of Eliza with bared ankles and calves flashed into Case's mind, bringing rise to all sorts of delicious thoughts. Before his imagination could arouse him further, he reached for his cup of water and drank it down, though he would have preferred to douse himself with it.

When Eliza finished eating she lay back on the blanket, folded her arms beneath her head, closed her eyes, and sighed contentedly, as if she'd just feasted at a banquet. The kittenish smile on her face was so beguiling that Case was hard-pressed not to lean over and sample that luscious mouth.

Maybe it wasn't the animals in the woods she ought to fear.

"We'd better get moving. I want to reach the river by sundown."

"I think I'll walk alongside the wagon for a while," she said as she pinned her hat in place. "I'm too stiff to sit any longer."

"Let me see your shoes."

Eliza turned on her side in a pose not unlike the one he had imagined on the pink sofa. Holding out one foot, she raised her skirt, revealing not only her leather slippers, but also a well-turned ankle. Case fought to keep his gaze from roaming further.

He examined the slipper and leaned back on his elbows. "You won't walk far in those."

"I'd only intended to go as far as the wagon to retrieve my walking boots." She stood and shook out her skirts. "Ready?"

Muttering under his breath about how much easier it was to travel alone, Case gathered up the food in the blanket and followed her.

But he did enjoy the way her hips swayed when she walked.

* * *

Eliza walked for exactly two hours. She made herself do it, though her heels blistered in her hot walking boots. She wasn't about to complain and have Case think she was a mollycoddled crybaby.

After surreptitiously checking her watch for the sixth time, she said, "Well, that's enough exercise for a while," and climbed onboard the wagon.

"How are your feet?"

"Oh, they're fine." She couldn't wait to take off her boots, but she didn't dare in front of Case. She decided to get her mind off them, instead. "Would you mind if I sing now?"

"Tell me about your friend Eileen."

Case was actually asking her to talk! What a relief to do something besides stare at trees, trees, and more trees.

"Eileen Neeley and Emeline Sullivan were my best friends growing up. Everyone called us the Three E's, but we preferred—"

"You said before that Eileen's father is well-to-do."

Eliza let his rude interruption pass. "Yes. He has a lot of fertile farmland. But the poor man has been in ill health; he's not expected to live out the year."

"Will your friend inherit everything?"

"Yes. She's his only child."

"And Caroni knows that, doesn't he?"

"I would imagine he does."

"I guarantee he does. It's the way he operates."

"I don't understand."

"For the past three years, Frank Caroni has made his living by marrying wealthy young women and taking their inheritances. In all instances, the young women were the sole beneficiaries, and their fathers were on their deathbeds."

"But Francis told us he'd never married."

"He's 'never married' four times, to be exact, and has yet to be divorced. Before that, he ran a bogus railroad bond scheme, targeting widows' life savings."

Eliza shook her head. "You must have someone else in mind. Francis grew up in California and has only been in our part of the country for a year. Before that he panned for gold in Colorado."

"The gold rush has been over for quite some time, Miss Lowe. I imagine his search for a fortune took him no further than some young lady's rich daddy."

"You can imagine whatever you wish, but I still say you're wrong."

"Medium height, stocky build, curly brown hair, neatly trimmed mustache—"

"That could be anyone."

"One blue eye, one green."

Eliza's mouth dropped open. That couldn't be anyone *but* Francis. "How do you know so much about him?"

A muscle in Case's jaw twitched, and his gaze grew cold. "He's been wanted for ten years."

"But ten years ago he would have been fifteen years old!"

"Nineteen."

Eliza scratched her nose. His description matched Francis exactly, yet his facts were in complete opposition. "All I know is that Francis and Eileen love each other dearly. He's a charming man; he simply wouldn't take advantage of her."

"You told me Eileen only knew him for four days before they ran off together. *Four days*, Miss Lowe. Hardly long enough to really get to know someone, let alone fall in love with them."

A horrible thought occurred to her. "*You're* not looking for Francis, are you?"

Case was silent.

A cold knot of alarm began to form in Eliza's stomach. "You were hired to help *me*. You can't be after him; that would be unethical."

She saw a muscle twitch in his jaw.

"Eileen loves Francis, Mr. Brogan, and she's carrying their child. I promised her I'd help them; I can't break my promise. If you have any intention of trying to stop me, I'll find a way to go on without you."

"What if everything I told you about him were true?"

"But it's not."

"What if it were?"

"If it were true, I wouldn't give him the money. I'd help Eileen leave him instead."

That seemed to satisfy him. But was he after Francis or not? She turned his question back on him. "What if everything *I* told you about Francis were true?"

"It's not."

"What if it were?" she insisted.

He fixed her with a piercing look. "I don't make mistakes like that."

Eliza folded her fan and tapped it against her palm. She had to convince Case of Francis's innocence before the two men came face to face. She'd given her word to Eileen that she'd help them, and she meant to keep it.

Regardless of her sore feet, by dusk Eliza's backside hurt so much that she was ready to hop down and walk again. Luckily, at that moment Case decided to guide the horses off the road to a clearing among the trees.

"Where are we?" she asked.

"If my map is accurate, the Green River should be just ahead. We'll set up camp nearby."

"Thank goodness! I'm famished."

While Case unhitched the horses and led

them down to the water, Eliza spread the blanket, sat down, and removed her boots.

"Just what I feared," she muttered, examining her bleeding heels. She tucked her feet underneath her as Case approached carrying a shotgun.

"I'm going to find a rabbit."

"Oh, not a rabbit!" she cried, jumping up. "They're so helpless."

"You're hungry, aren't you?"

"Not that hungry."

"All right, a squirrel."

"Not a squirrel, either. Nothing with a cute face."

Shaking his head in disbelief he headed for the forest. "I'll look for a homely deer."

"Mr. Brogan!"

Case swung around.

She gave him an imploring smile. "We have bread, cheese, and jerky."

"Will that be enough food for you?"

"Maybe I can find some berries in the woods."

"Maybe you'll run into a friendly bear, too. You can ask him where to look for berries."

Eliza crossed her arms and gave him a disgruntled look.

Case shook his head resignedly. "There's canned beans in the wagon. Why don't you see about fixing them while I start a fire?"

While he gathered wood, Eliza rummaged through the wagon and found beans and a dented tin pan. She opened the can, sniffed the contents, decided they smelled pretty darn delicious, and dumped them into the pan.

Never had beans, bread, and cheese tasted so good. To her delight, Case even ground coffee beans and brewed coffee. Although bitter without sugar, Eliza enjoyed every drop.

"I'm going to roll out your bedroll in the back of the wagon," he told her as they washed their plates in the river.

"I'm not sleeping in that stuffy wagon. I'll sleep outside by the fire. *You* may have the wagon."

"And have some bear carry you off for his next meal? Not on your life," he said as they tramped back.

"He won't come near the fire."

"You can't be sure of that."

"He could just as easily crawl into that wagon," she reasoned, "especially if he smells food."

Case scowled as he contemplated the situation. "We'll both sleep by the fire," he finally said. "I'll have my shotgun right beside me."

"Fine. I'm going to wash first." Eliza climbed into the wagon, removed a towel and bar of soap from her trunk, and headed for the river.

Striding after her, Case grabbed her arm and

pulled her to a stop. "You're not going in the water now. It's almost dark."

"I won't be able to sleep with all this dust and grime on me."

"You'll survive."

"When I can't fall asleep, I sing." She gave him a beguiling smile.

Case glared at her, realizing he'd lost the argument. "The only way you're going near that river is if I'm there to watch over you."

For a moment she glared back, then a wily look came into her eyes. "All right, watch if you must. I'm sure Auntie Vi will be most interested to know about it."

Case counted slowly to eleven, adding the last number for good measure. "We'll compromise. You sing while you're bathing so I know you're safe. If you stop singing, I'll come running."

"It's a deal."

Case walked Eliza down to the sloping riverbank and checked the site out while she removed her shoes. The river was narrow and seemed fairly shallow. Still, who knew what lurked beneath that dark surface? Eliza could be singing one moment and gone the next. He swung around to tell her he'd changed his mind, but she'd disappeared.

"Miss Lowe!" he shouted.

He heard the rustle of leaves, then saw her skirt come up over the top of a bush. Instantly, a picture of Eliza unclothed darted through his mind.

"I'm ready," she called. "You can leave now."

"Start singing."

He strode away as she trilled out a song in Italian. Despite his best efforts to keep his thoughts off her, in his mind's eye he could see Eliza standing in chest-high water, the peaks of her breasts gleaming in the shafts of moonlight that spilled across the black surface, her pearly arms lifted, dripping with water droplets as she lathered her hair. Damn it! He hated being aroused when there was no outlet for it.

Then he realized she'd stopped singing.

With his heart pounding like a kettle drum, Case ran down the slope, scanning the water for her, but she was nowhere to be seen. Yanking off his shoes, he plunged into the cool water.

At that moment, Eliza emerged from the depths like a goddess rising from the moonlit sea, her long black hair cascading over her ivory shoulders, water streaming down her curvaceous body. Alerted by the sound of heavy splashing, she quickly scrubbed the water from her eyes, took one look at Case charging toward her, and shrieked.

Without hesitation Case swept her into his arms, swung around, and waded back.

"What are you doing?" she cried indignantly, trying to cover herself.

"You were in danger."

"I was not!"

"You stopped singing."

"I had to rinse my hair. Put me down! Oh, no, don't put me down. You'll see more than you already have."

Case tried to keep his gaze high while he figured out what to do with her. He knew what he *wanted* to do, and despite the chill of the water, he was more than ready to do it. But he was supposed to protect her, damn it!

"Take me to my towel," she said, pointing behind him.

Case swung around, his own clothing now plastered to his body. He bent his knees and lowered her, trying to keep his balance as she stretched out a hand.

"A little lower," she directed, "and close your eyes."

"Just stretch your hand out farther."

"I can't and keep my modesty. You're not closing your eyes!"

Little did she know, she had more to worry about than keeping her modesty. With his eyes shut, Case could feel one of her hardened nipples pressing against his sodden shirt, tantalizing him beyond endurance.

He gritted his teeth, willing himself to ignore the lust sweeping through him. "Now can you reach it?"

"I . . . think . . . so. Just a little closer—oh!" she cried, as they toppled over. Case landed right on top of her, one arm still around her back.

For a stunned, breathless moment, they simply gazed at each other. Slowly Eliza became aware of the weight and heat of his body in contrast with the coldness of his wet shirt and pants against her naked flesh. One knee rested between her legs, sending electrifying tingles from her breasts to the very heart of her womanhood. She lay unclothed and helpless, pinned beneath his strong torso, and for some reason that thought aroused her enormously.

As though his awareness grew with hers, Case's eyes darkened and his heart hammered against her chest. He lifted his head to let his gaze sweep down over her breasts, bringing a delicious throbbing between her legs. Then his head dipped lower, his lips dangerously close to hers.

She was positive he was going to kiss her.

Chapter 4

~~~~~~~~~~⚬⚬~~~~~~~~~~

He could already taste that kiss; he knew just how those lips would be: sweet, hot, and responsive. But if Eliza responded, could he stop at a single kiss? Two?

Not likely. Especially not with her lying nude beneath him.

Cursing to himself, Case rolled off and got to his feet while Eliza scrambled for her towel.

Holding it before her like a shield, she said, "Turn around while I get my clothes."

With a frown, Case turned. How the hell was he going to get any sleep tonight? Now he was randier than a buck, and grumpy besides.

"All right. I'm dressed."

Case swung around as Eliza marched past

54

him and headed for the wagon, her shirtwaist untucked, her shoes and stockings in her hands.

"Aren't you coming?" she called.

"I'll be there in a while."

He waited until she was out of sight, then he stripped down and stepped into the cool water, wading out until he was immersed to his waist.

Why couldn't she have been an ugly old hag?

Eliza's curiosity bested her. After the lecture Case had given her, surely he wasn't going to bathe! She stepped behind a wide tree trunk and waited a moment, then peered around it. Stifling a gasp, she quickly pulled back.

He was *magnificent*.

Go back to the wagon, Eliza, she chided herself. *You're not a silly sixteen-year-old, all agog over the sight of an unclothed male.*

True, she wasn't silly or sixteen—but good heavens, was she agog! Oh, the splendor of his body—sleek, bronzed, and muscled, with moonlight playing off his wet skin.

Maybe just one more glimpse.

Eliza watched in utter fascination as Case rubbed the soap into his chest, lathering the dark, curly hair, then moving down to his belly. When his hands slid below the water, she felt that tingling all over again, imagining what he was washing next.

She smiled dreamily, remembering how he'd

swept her out of the water and into his arms, rescuing her like some valiant knight of old. And, oh, what delicious thoughts had raced through her mind as he'd laid atop her!

Just the thought of that glorious, masculine body on top of hers gave her tingles all over again. She'd wanted him to kiss her; perhaps she'd even wanted more than that. Perhaps she'd wanted him to touch her, too, in places too secret to even say aloud.

Ye gods! What would Auntie Vi say if she knew the thoughts going through her niece's mind?

Eliza had just decided to leave when Case dipped his head beneath the water, then rose up, shaking droplets off much as a dog would. The moon slid behind a cloud, and she lost sight of him.

What if he came out of the river and caught her watching?

Eliza hurried back to the wagon, bruising the soles of her bare feet on sharp twigs. She'd just reached the fire when she realized she was carrying the towel, along with her shoes and stockings. She thought about returning it, but what if he'd already started back? Naked?

Nonsense. He'd put on his clothes, even if they were wet. He was too pragmatic to do otherwise.

Eliza hurried toward the river, leaving behind

the friendly glow of the fire to make her way among the trees, where little moonlight filtered through the leafy branches. A sudden rustling in front of her made her pause.

It's nothing. Don't be afraid. Back home in Coffee Creek, the worst you could run into were skunks and an occasional fox. She'd probably only heard a squirrel moving from branch to branch.

But what if there were truly bears in those woods?

She started singing, softly at first, then increasing her volume. A dark shape moved not far ahead of her, and she stopped again. That had definitely been too large for a fox.

"Mr. Brogan, I'm bringing you a towel," she called out.

"It's about time."

Eliza gasped as the shape stepped out in front of her, snatched the towel from her hands, and thrust a pile of soggy clothes in her arms.

Before she could utter a word, Case wrapped the towel around his middle, took her elbow, and steered her back the way she'd come. "You could have brought a dry one."

"Ouch." She stopped to rub her big toe where she'd stubbed it on a log.

"Are you barefoot?"

"Yes."

He stopped and swung her up in his arms.

"You've done enough damage to your feet for one day. I saw those blistered heels."

How could he have seen them? She'd deliberately kept them hidden. Yet wasn't it exciting to have him play the role of knight gallant once again? She could easily fall in love with a man like that.

Eliza shook those crazy thoughts from her mind. Case Brogan wasn't a knight, he was a Pinkerton, and an especially stern and stubborn one.

Her knight would have to share her passion for opera, or at least for music of some sort. He'd have to be fun-loving and romantic, too. And he definitely would be of a trusting nature.

Case strode on, carrying her as though she weighed nothing, seemingly oblivious of the rough ground. Eliza's left arm was around his neck for balance, and she suddenly noticed how firm the muscles in his shoulder felt beneath her fingertips, and how smooth his skin was. She had to stop herself from running her other hand over that springy hair on his chest. But she itched to feel it.

As they came out into the clearing near the fire she heard him curse under his breath.

"What's wrong?"

"The towel fell off."

The towel fell off? Eliza caught her lip between her teeth and curled her toes, trying to keep from giggling. She knew she should swoon in a situation like this—but Eliza wasn't inclined to swoon at all.

Case stopped and swung around, trying to decide what to do with the warm, soft female in his arms. If he put her down, she'd probably be so mortified by his state of undress that she'd faint, and then he'd have to catch her, and carry her to the blanket, and who knew where that would lead? Better to deposit her in the wagon, where at least the wooden back would hide him from the waist down.

"I'm going to set you inside," he told her. "Stay put until I return."

"Yes, sir," she said.

Case lowered her into the wagon, then reached into his satchel for dry clothes. He could have sworn he heard a muffled giggle as he walked around the side.

He dried off and pulled on clean long johns, pants, and a shirt. After adding more wood to the fire, he headed back to retrieve their bedrolls. "You can come out now."

"Will you help me down?"

Eliza had changed into a night robe that might have been suitable for a fancy hotel, but not for the deep woods. It was flowered and shiny, with long, flowing sleeves trimmed in white, and a white sash that seemed to be its only means of staying closed. One tug would probably open it. He assured himself that she undoubtedly had layers of female items underneath.

She reached out to take his hands, but Case put his hands beneath her arms and lifted her down instead. A jolt ran through his body as he realized he could feel her ribs. She wore no corset! Did that mean she had *nothing* on beneath that robe?

How the hell was he going to get any sleep lying near her all night, wondering if she was naked, remembering how beautiful she'd looked emerging from the river, and how she'd felt lying beneath him?

Annoyed, he yanked out his blankets, purposely leaving hers behind. "You're going to sleep in the wagon."

"We've already discussed that. I'm sleeping by the fire."

"Your aunt hired me to keep you safe. I can't keep you safe unless *you're* in the wagon and *I'm* by the fire."

"I won't be in any danger," she scoffed. "Besides, the wagon is too stuffy. It doesn't make sense for me to—"

Case clasped her shoulders and brought her against him, dropping his head to catch her lips in a crushing kiss, intending to show her exactly the kind of danger she was in. But as he tasted her, as he felt the silken texture of her lips and the wet warmth of her mouth, he forgot the lesson he was trying to teach and began to kiss her in earnest.

His hands slid down her arms and up again, massaging her shoulders, then moved around to her back, gliding down her spine and coming to rest on the curve of her shapely bottom. He pulled her against his swollen member, his blood throbbing so thickly he thought he'd explode. Sweet Jesse, how he wanted her! His lust threatened to overcome what common sense remained.

Riley's voice echoed in his head: "... *her aunt is an old friend of mine who's entrusting me with the safety of her niece.*"

Case broke the kiss, a string of oaths on his tongue. What was it about this young woman that brought out all his animal lust? And why the hell hadn't she tried to resist?

He gazed down at Eliza, who had her eyes closed and a rapturous look on her face. She opened her eyes and smiled guilelessly. "Would you do that again, please?"

He groaned. Lord, how he wanted to oblige. Shaking his head firmly, he stepped back. "No. Uh-uh. You wouldn't like where it led."

"It wouldn't lead anywhere. You wouldn't let it."

"*I* wouldn't let it?" Case laughed harshly as he strode to the fire and knelt down to unroll his blanket. "Don't count on that."

"I count on *you*," she said simply.

"Maybe one of these days you'll learn not to be so trusting."

Eliza said nothing, but as he smoothed out the wrinkles, he could see her bare ankles as she stood at the end of his bedroll. "Would you put some shoes on?" he snapped. There were limits to a man's willpower.

She marched back to the wagon, slipped on a pair of shoes, and returned carrying her blankets. Spreading them on the opposite side of the fire, she curled up inside them, facing away from him. "It must be terrible not to trust anyone."

For a long time afterward, Case sat cross-legged on his blankets in front of the fire, the shotgun on his lap, trying to figure her out. Eliza seemed intelligent enough, and she had to know how very attractive she was—if she hadn't had a dozen beaus or more he'd be surprised—yet she seemed completely unaware of her desirability. Could she be that naive when it came to men, or was she purposely testing him?

"It must be terrible not to trust anyone."

Not as terrible as trusting and being betrayed.

Suddenly Case heard a thrashing in the woods to his left. With a racing heart he jumped to his feet, aimed his shotgun, and waited. An owl hooted overhead. Leaves rustled. He shifted from one foot to the next, but nothing appeared.

Cautiously he sat down again, facing in the direction of the noise. He didn't like not knowing what was out there. He wondered if rats inhabited woods, or if they were only city creatures.

Case hated rats. In Chicago, black rats, some the size of small dogs, prowled the alleys, their beady red eyes and sharp little teeth shining like evil beacons in the gloomy stench of those narrow passageways.

A voice from the past whispered in his head, *"You're not scared of a few little rats, are you, fraidy cat?"*

It had happened over ten years ago, but Frank Caroni's taunting words still echoed in his mind.

Frank had lived with them back then. He'd been taken in by Case's father, Charles Brogan, a Chicago policeman, who'd caught Frank picking pockets at the railroad station. The nineteen-year-old had been arrested many times before, and was on the verge of being sent to prison.

When Case's father learned that Frank had been orphaned at the age of eleven and had lived on the streets for years, trying to survive on his own, he'd opened his home to him, found him steady employment, and even given him a bed in Case's room, thinking he could reform the boy.

"I'm giving you one last chance to turn your life around, Frank," Case's father had cautioned. "Don't bungle it, or you'll be back in jail before you can blink twice."

Frank had thanked Case's father profusely and had promised to lead a virtuous life. For several months afterward he had done just that. He'd shown up at his job promptly, treated Case's parents courteously, and designated himself Case's guardian.

Two years Case's senior, Frank had been streetwise and savvy, with a quick mind, an easy grin, and charm that drew girls like a magnet. Initially Case had admired him. Case's brother Connor, who'd left home at the age of sixteen, had been two years older, just like Frank.

Then, one spring evening at dusk, he and Frank had walked home from the park where Frank liked to meet girls. An old man had been walking in front of them, and when he'd turned down an alley, Frank had followed.

Case had stopped short. "Where are you going?"

"I'm taking a short cut."

"There's rats down there," Case had cautioned.

"You're not scared of a few little rats, are you, fraidy cat?"

At his taunting, Case had started after him, only to see Frank sneak up behind the old man and hit him on the head with a blackjack, knocking him to the ground.

"What did you do that for?" Case had yelled in a panic, as Frank rifled through the man's coat pockets.

"Shut up!" Frank had hissed as he fled the alley, dragging Case a good half block before he'd stopped. Then he'd opened a coin purse and dug through it.

"Here," he said, handing Case a quarter, "go buy yourself a cherry phosphate."

Horrified, Case had pushed his hand away. "You stole the old man's money!"

"Shut up, will you? It's none of your business what I did."

"But my father told you what would happen if you—"

Frank had grabbed Case by his shirtfront and pulled him up until they were nose to nose. "Your father isn't going to find out, is he?"

At that moment Frank had spotted a policeman peering into the alley. When the policeman went in farther to investigate, Frank had cried, "Come on!" and had dashed away, leaving Case standing in the street.

For a moment Case had stood there paralyzed, torn between guilt at what Frank had done and his fear that Frank would be sent to jail. He'd finally run away, too, but he'd never gone anywhere with Frank again, nor had he trusted him.

What he'd failed to do was to tell his father about the incident, and that omission would torment him forever. If his father had been alerted to Frank's true nature, he might not have died by Frank's hand.

Eileen Caroni lay on a thin, lumpy mattress in the dingy hotel room, listening hopefully for the sound of her husband's footsteps. The musty smell of the room made her want to gag and the stains on the worn coverlet gave her gooseflesh, but she and Francis couldn't afford to stay anywhere else.

She'd never in her life seen such dirty places as she had since they had fled Wyoming. Now they were in Nebraska, in some tiny little town on the North Platte River, far, far away from her home in Indiana. But she could hardly blame her husband for their circumstances; it wasn't Francis's fault the police had accused the wrong man. Francis could never have done what they'd said he'd done. He wouldn't have cheated innocent widows out of their life savings; he was a good man.

Eileen sighed miserably. Poor Francis. He was trying so hard to provide for her. He'd been out since dawn looking for work, even though they were only planning to stay until they received Eliza's reply to their last wire. Eileen glanced up at the ceiling, scouting for bugs, praying Eliza's reply would come soon.

The thought of her best friend brought tears to Eileen's eyes. She couldn't wait to see Eliza again. She was terribly homesick; she hadn't seen a familiar face in months, and she longed for news from Coffee Creek. Her father's health hadn't been all that good when she'd left, but, thankfully, she'd heard just a few weeks ago that he was doing better.

She prayed daily for her father. They had become very close after her mother died, and she knew she'd hurt him deeply by running off with Francis. But how could she have passed up an opportunity to marry the only young man who'd ever noticed her?

Eileen pushed herself to a sitting position. She felt so weak and queasy from the baby she carried that sometimes she wished she weren't pregnant. When she had those thoughts, she got down on her knees and prayed for forgiveness and for her good fortune at finding a man who actually wanted her.

Eileen heard footsteps coming up the wooden steps and quickly swung her legs to the floor and pinched her cheeks for color.

"Hello, my pretty baby," Francis called cheerfully, sweeping off his hat as he entered the room.

Eileen caught her breath, smiling happily. She knew she wasn't attractive, yet Francis didn't seem to mind. She still couldn't believe this handsome, charming man had fallen in love with her.

He tossed his hat on the only chair in the room and came over to give her a loud smooch on the cheek. "How are you feeling?" he asked, patting the small bulge of her abdomen.

"A little hungry," she said, though the thought of food made her sick.

Francis opened his coat and pulled out a lady's black satin handbag. "Then my pretty baby shall eat." He rummaged through the contents of the bag, found a coin purse, and opened it. "Ha! Looks like you'll have a feast tonight."

"Francis, where did you find that?"

"Doesn't matter. You know the old saying: finders keepers, losers weepers."

"But someone will be missing it."

"Whoever owned this bag can afford to lose a little money." Francis pocketed some coins and clapped his hat on his head. "Come on, pretty baby, let's go eat."

Eileen slid off the bed, careful not to jostle her stomach. She didn't like the idea of eating off someone's lost money, but neither did she want to ruin Francis's cheerful mood. "Did you find work?"

"Nah."

"Where were you all day?"

He ushered her down the narrow steps to the seedy hotel lobby. "I met some fellows by the river who invited me to join their card game. Ha! I really took them, too. But then I had a bad run of luck and lost it all."

"You played cards all day?"

"There's no work in this town, sweetheart."

"None at all?"

"Are you doubting me?"

The sudden sharpness of his tone startled Eileen. She shook her head. "Never, Francis. I'd never doubt you."

"It's too bad your friend Eliza doesn't feel the same."

"She doesn't doubt you, Francis. Why would you think that?"

"She doesn't trust me enough to wire the money, does she?"

Eileen bit her lip. It was her fault Eliza was coming, but she couldn't tell Francis. He didn't like it when she didn't do exactly as he'd instructed.

"Now we've got two people involved," he complained irritably.

"Two?"

"Your friend won't come alone, you can bet on that—not carrying that amount of money."

Eileen pressed a hand against her queasy stomach to calm it, trying to keep a cheerful tone in her voice. "She'll probably bring her aunt. That's who's lending us the money, after all. And Violet Lowe is a sweet old thing. You'll like her, Francis. But if you're worried, we can send another wire and ask her who she's bringing."

Eileen held her breath, hoping her idea would pacify her husband.

"That's a good idea, sweetheart," he said, suddenly cheerful. "Let's go wire Eliza now."

Chapter 5

The morning light seeped behind her eye-lids, waking Eliza from a sound rest. For a moment she lay still and listened to the birds singing—cardinals, orioles, yellow-winged spar-rows, and wood thrush—and, wait—even a bob-white. How she'd missed those cheerful, folksy sounds in Chicago.

Eliza turned onto her back and groaned from the stiffness that had set in. She pushed herself to her elbows and looked around. Case's bedroll was empty, and she saw no sign of him near the wagon. But a fire crackled in the shallow pit he'd dug the night before. He had probably gone down to the river for water.

Recalling their heated embrace, Eliza lay

71

down again with a smile. What a kiss! What a mouth! So firm, so demanding, so hot and sensual. She quivered inside just thinking about it. But she wasn't sure Case had liked it as much as she had. After all, he'd refused when she'd asked him for more.

"You wouldn't like where it led," he'd told her.

How would she know unless she tried it?

Eliza pulled her satin wrapper over its matching gown. She'd certainly brought the wrong kind of clothing for this trip; she'd have to buy something more serviceable when they reached the next town.

As she walked to the wagon she still saw no signs of Case. She climbed inside, rummaged through her trunks for something simpler, and found a blue skirt and jacket with white piping at the hem, neckline, and cuffs. As she dressed and pinned up her hair, the aroma of coffee wafted into the wagon, and she sniffed appreciatively. Case was back.

"Good morning," she called, walking to the fire, where he tended a pot of coffee.

"Morning."

Although Case had shaved and combed his hair, he still looked rumpled, as though he hadn't slept a wink. He eyed her as he handed her a cup of the fragrant brew.

"How did you rest?"

"Soundly," she told him, "though I am dreadfully sore this morning. How did you sleep?"

"Sitting up," he replied, taking a sip from his tin cup.

Eliza shook her head in exasperation. "Do we have any breakfast food?"

"Bread, jerky, and—"

"I know. Cheese." She marched back to the wagon, thinking she should have brought her own food supply. He simply didn't understand how to pack for a trip. How much effort would it have taken to bring eggs, a dollop of lard, and a skillet?

After a quick breakfast, they headed west once more. Eliza shifted from one hip to the other on the wagon bench, trying to find a position that didn't hurt. She consoled herself with the possibility of sleeping in a real bed that night, eating a good, wholesome meal, and even taking a hot bath.

At least the journey was a little more interesting today. They crossed several rivers—once at a shallow ford, once on a rickety bridge that made her cling to the bench with white knuckles, and once on a barge.

They stopped at noon to eat, and before Eliza had even finished her hunk of bread, Case was fast asleep, his back propped against an accommodating tree trunk. Eliza packed up their supplies, slipped off to relieve herself in the woods, then came back to find him still sleeping.

She cleared her throat several times, and when that failed to wake him, she decided he needed the rest. Hands on her hips, she looked around for something to do that didn't involve sitting. Unfortunately there wasn't much to do in a forest.

Eliza gazed up at the pine trees surrounding the clearing, spotted a black walnut tree among them, and smiled.

Case opened his eyes and sat forward, rubbing his aching neck. He checked his watch and was surprised to see he'd slept a whole hour. But he did feel better; he'd struggled all morning to keep his eyes open.

He climbed to his feet, stretched leisurely, and looked around. Figuring Eliza had stolen off to nap in the wagon, he strode over and peered inside, but she wasn't there. Puzzled, he turned and scanned the area.

"Miss Lowe?"

Hearing nothing, he cupped his hands around his mouth and called, "Eliza!"

A round green nut landed near his feet. He stepped over it just as another came sailing across the small clearing, almost hitting him. He ducked as a third flew past his shoulder, accompanied by a peal of laughter.

He searched the branches for movement, trying to remember what color her dress was. "Where are you?"

"Guess."

"We don't have time for games."

"But we do have time for naps?" she called.

Case's neck began to ache from craning it. "Get down here right now—please."

"I would, but my foot is caught."

He followed her voice and finally spied a bright blue form high up in a walnut tree. Sure enough, her foot was wedged in a vee formed by two branches. "How did you do that?"

"Does it matter? It hurts."

He hoisted himself onto a heavy limb and stretched his hand up, trying to reach the trapped foot. How the hell had she climbed so high? He pulled himself onto another branch and had just gained a foothold when Eliza announced, "Never mind."

"Never mind?"

"I slipped my foot out of my shoe. I don't know why I didn't think of that earlier."

"Why did you climb the damned tree in the first place?"

"You were sleeping, I was bored, and there wasn't anything to do except climb or sing. I assumed you'd rather have me climb."

He couldn't argue with that reasoning. Besides, she looked so angelic in her baby-blue dress, with those smiling blue eyes and glossy black curls, that he would've had a hard time chastising her anyway. "Do you need help getting down?" he asked crossly.

"You're speaking to a former Coffee Creek Tree-Climbing Champion."

Case lowered himself onto the branch below. "You entered a tree-climbing contest?"

"Of course."

"Isn't that a boy's activity?"

"I've yet to see a sign posted on a tree that said no girls allowed." Her foot hit the top of his head. "Oops," she said with a giggle. "Sorry."

Case jumped down and turned as Eliza prepared to lower herself from the last branch. Instead of letting her drop the last few feet, he caught her about the waist and set her down, allowing her body to slide against his.

That was all it took for Case's mood to change from irritated to aroused. He searched her lovely eyes and saw an answering glimmer of interest before she shyly averted her head. He lifted her chin and gazed at her, imagining laying her on the ground and raising her skirts to expose her creamy thighs, exploring her womanly delights until they were both breathless with desire and ready to act on it.

Eliza asked impatiently, "Aren't you going to kiss me?"

His mind was so intent on his erotic daydream that he only slowly understood what she said. When he did understand, it only made sense to answer yes. What harm would it do?

But as Case took his kiss—a long, slow, deeply stimulating kiss that made him so hard with need he throbbed painfully from it—he saw the flaw in his logic. A kiss was harmless enough on its own, but combine the kiss he'd just had with this particular young lady, whose lips brought all sorts of pleasurable images to mind, and whose body he'd already seen naked, and that kiss became as dangerous as a loaded revolver.

Eliza had to know it, too.

Case broke the kiss and stepped back, eyeing her distrustfully. What was her plan? To tell her aunt that he'd ravished her and get him fired? Did she want revenge for having had to accept his protection?

"That was"—she sighed dreamily—"wonderful."

She was playing a part. She had to be. No female was really that naive.

Eliza watched, stunned, as Case pivoted and strode rapidly back to where the horses were tethered.

"Are you ready to go?" he called brusquely.

For a moment all she could do was stare at him in disbelief. What on earth had happened?

One moment he'd kissed her with all the tenderness in the world, the next he'd turned into an ogre.

She ran her fingertips over her sensitized lips as she climbed aboard the wagon. Perhaps lack of sleep was the reason for his irritability.

"I'll wager you didn't sleep last night," she said as Case guided the wagon onto the road.

"Someone had to stand guard," he grumbled, "since someone *else* wouldn't sleep in the wagon."

"I wouldn't then and I won't tonight, either."

"We'll be staying at a hotel tonight."

Eliza could have kissed him for that. But given his current frame of mind, she figured it wouldn't be wise.

For an hour Eliza withstood his silence, then she reviewed her options. Her heels were too sore to walk, and Case probably was in no mood to hear her sing. That left only conversation.

"What does Case mean?"

He glanced at her with a look of total befuddlement.

"Your name," she explained. "What does it mean?"

"It's just a name. It doesn't mean anything."

"Yes, it does. All names have a meaning. Yours is probably a shortened form of Casey, or even a male version of Cassandra."

"It's not Cassandra," he said firmly.

"All right, then let's say it's Casey. I know that's an Irish family name, but I don't know its meaning. Now, my name is a shortened form of Elizabeth that was used by sixteenth-century poets writing about Queen Elizabeth. And Elizabeth comes from the Hebrew Elisheba, which I think means 'oath of God,' or 'God is perfection.' "

Case gave a little "huh" in response, but didn't tell her to stop.

"And since you're Irish, you might be interested to know that Eileen's name comes from the Irish Eibhlin, which probably came from the English Helen or Evelyn."

"How do you know all this?"

"It was a hobby of mine in school. Take the name Francis, for instance, which means Frenchman, or Frank, in Latin."

"Enough!"

Eliza glanced at Case, instantly noticing the change in his expression. His features had set like plaster and his eyes had narrowed to dangerous slits. She'd seen that same look the last time she'd mentioned Francis.

"I wasn't going to talk about Francis Caroni."

"It's *Frank* Caroni."

"I know him as Francis."

"If you really knew him, Miss Lowe, I guarantee you wouldn't be rushing to his aid."

"What I *really* know is that Eileen loves him,

and she's going to have a child with him. That's enough for me."

"That's the dumbest statement I've ever heard."

Eliza gave him an indignant glare. "I beg your pardon?"

"What if I told you he was a murderer? Would you still want your friend to be married to him?"

"If you told me he was a murderer I wouldn't believe you."

"What would it take to convince you?"

Eliza's frustration mounted. "I can see that the only thing that will convince *you* is to meet Francis. Then you'll see you have the wrong man."

Eliza knew she hadn't changed his opinion. She would, though.

"Are we getting close to Moline?" Eliza asked as they rode into a small, dusty town.

"We've got over another day's ride."

"It's nearly dusk, and I'm hungry. Why don't we stop here? They're bound to have some kind of restaurant."

Case pulled the wagon to a halt in front of a barbershop and glanced around. He wasn't thrilled about stopping; the town looked seedy and there was no restaurant in sight.

What he did see was a general store, the

Seaton Sentinel newspaper office, a barbershop, and two saloons. From the nearer saloon, with the odd name of Redbud, he heard the loud guffaws of drinking men and the tinkling of an out-of-tune piano. The other saloon was farther down, across the street from the jailhouse.

"I don't see a restaurant," he told Eliza. "By my map, we're not too far from Peru, which should be a decent-sized town. Let's go there."

"Why don't I go ask that man?" Eliza suggested.

Case followed the direction of her gaze and saw a big, burly, unshaven fellow with a menacing frown and a flinty look in his eyes. He was leaning against a post outside the Redbud Saloon, watching them warily.

Case grabbed Eliza's arm as she started to get down. "Not on your life. I'll go."

Eliza looked over at the man, gave him a smile, and said to Case out of the side of her mouth, "He looks perfectly harmless to me." She jerked her arm free and climbed down.

As she approached the man and began to talk, he stepped toward her, his thumbs hooked in his belt, his gaze sweeping up and down her body. That was too much for Case. He grabbed his shotgun from beneath the bench and jumped down.

"Step back, mister," Case ordered, aiming the gun straight at the roughneck's barrel chest.

Eliza swung around, a shocked look on her face. "What are you doing?"

"Come over here, Miss Lowe."

"But—"

"You'd better put down that shotgun," the man growled.

"Give me one reason why."

"Because, Mr. Brogan," Eliza said, "he's the sheriff!"

Chapter 6

Case blinked several times as her words registered, then he lowered the gun, feeling like an idiot. Was it his fault the man looked suspicious? He could very well have meant Eliza harm.

"I apologize, Sheriff," Eliza said, flashing her bright smile. "He's only trying to protect me. He's a Pinkerton."

"A Pinkerton, huh?" The sheriff turned his head to spit, then gave Case and his shotgun an appraising glance. "You city boys are might quick on the trigger, aren't you?"

"Sorry," Case muttered.

"You tracking someone?"

"He's escorting me to meet a friend," Eliza explained. "She and her husband need money, you see, because they—"

"Any good restaurants around here?" Case cut in, before Eliza could reveal any more information.

"I was just telling the lady that there's a nice one around the corner."

Case hooked his arm through Eliza's. "Let's go."

Before she could utter a protest, he led her toward the wagon, calling back, "Thanks for your help, Sheriff."

"I told you he was harmless," Eliza whispered furiously.

"He didn't look harmless."

"You didn't trust me."

"It was *him* I didn't trust."

"No, it was my judgment you didn't trust, and that hurts my feelings."

"Better to have your feelings hurt than you."

Eliza tapped her toe against the sidewalk while Case stowed the gun in the wagon. "You interrupted me, too," she said.

"You were about to tell him how much money we're carrying."

"Ye gods! He's a sheriff."

"I suppose you believe all lawmen are honest."

Eliza shook her head in amazement as they

headed for the restaurant. "I suppose you believe they're all crooked."

"Not all of them. My father was a cop. A fine one, too."

Case revealed little about himself, and this made her even more curious. "Is he retired?"

There was a long pause, and then Case said, "He was killed ten years ago in the line of duty."

"I'm sorry." Though his words had been brief, she could tell he was holding back deep emotions. Clearly, Case had loved his father. And he'd been only sixteen years old when his father had died.

Eliza wanted to offer words of comfort—she knew the pain of losing a father—but she knew he wouldn't welcome them. He seemed to prefer keeping everyone at a distance.

But it simply wasn't fair for Case to say that all lawmen, with one exception, were dishonest. She'd known Sheriff Logan and several of his deputies back in Coffee Creek nearly her whole life, and more honest men couldn't have been found. What had happened to Case to make him feel as he did?

Eliza was beginning to realize she'd never argue him out of his cynicism; instead, she'd have to prove that his mistrust was simply unjustified.

* * *

After a hearty meal, they took two rooms at the Seaton Hotel—adjoining rooms, at Case's insistence. He thought the clerk looked untrustworthy.

The hotel, formerly a boardinghouse, was a deep, narrow, three-story building with four rooms on each of the two upper floors. The white paint on the wooden clapboard siding had peeled badly, and the wooden floors inside had warped, probably from years of a leaking roof, but the rooms were clean and tidy, if spartan.

Eliza's and Case's rooms were on the third floor. Both were furnished with just a narrow bed, a solitary pine chair, a washstand and basin, and a row of hooks near the door for clothing.

After carefully checking Eliza's room, Case propped a chair against the door to prevent anyone from getting in. Then he let himself into his room through the connecting door.

He stuck his head back in. "Lock this behind me," he instructed.

"Don't you trust me?" Eliza teased, gazing up at him.

Case lifted her chin, his eyes darkening with a hint of danger that made her skin tingle. "Leave it open then—if you dare."

"If I dare what?" she challenged.

His gaze traveled down to her mouth, lingering there for a long moment before moving down to her bodice, where Eliza suddenly felt as though her breasts were swelling from the intense heat of his gaze.

"If you dare trust me."

Eliza couldn't resist the challenge. "Kiss me," she whispered, "and I'll show you how much I trust you."

Case's palm glided up the side of her face as he gazed deep into her eyes. The scent of his bay rum swirled around her, and the air vibrated with electricity as he dipped his head closer.

In anticipation of his kiss, Eliza ran her tongue over her lips to moisten them.

A wry grin spread slowly across his face. "You're a lot smarter than I thought, Miss Lowe."

Eliza's smile disappeared. She had a feeling he wasn't complimenting her. "Smarter how?"

"Sly and conniving—like most women."

Eliza slapped his hand away and stepped back, bringing the door around to close it. "You've become blinded by your distrust, Mr. Brogan."

He jerked back just before she slammed it in his face.

Case's internal clock always awoke him at dawn. So when he took one look at the sun shining through his window the next morning, he leaped out of bed. "Seven-thirty?" he cried, blinking at the numerals on his watch.

He tapped on Eliza's door. "Miss Lowe?"

Receiving no answer, he knocked harder, then barked, "Eliza!"

She must be gone, he thought, pulling on his pants. No one could sleep through that. What if she'd left for Moline without him? He sure wouldn't put it past her; she'd been pretty angry with him last night.

"You've become blinded by your distrust, Mr. Brogan." Didn't she understand that she was the one who was blind?

After tucking in his shirt, splashing water on his face, and dragging a comb through his hair, Case locked his room and raced down the stairs.

The elderly man at the front desk looked up in alarm as Case strode over and demanded, "Did you see a young lady come through here? She's about this tall"—he gestured—"with black hair and blue eyes and—"

"Is she yer lady friend?" the old man asked with a wink.

"No."

"Then why you travelin' with her?" He peered at Case suspiciously from under bushy white brows. "You up to no good with her?"

"Have you seen her or not?"

"Nope."

Damn! She better not have taken the wagon.

Case pulled out his wallet. "What do I owe you for both rooms?"

"That'd be yer lady friend's room, too?"

Case clenched his jaw. "Yes."

The man rubbed his ear. "Let's see here. One room's gonna cost you . . ." He paused to count on his fingers.

Case took out two bills and plunked them on the counter. "That should cover it."

The clerk's eyes bugged when he saw the money. "Thanks, sonny! You know, now that I think on it, I do remember seeing a purty young girl come through here."

"When?"

The old man rubbed his ear again. "Can't say. You could go ask her, though. She's right around the corner in the restaurant."

Muttering curses under his breath, Case strode out of the hotel and around the corner. He stood in the restaurant doorway and scanned the room crowded with chattering diners. Seated at a small table covered in a red-and-white-checkered cloth near a front window, Eliza calmly munched on a piece of crisp bacon as she read a newspaper.

"Would you look at this?" she said nonchalantly as he yanked out a chair and sat down. "The Moline police apprehended a thief yesterday. His name is Frank Cassidy and he's from Wyoming."

"What do you think you're doing?"

She glanced at him as though he'd suddenly lost his mind. "Having breakfast."

"You could have let me know you were coming here."

"I didn't want to wake you."

"How about a note under my door?"

"Next time I will. Why are you so upset?"

"I figured you'd gone to Moline."

Eliza gave him a quizzical look. "Why would you think that?"

"You weren't too happy with me last night."

"Even so, I wouldn't up and leave without telling you." She tapped the news item. "See this? Frank Cassidy. I'll bet he's the man you really want."

Case gave his breakfast order to a waitress, then settled back to study Eliza. He still couldn't get over the fact that she hadn't left.

"Cassidy and Caroni aren't the same man," he assured her. He thanked the waitress for the coffee and took a sip.

"How can you be sure? There could have been a name misunderstanding. Do you even know what crime Francis is wanted for in Wyoming?"

"The latest charge is fraud."

"What's fraud?"

"In Caroni's case, he sold counterfeit railroad bonds to widows."

"Don't you think it's a bit of a coincidence that a Frank Cassidy, from Wyoming, was apprehended for thievery?"

"Frank is a very common name, as you should know, since you're so well versed on the subject. But if it will make you feel better, when we get to Moline we can stop by the jail and take a look at him. If he has one blue eye and one green, then we'll discuss your theory further."

Eliza sighed in resignation. It had been a longshot, but she'd figured it was worth a try.

After another day on the road and another night at a nondescript inn, they reached Moline around noon. It was a sprawling city on the far west side of Illinois, built on gently sloping hills and fertile grasslands. It sat beside the Rock River at a point where the rock bottom was shallow for easy crossing. Not nearly as large as Chicago, but much more civilized than the tiny hamlets they'd been through, to Eliza it was a welcome sight.

The first stop they made was at the telegraph office. Eliza opened the wire that was waiting for her and read the brief message.

HEADING EAST TO IOWA. STOP. WILL LEAVE WORD AT DES MOINES TELEGRAPH OFFICE WHERE TO MEET. STOP.

She handed it to Case. "Looks like we'll be traveling a while longer."

"Young lady?" the elderly gentleman behind the counter called. "There's another wire here for you."

Eliza tore it open and read it, surprised to see it contained only one line. The new wire was dated two days after the first, and was clearly written by Eileen.

IS AUNT VI TRAVELING WITH YOU? STOP.

"I wonder why she wants to know," Eliza murmured, showing the wire to Case.

"*She* doesn't want to know. Caroni wants to know."

"Nonsense. Eileen probably wants to secure hotel rooms for us in Des Moines."

"Right. And Caroni is planning a banquet in your honor."

"Tease all you want," Eliza said, picking up a pen to write out her reply. "It doesn't bother me in the least." She glanced around at Case, who was looking over her shoulder. "I can't think with you hovering."

While Case stood at the window looking up and down the street, Eliza wrote, "Leaving today for Des Moines. Traveling with a Pinkerton for protection. Hope you are well." She handed the message to the telegraph operator, then wrote out a message to her aunt, letting her know where they were headed. She paid the man and walked to the door.

"What did you write?" Case asked as they strolled down the sidewalk.

"I wrote to my aunt that we are well, and I wrote to Eileen that we're leaving today for Des Moines," she said, pulling on a pair of white gloves, "and that I'm traveling with you."

Case came to an abrupt stop and gaped at her. "You wrote *what*?"

Without waiting for her reply, he turned and dashed back to the telegraph office.

Chapter 7

 ~~~⌒∞⌒~~~

Case strode into the telegraph office and straight up to the counter. The elderly operator was nowhere to be seen. "Hello?" Case called. "Anyone here?"

"What are you doing?" Eliza cried, fast on his heels.

"I've got to get that message back before he sends it. Hello?" he called again.

The old gentleman poked his head around the door. "Can I help you?"

"I need the messages back that Miss Lowe gave you."

"Not much use in that," the man said, scratching the top of his snowy head. "Already sent one and most of t'other."

"How much of the other?"

"All but her name," he replied, nodding in Eliza's direction.

"What's wrong with my telegram?" Eliza demanded.

"Damn," Case muttered. "I should have checked it first."

"Want me to finish?" the man asked.

Case sighed. "You might as well."

"What's wrong with my telegram?" Eliza repeated.

"Did you give Caroni my name?"

"No."

Case mumbled something under his breath that Eliza was sure she wouldn't like.

"If it makes you feel any better," she told him, "I wrote that I'd brought you for my protection. Unlike *you*, they trust my judgment. They know I wouldn't do anything to hurt them." Eliza gave Case a pointed look.

"Next time—if there is one—let me read your message before you send it." Case strode ahead and opened the door for her.

"Fine," she said in exasperation. "In fact, I'll just let *you* write it. Can we get some food now?"

Case shook his head in wonder. "For someone of your stature, you sure do your share of eating."

Eliza came to an abrupt stop on the sidewalk outside. "Are you implying that I'm overweight?"

"How did you get that out of what I said? I said for someone of your *stature*, not weight." His gaze followed her curves from shoulder to hip. "Believe me, it wasn't an insult," he said huskily.

Eliza looked down, feeling her cheeks grow warm. He'd actually paid her a compliment! "Well, then, thank you."

"You're welcome."

Eliza walked quietly at his side, basking in a warm glow. She had a feeling that he rarely complimented anyone. How absurd, really, that one little snippet of praise should mean so much to her, but there it was.

Case Brogan was stubborn, opinionated, bossy, and terribly cynical, yet she'd seen glimpses of another man inside him—an honest, loyal, and extremely attractive man who intrigued her. She just wasn't sure what to do about it.

After locating a livery stable for the horses, they found a restaurant that served a tasty chicken soup and hearty dark bread. Then, while Eliza savored a last cup of coffee, Case left, promising to be back in a short while.

He returned to the telegraph office and sent a wire to Assistant Chief Riley, letting him know the latest development on Caroni and telling the chief to forward any news to Des Moines. Then he got instructions on the best route across Iowa and headed back to collect Eliza.

As Case neared the restaurant, he heard the strains of a high soprano voice and a deep bass voice singing in harmony. He recognized the old Irish tune, although he couldn't remember its name. His mother used to sing it as she worked about the house.

It wasn't until he opened the door that Case realized the soprano was Eliza. He stood just inside, watching in amazement as she and an old man with long gray hair and a thick handlebar mustache leaned their heads together and produced music that brought tears and sniffles to the other patrons' eyes.

Well, well, Case thought, shaking his head. It seemed Eliza could sing something besides opera. He wondered why he hadn't noticed before how sweet and pure her voice was.

He peered again at the old man. He had the strongest feeling he'd seen that face before—had it been on a wanted poster? Case rubbed his jaw in puzzlement, trying to come up with a name to match the face. But Eliza was too powerful a draw to keep him puzzling for long.

Case conceded grudgingly that he'd been wrong about her. She wasn't an eyelash-fluttering, whining, spoiled diva. She was brave, optimistic, talented and beautiful.

Realizing that he was stepping into dangerous territory, he hastily added: irritating, headstrong, naive, and too attractive for her own good. With a frown he turned around and left.

Frank Caroni picked up the telegram and walked outside the office into the hot, dusty air. "A Pinkerton," he sneered, reading the brief message. That little bitch was bringing a hired detective from Chicago. He knew he shouldn't have trusted her.

Frank stormed down to the river, to a tavern he'd been frequenting since he'd arrived. Ever since he'd hooked up with his dull-as-a-doorknob wife, he'd had a disastrous run of luck. Why hadn't he stuck to the big cities to do his fishing?

It was Eileen's fault they had no money. She'd led him to believe her father was on his deathbed, but the stubborn old geezer had hung on just to spite him, forcing him to revert to his old ways.

He'd done pretty well, too, until one of the biddies he'd scammed had turned out to be the sheriff's mother. He'd barely managed to grab Eileen and flee. If it hadn't been for her rich friend, Frank would have gladly left his wife behind.

Now his scheme to milk Eliza for money was in jeopardy, too, thanks once again to Eileen.

Somehow he had to pull this off. One thousand dollars was a small fortune. With that kind of money he could live like a king down in Mexico.

Frank downed a shot of whiskey and plunked the glass on the bar. "A Pinkerton," he muttered in disgust. He hated Pinkertons—or anyone resembling a cop. Well, he'd just have to be extra cautious, that's all. He wasn't going to let a hired beagle ruin *this* plan.

Eliza hugged her singing partner and kissed him on the cheek while the people in the restaurant clapped. She turned and curtsied, then glanced around for Case, whom she'd seen earlier standing near the door. Had he left the restaurant?

She found him leaning against the wagon. "Is your concert finally over?"

Eliza chose not to reply as she pinned her hat to her hair. Case was clearly unhappy that she'd held up the trip, but she'd grown bored waiting for him to return, and the opportunity to share a lovely song had been irresistible. She supposed Case wasn't going to be any happier about her next announcement.

"I need to buy some clothes before we leave. It won't take long."

"Aren't your fancy traveling outfits holding up?"

"There's no need to be sarcastic," she replied evenly. "Had I known we would be using anti-quated transportation, I would have packed differently. I spotted a dry goods and millinery shop about two blocks back, so I'll see you in half an hour."

"Get a new hat while you're there," he called.

Eliza threw him a smile over her shoulder. What a splendid idea. And how uncharacteristi-cally kind of him to suggest it. Imagine Case Brogan appreciating the importance of coordi-nating one's hat with one's outfit.

Case left the wagon parked by the telegraph office and made two complete circuits of the block around the millinery shop, stopping once to peer in the large front window, where several manikins displayed the latest in country style. He finally stepped inside to see what was going on.

The store was as wide as it was deep, with shelves on one side wall filled with thick, color-ful bolts of material, racks of ready-made cloth-ing down the middle, and a huge display of men's and ladies' hats on the opposite wall. A counter at the front held a glass display case full of ribbons, combs, and other feminine trap-pings, which several ladies were examining.

A tall cheval glass at the back caught his eye. In front of it stood Eliza, wearing a simple dress of cream-colored calico with little blue flowers on it. The material was summer-weight, with lightly puffed sleeves and a neckline that was vee-shaped instead of the high-buttoned style popular in the city, which seemed sensible to Case.

He watched as Eliza swiveled to study the dress from different angles. All of her angles looked good to him.

A seamstress hovered nearby, a tape measure around her neck and a pincushion on her wrist. "If it's a bit snug in the hip I can let it out for you."

"Thank you, but it's quite comfortable. I'll take this one and the green one—and the hat, too."

While the lady hurried off to wrap her dresses, Eliza turned and spotted Case. "That didn't take long, did it?"

"Long enough."

He followed her to the front counter, where he spied a monstrosity that looked more like the backside of an overweight ostrich than a lady's hat. As Eliza ran her fingers over the feathers he said, "You're not serious about that hat, are you?"

"This one? I think it's beautiful. Don't you like it?"

"Do you think there'll be room in the wagon for all three of us?"

A loud harrumph caused Case to turn. A portly matron stepped up to the counter, snatched the hat, and placed it carefully on her head. Throwing him an icy look, she marched out of the shop, muttering about the rudeness of strangers.

Eliza covered her mouth to muffle her giggle. "Now do you want to see the hat *I* chose?"

She reached behind the counter and brought out a more sedate version of the ostrich hat. Case took one glance at it, strode over to the shelves, selected a simple straw hat with a long front and side brim and a single black ribbon that hung down the short back brim, and handed it to her. "Try this one. It'll protect your face better."

She wrinkled her nose. "But it's so plain."

"You don't need a fancy hat. You're pretty enough."

Eliza's eyes widened.

Now he'd done it. Now she'd turn all mushy on him and want to know in minute detail exactly how she was pretty.

Instead she turned to a looking glass on the counter and placed the hat on her head to take a look.

"That looks marvelous on you," the seamstress gushed, putting the wrapped dresses on the counter. "It's one of our latest summer styles, you know. It's called a Newport. Very popular on the East Coast."

Eliza gazed at her reflection for a moment, then turned to Case. "Do you really like it?"

Oh, he liked it all right. He especially liked the way it gave her eyes a very sultry, very mysterious look. He liked it so much that he told her not to buy it.

"But you chose it," she said in bewilderment.

"Don't trust my opinion. I don't know anything about hats."

Eliza smiled at the lady. "I'll take it. Would you box my old hat so I can wear this one now?"

They crossed the Mississippi River, made their way through Davenport, Iowa, passed several tiny villages, and headed for Iowa City, hoping to make it before nightfall. But only two hours outside of Davenport, one of the wagon wheels came loose.

Eliza walked up and down the dirt road to stretch her legs while Case worked on the wheel. As far as the eye could see, the narrow road wended across the rolling plains like a sable ribbon unfurling on a great expanse of muslin. On either side of the road, prairie grass rippled in giant waves, with an occasional tree dotting the horizon like bright green sails on a ship. Eliza took a deep breath and let it out, thinking there wasn't anything that man had built that could rival what God had created.

"We'll have to go back to that last village," Case told her, moping his brow. "It's not much more than a whistle-stop, but they're bound to have a blacksmith. Put on your walking shoes; we'll need to walk to lighten the load."

Eliza buttoned her shoes, retrieved her ivory-handled fan, and set off beside the wagon, grateful for the coolness of the calico dress. Although her new hat was terribly ordinary, it did sit lighter on her head and kept more sun off her face than her fancier hat had. She was grateful for that, and told Case so.

He glanced at her skeptically. "You're admitting I'm right?"

"*Admitting*? You make it sound as though I'm confessing to a crime. I like the hat you chose, that's all. Why wouldn't I say so if it's true?"

"Because you're too proud to concede I might be right."

"But you *are* right, and I *did* concede it." Eliza huffed in frustration. "If you'd stop being so mistrustful you might see that I was complimenting your taste."

Case grumbled something under his breath.

"What was that?" Eliza asked.

"I said thank you."

"If you'd said that at the beginning, we

could've avoided this conversation and talked about something pleasant."

Case didn't reply, so Eliza continued. "Let's talk about music. Did you like the song I sang at the restaurant?"

"That reminds me: when I left, you were sitting alone. When I returned, you had your arm around a complete stranger and were singing with him like you were old friends."

"Music will do that to you. Did you like the song?"

"I'll wager you didn't even find out his name. For all you know, he could've been a hired gun."

"William Cody."

"What about William Cody?"

She blew an errant curl off her forehead. "That was the man's name."

Case came to an abrupt halt. "William *Cody*? As in *Buffalo Bill* Cody?"

"He only said William."

Case began walking again, muttering, "Come to think of it, he *did* look like an older version of Buffalo Bill. But he's supposed to be retired and living on a ranch in Wyoming."

"William did mention that he was on his way back to his ranch in Wyoming. Did you like the song?" she asked again.

"As I think more about it, his hair and mustache were the same, only thinner and whiter."

He stared at Eliza in amazement. "You sang with Buffalo Bill Cody!"

"So you liked the song?"

He hesitated a moment, then, his voice heavy with sentiment, he said, "I liked the song. My mother used to sing it."

Eliza smiled, feeling as if she'd just won a major victory. She wanted to ask him more about his mother, but he was already back to a subject that clearly excited him.

"My father took me to see Buffalo Bill's show back in '84 when his touring company came through Chicago. I must have been about twelve." Case shook his head. "What a showman Buffalo Bill was. I'll never forget seeing him ride backward on a horse, shooting at a target over his shoulder using only a hand mirror. I wanted to do that for the longest time."

Eliza held her breath, hoping he'd tell her more.

In a quiet voice he said, "There were only two men I ever genuinely admired: Buffalo Bill was one, my father was the other." His voice broke slightly as he added, "They were my heroes."

The poignancy of his words and the sadness in his expression were almost too painful to bear. His vulnerability made him more human, so unlike the stony, unapproachable man he presented to the world.

She yearned to comfort him, to assure him

that his father would always be with him. But he would only throw up that impenetrable shield to keep her away.

Eliza squared her shoulders. Somehow she would break down that shield and make him trust her. She had to do it, and not just for Eileen's sake.

For whose sake, then?

Eliza glanced at him, and her heart stood still. "Oh, no."

"Is something wrong?" Case asked.

Dear heavens, yes, something was wrong. She was starting to feel things for Case Brogan that she shouldn't. She wouldn't! She fanned her face to cool her cheeks. "How many days have we known each other?"

"Five."

Five days. Eileen had known she was in *love* with Francis in just four days. Well, thank goodness that hadn't happened to her. All she felt for Case was—pity. Yes, that's all it was: pity for losing his father. That and a healthy dose of physical attraction.

And that was bad enough.

Chapter 8

❦

Eliza fanned her face so hard her wrist ached. How could she be attracted to Case Brogan? He was a practical, stodgy Pinkerton, for heaven's sake. That was no match for someone with her artistic temperament.

The man of her dreams would be kind and sensitive. He'd tell her his innermost secrets and burning desires; he'd surprise her with flowers, and bonbons, and long serenades on moonlit nights. That definitely wasn't Case.

"Are you sure you're feeling all right? You look flushed," he told her. "Maybe you're overheated. Let's stop and get you some water."

His rare show of concern touched her. Maybe

she'd misjudged him. "No, really, Mr. Brogan, I'm fine."

"Do you want to ride in the wagon?"

"And risk damaging the wheel? That's very considerate of you, but I'll walk. Thank you for asking."

"I wouldn't want you to complain to your aunt."

Eliza's fan came to a sudden stop. So much for his concern! There was absolutely no way she could ever be happy with a man like him. Case didn't have a compassionate bone in his body.

She took out her handkerchief to blot the perspiration on her neck. "Will we make it to Iowa City tonight?"

"No. We'll have to find a place to stay in the village."

Just as well, Eliza thought. She was hungry again.

By the time they reached the tiny farming community of Braggerton, population two hundred twenty-nine, Eliza's stomach was growling loud enough to scare away the birds. They located the smithy's shop only to find it had already closed.

"Let's find somewhere to eat," Eliza suggested.

"We need to find a place to stay for the night first. Your stomach can wait awhile longer."

Neither of their ideas worked. The village proper was nothing more than a gristmill, a general store, a blacksmith shop, and a narrow, whitewashed, steepled church, all on the same dusty dirt road. Knowing how disappointed Eliza would be, Case prepared himself for a heavy round of complaining as he pulled the wagon to a stop.

"The general store is open," Eliza remarked good-naturedly, astounding him. "Let's buy some food and set up camp. We should be able to find a place to park the wagon somewhere near the blacksmith shop."

Case was further amazed at her cheerful mood as she perused the store's aisles, selecting a half-dozen eggs, a slab of bacon, fresh bread, and a cast-iron skillet.

Was Eliza up to something? Was she trying to make him believe she didn't care that she'd be sleeping and dining outdoors again, so she could turn around and blame him in the end?

Even as he posed those questions, Case knew better than to believe them. Eliza simply wasn't like other women. She made the best of every situation, and he had to admire her for that.

As they waited for the grocer to wrap the packages and tally the cost, Case noticed a crowd gathering outside in the street.

"What's going on?" he asked the grocer.

"Some of those Iowan Injuns are in town to get their wheat ground."

"Those aren't Indians I see gathered outside."

"They're out there, take my word for it. The folks hereabout try to discourage them from coming in, that's all. We don't much care for them and their strange ways." The shopkeeper turned and spit tobacco juice in a spittoon for emphasis.

"What nonsense!" Eliza said, and immediately headed for the door.

"Don't go out there," Case ordered, then sighed as she vanished from his sight.

The grocer clucked his tongue and shook his head. "Women—they're near as bad as Injuns."

Eliza huffed at the grocer's provincial attitude as she marched straight for the crowd. Hearing a woman's distressed cries coming from the center, she quickly pushed her way in far enough to see an Indian woman kneeling on the ground, bending over an infant. Several children stood around her, clutching her clothing, wide-eyed with fear as they gaped at all the strange faces staring at them.

"What's happening?" Eliza demanded.

"One of the Indian brats is sick," someone told her.

"Has someone sent for a doctor?"

"You mean a medicine man?" a man beside her scoffed, causing others around her to guffaw. "We don't have any of those heathens in our town."

"You must not have any consciences in your town, either," Eliza retorted sharply, throwing icy looks at the people nearest her. She quickly hurried to the frantic mother, who was probing the baby's throat with her finger while she called something in a foreign tongue to her other children. The baby, who appeared to be about four months old, was blue around the lips.

Realizing the child was choking, Eliza pushed the mother's hand aside. "I can help," she said, and picked up the child, trusting that the woman understood.

The crowd gasped as Eliza turned the baby upside down, held it by the heels, and rapped it between the shoulder blades as hard as she dared. She'd once seen her father save a child that way; Eliza prayed it would work for her.

"Can you hurry that up?" Case growled as the grocer wrapped a length of string around the package. Case glanced nervously out the window, but couldn't see a thing. Damn it! The old coot was moving slower than molasses. "Just give it to me," he finally said. "I don't need it tied."

He had a bad feeling as he grabbed the supplies and left the store. That feeling grew stronger as he stepped into the milling crowd and heard snatches of angry comments: "Who does that woman think she is?" "It's just a danged Injun." "She's a stranger here. She oughta mind her own business."

He just knew they were talking about Eliza.

Shifting the bundle to his left side, Case pulled out his gun. "Move back," he shouted. "Everyone move back *now*!"

Heads swiveled at his authoritative tone, and a wide aisle opened between him and the commotion in the middle. He saw Eliza pounding on an infant's back, with no regard for what was happening around her.

At that moment, a large, male Indian came out of the gristmill down the street, took one look at Eliza whacking the upside-down child, let out a bellow, and charged toward her.

Case swore soundly as he raced in to protect Eliza. He didn't want to have to hurt anyone, but he wasn't about to let Eliza get hurt, either.

"Stop right there," he commanded, but the Indian either didn't understand or didn't care. He dashed straight past Case as if he were invisible.

Case followed, prepared to launch himself at the Indian. To his surprise, the baby's mother stepped in front of Eliza, cutting off the big male, and began talking rapidly to him in her own tongue.

Suddenly the infant coughed and then began to wail loudly. Case watched, stunned, as Eliza tearfully hugged the baby to her bosom. Then, smiling through her tears, she handed the baby to its mother, gently smoothing back the dark hair on its head. Only then did she seem to notice the enormous, scowling male standing behind her.

"Your baby will be all right," she assured the father, patting his muscular arm in a motherly manner, even as she swiped tears from her cheeks.

Warily Case moved closer.

The man conferred with his wife in a low voice, his hand tenderly cradling his child's head. Then he turned to Eliza and placed his large hands on her shoulders. Case tensed.

"You are a brave, kind woman," the man pronounced gravely. He removed a pouch from around his neck, opened it, and said, "Give me your hand."

Case opened his mouth to warn her not to do it. But without hesitation, Eliza held out her hand, palm up. The Indian placed something in it, then covered it with his own hand.

"You have given me my son's life. Take this and keep it close to you. It will help you find the one you seek."

As he slowly uncovered her palm, Eliza peered at the oblong crystal in its center. One end was smooth and round and clear, while the other was rough and opaque. She glanced up at the Indian in amazement. "How do you know I'm seeking someone?"

His piercing dark brown eyes seemed to bore into her. "Your eyes reveal what is in your soul," he said quietly.

His words raised gooseflesh on her skin. For a moment, all Eliza could do was stare at him in wonder. Then she glanced down at the crystal charm and slowly closed her hand around it. "It's beautiful. I'll treasure it forever. Thank you."

He gave a solemn nod, then turned to usher his family away, ignoring the murmurs and stares of the people around him.

Oblivious to the glares directed her way, Eliza walked over to Case and showed him the gift. "Isn't this beautiful? How kind of him to—Why is your gun out?"

"Let's get out of here," Case said, taking her arm and leading her through the crowd. "These folks aren't happy about what you did."

"Saving a baby's life?"

"They don't like Indians."

"It's more likely that they fear them. People fear what they don't understand. Take you, for instance—"

"No, *don't* take me," Case grumbled. "Just keep moving."

"Miss?" A young woman holding a child in her arms reached out to touch Eliza's sleeve. "I just wanted to say God bless you; you have a generous heart. No one wanted to help those people."

"Thank you," Eliza replied. She started to turn away, then paused to add, "Promise me something. If a situation like that ever happens again, *you* step in to help. That could have been your baby dying."

The young woman's grip tightened on her child as tears came to her eyes. "I will," she whispered.

"Now then, as I was saying," Eliza began, as Case steered her toward the wagon.

"Not even counting the townspeople's reaction to what you were doing," Case interrupted, "did you ever stop to consider how your actions might have looked to those Indians? You were holding their baby upside-down and hitting it!"

"Saving that child was my only consideration. I just had to trust that the parents would understand."

"That Indian didn't look too understanding when he charged toward you," Case replied, stowing their supplies in the back of the wagon.

"Is that why your gun was out?" she asked, following him around the wagon. "You were going to shoot him for defending his own child? How *could* you?"

Case climbed up onto the bench and glanced down at Eliza, standing on the battered wooden sidewalk with her hands on her hips. "I would have shot him if he'd tried to hurt you. That's my job."

Eliza let out an exasperated sigh. "You always think the worst of people."

"You always assume the best of people," he retorted. "You're blind to their faults."

"You're blind to everything else about them. I saw a mother trying to save her dying child, and a father trying to defend his son. If I had looked at that situation through your eyes, that baby would be dead. Now, which one of us was blind and which was right?"

Case gritted his teeth as he took up the reins. Eliza was just lucky that the situation had worked out the way it had. "Are you coming or are you going to stand there all day?"

"The wheel is broken," Eliza reminded him, giving him that beguiling smile.

Case swore to himself as he climbed down. Damn it! He hated it when she was right.

After parking the wagon in the empty field behind the blacksmith shop, Case took care of the horses, then gathered wood for a fire. He could hear Eliza humming as she cut the bacon into thick slices and set them in the skillet.

As soon as the fire was hot, Case watched

hungrily while she turned the meat with a long-handled fork until it was sizzling, then cracked the eggs over them and let them bubble in the bacon grease until they were done.

He had to admit, for someone who lived a pampered life, she handled the food quite expertly.

"Very tasty," he conceded, swallowing a mouthful of juicy fried egg.

"Thank you."

"I didn't know you could cook."

She gave him one of her tantalizing glances. "There's a lot you don't know about me."

He knew the way she looked rising naked from the dark water, and the sweet, enticing way her mouth tasted—and he'd like to know a lot more.

Case moved to a safer subject. "How did you know what to do for that child?"

"My father was a doctor, remember? He was an excellent doctor, too. Very compassionate and wise. Everyone in town loved him." Eliza paused for a drink of water. "After he died, my sister Mariah took over his practice."

"Unusual for a woman to be a doctor."

"Mariah's an unusual woman. My brother Ben would have been a doctor, too, but he died when he was seventeen."

Case wanted to halt the conversation right there. He already knew enough to feel sympathy for her: she'd lost her father, mother, and brother. Yet she seemed to handle it well. How did she keep such an optimistic view of life?

Case took another bite. Against his will, he asked, "How old were you when your brother passed on?"

"Thirteen."

"How did he—?" Case decided not to finish the question. He really didn't have any right to ask it. "Never mind."

Eliza looked down with a sad sigh. "No, it's all right. My brother drowned. He and some friends drank too much whiskey and jumped into a lake, but Ben couldn't swim."

"Must have been rough on you," he said quietly.

She raised her head, her blue eyes swimming in tears. "It was. I looked up to Ben. It took me a long time to see the gift in his death, but I did, and it helped me immensely."

"Gift?"

"Something good that came of it," she explained, dashing away a tear that had rolled down her cheek. "I'd never felt close to my family. They were all very bright and studious, and I—well, I couldn't be bothered with schoolwork. That frustrated my family no end, and caused all sorts of arguments and hurt feelings. After Ben died, we realized what really mattered was that we loved each other, no matter what our failings. Ben would have liked knowing he helped us. It was his gift to us."

Case pondered the idea briefly, but as far as he could see, there'd been no gift in losing his own father. Had she witnessed her brother's death, as he'd witnessed his father's? He couldn't ask her, because there was no way he could talk about that horrible time to anyone. Only one other person knew what had transpired that day—and that person was going to pay with his life.

"Are you going to sit up all night again?" Eliza asked as she laid out her bedroll.

"If you'd sleep in the wagon I wouldn't have to."

Eliza shook her head in vexation and rolled her blankets up again. "All right. I'll sleep in the wagon."

She made the bed as comfortable as was possible on such an unforgiving surface, changed into her nightclothes, then peered out the canvas opening to see what Case was doing. To her surprise, she saw him sitting on his blanket next to the fire, the shotgun on his lap.

"You said you weren't going to sit up all night."

"Go to sleep. I'm fine."

"I can't go to sleep thinking about you sitting out there all night."

"You're not going to start singing, are you?"

"I might."

She heard him curse softly as he stood up and came toward her. "What do you want me to do?"

"You can sleep in here. I'll lay a barrier between us."

Case shook his head in disbelief. Her naiveté was unbelievable.

On the other hand, he *could* protect her better if he was near her.

"All right," he said, "make a barrier."

He watched as Eliza rolled up clothing and shifted supplies, creating a long, low wall down the middle. "Give me your blankets," she commanded.

Case waited as she carefully laid them out, then he climbed inside, drew the canvas cover closed in the front and the back, and settled down to try to get some sleep.

"Good night," she called softly.

"Night," he murmured, turning away from her. Ha! As if he could forget that Eliza was lying only a few feet away, wearing that silky thing again that probably had nothing underneath it.

But instead of conjuring up lustful images, he kept remembering how she'd saved that baby without a moment's thought to her own safety. Although it was one of the most foolish acts he'd ever seen, it was also one of the bravest. He admired bravery.

Eliza had been correct; if she'd looked at the situation through his eyes, that baby would have died. Case had thought only of protecting his charge.

For some odd reason, he found himself wishing he could be a little more like Eliza in that respect.

Eliza lay quietly on her back, holding the crystal in her hand. She rubbed her thumb over its smooth contours, thinking about the Indian's words: *"It will help you find the one you seek."*

Naturally he'd been referring to Eileen. Now she felt more strongly than ever that helping her friend was the right thing to do. So her next goal was to change Case's mind about Francis Caroni.

Eliza was still awake when Case began to toss fitfully. She waited awhile to see if he'd go back to sleep, but he became more agitated instead. Realizing he was in the throes of a bad dream, she slipped quietly from the wagon and went to the fire, where the pot of cold coffee still sat. Pouring him a cup, she returned and gently tried to wake him.

The Indian was back, tall, unsmiling, forbidding, motioning for Eliza to follow him.

"Stay here with me," Case told her.

Eliza smiled. "I'll be fine. He means no harm. He probably just wants to thank me."

Case started after her, only to find himself bound by chains at the ankles. "Eliza! Come back."

"Trust me. I know what I'm doing."

He strained against the chains until they broke, then he ran after her just as she disappeared down a dark alley. Case stared into the gloom, his heart pounding in dread. Something bad was going to happen to her.

Suddenly he heard a cry of surprise, then a long groan of pain, but it wasn't Eliza's voice. He blinked hard as a dark figure staggered toward him, dropping several yards away.

"Father!" With a sob of anguish, Case knelt down beside his dying father, cradling his head, pleading with him not to die. "I need you. Don't leave me."

He gasped as Frank Caroni stepped out of the shadows, laughing at him.

"You're not scared of a few little rats, are you, fraidy cat?"

As Frank ran off, Case glanced down at his father in horror, where black rats were biting his hands. Case tried to fight them off but they bit him, too, crawling over both of them until he was too exhausted to struggle.

He'd failed completely: he'd lost Eliza and he'd lost his father. And Frank Caroni had escaped once more.

He lay down next to his father, prepared to die at his side, but suddenly the bites became gentle caresses—soft fingertips brushing across his cheeks, smoothing his hair. He reached up and caught a small hand.

"It'll be all right," Eliza's voice said soothingly near his ear. "It's only a dream."

"Wake up now. I have some coffee for you. Why don't you sit up and have a sip?"

Case opened his eyes and blinked in confusion, trying to decide if he was still dreaming or if Eliza was really kneeling beside him.

"This will clear away those bad dreams," she said, offering him a tin cup that smelled of strong coffee.

With immense relief, Case pushed himself up on his elbows and accepted the cup, taking a long drink.

"Feeling better?" Eliza asked, her concern evident in her expression.

He noticed then that her barrier had been pushed aside, and that all she wore was a long, clinging shift that permitted a tantalizing view of the tops of her breasts. Her black hair was loose and tumbled over her shoulders. Her gaze was sleepy, which gave her an erotic look, and her eyes reflected slivers of moonlight.

"That must have been a terrible dream. You were crying out for your father."

"It's over." He didn't want to think about the

dream. He only wanted to think about the desirable woman beside him. She was simply too luscious to resist.

He set the cup aside and leaned over her, gazing deep into her eyes, waiting to gauge her reaction. But Eliza showed not the least bit of trepidation as he lowered his mouth to hers.

Chapter 9

Thrills of desire raced through Eliza as Case took her down to the blanket, his arms behind her back, his lips warm and seeking. He nibbled teasingly at first, then kissed her with more passion. She wound her arms around his neck and reveled in the firmness of his mouth, the scratch of his chin against hers, the pressure of his hard chest against her nipples.

A jolt shot through her as his tongue edged between her lips, then probed the depths of her mouth, inflaming her passion until she moaned and lifted her hips to rock against him, seeking more.

Case broke the kiss to glide his mouth down her throat, while his fingers slipped the thin straps of her chemise over her shoulders. Eliza knew he was about to bare her breasts, and her skin tingled in anticipation of his touch. The night air brushed across her nipples before his hands covered them, rubbing across them, then molding her breasts beneath his palms.

When his mouth took over where one palm had been, Eliza arched back with pleasure, thrusting the nipple further inside his hot, wet depth. A tiny voice inside cautioned her to stop, but Eliza was so overcome with desire that she ignored it.

She gasped in pleasure as Case ran his tongue around the soft tip, flicking it until it tightened, shooting a current of desire all the way to her toes. His lips closed tight around the sensitive bud, then he suckled, bringing on an intense throbbing between her thighs. He shifted to the other breast, circling, stroking, making her desperate for more.

As he continued the delicious assault, his hand slipped beneath her shift and raised it up to her hips. As he lifted his mouth to capture hers once again, his fingers ran lightly over the curly hair at the juncture of her thighs, then pushed down through the middle into the valley, seeking the taut nub of her passion.

Eliza arched her hips upward with a moan, pressing against his hand, needing something that she couldn't name. She'd never felt such exquisite delight, and as the stroking grew longer, harder, deeper, she thought she'd burst from the sheer joy of it.

Suddenly his lips were skimming up the smooth surface of her inner thighs, pressing hot kisses higher and higher. Eliza's eyes flew open in shock. Oh, heavens—his tongue!

His boldness stunned her, yet aroused her to even greater heights. As the tension inside her built, she thought she could bear the ecstasy no more. Then, like a storm breaking, her release came—wave after wave of pleasure, causing her muscles to spasm until she sank back, exhausted, and closed her eyes.

She'd never imagined such pleasure was possible. She basked in the afterglow, feeling her heart swell with tenderness and gratitude. To caress her so gently, so intimately, so lovingly, Case surely must have very strong feelings for her.

Dreamily she opened her eyes and reached out to him.

Case was gone.

Standing in the shadows behind the blacksmith shop, Case gritted his teeth, determined to bring his raging passion under control. Damn! Why hadn't he finished it the right way? God knew Eliza would probably have let him.

But how could he justify taking her in the heat

of passion? It was just so damned difficult to resist her.

After tonight they would sleep far apart. He couldn't put himself through such torment again.

In a black mood, Case climbed back into the wagon, pulled a blanket over himself, and turned away from her.

"Case?" Eliza called softly.

He ignored her, trying not to let the sweetness of her voice tempt him. He was better off staying angry.

Eliza waited a few moments, then dropped her head back to the pillow. Why wouldn't he answer? Was he angry? How could he be angry after the extraordinary thing they'd just shared? She rubbed the crystal, thinking hard.

Aha! She had it.

"Case," she said softly, "you needn't feel guilty. You didn't lead me on. I played a part in it, too."

When he still didn't answer, she said, "If it eases your conscience any, I found the experience heavenly."

At Case's continued silence, Eliza frowned into the darkness. Perhaps she was wrong about his guilt. Perhaps she'd appalled him, letting him touch her so intimately. Indeed, she'd

stunned herself by allowing him such liberties
when they weren't married, or even engaged!

But all those new, exciting emotions had simply overwhelmed her. That she'd completely
lost her good sense befuddled her, since she
wasn't prone to that kind of behavior at all. And
Eliza was absolutely certain there could never
be anything between them. Yet it had happened,
and there was no taking it back.

"Case, I'm sorry if my behavior shocked you.
I simply let myself get carried away. Let's put
this behind us and never speak of it again, all
right?" She waited to see if he would answer,
then added, "I'm glad I can trust you. I knew
you wouldn't take advantage of me."

She stopped and waited again, hoping for
some sign that he'd heard. Instead she caught
the sounds of deep breathing. Her intuition told
her he was pretending to sleep. But her intuition
also told her to leave him alone.

Case kept up the snoring until he was sure
Eliza was asleep, then he turned on his back and
lay staring at the canvas overhead, thinking
about what she'd said.

*"I'm glad I can trust you. I knew you wouldn't
take advantage of me."*

Damn it, he'd come so close to doing what she
trusted him *not* to, that he'd scared himself.

Case lifted his head to peer at her. Eliza was

on her side facing him, a little frown turning down those luscious lips, a crease of worry between her eyebrows. She stirred in her sleep, brushing away a stray curl with the back of her hand, then snuggling deeper into her blanket.

Case lay back with a heavy sigh. Taking advantage of her would go against his honor. No matter how much he wanted her, he would not give in to those lustful urges again.

"I've been thinking, Eileen," Frank said to the sallow-complexioned woman sitting across from him. "We need to find out the name of the Pinkerton your friend hired."

He waited as she swallowed a spoonful of chicken soup, which was about all she'd eat these days. She hadn't even touched her meat and potatoes.

"Why do you need his name?" she asked.

Frank took a potato from her plate and stuffed it in his mouth. "I know some of them." He stopped to lick the butter from his thumb and finger. "Could be the one she hired is planning to bring me in."

"Eliza wouldn't betray us like that. She only wants to help."

"Maybe she doesn't know what the cops have planned. They're tricky sons of bitches, and could easily have duped her." Frank stabbed a bite of her meat, then chewed it thoughtfully.

"Eliza should be reaching Des Moines in another day or two, so we should send that wire
today."

"Where are we going to meet them?"

"I'm not sure yet. Maybe Omaha." He finished off her potatoes and meat, and drank his
whiskey in one gulp. Omaha was right on the
Missouri River, so once he had the money, he
could hop on a southbound boat and head to
Mexico—without the sickly peahen sitting
across from him, thank God. He was tired of
waiting for her daddy to kick the bucket. Besides, there'd be more bait down Mexico way.

First, though, he needed to find out about that
Pinkerton. Ever since they'd received Eliza's last
wire, Frank had had an uneasy feeling. The
chance of the man being Brogan was slim, but it
was a chance Frank wasn't about to dismiss.

Eliza fixed the rest of the eggs and bacon for
breakfast while Case took the buggy to be re-
paired. He returned and sat down cross-legged
by the fire, watching as she dished out the food.
She had on the cream-colored calico dress, but
was minus her shoes. As Case munched on crisp
bacon, he found himself staring at her bare toes,
recalling the look of her legs, the feel of her
thighs, and the salty, tart taste of her.

*"If I were really comfortable around you, I would
take off my shoes and stockings."*

Clearly she was comfortable now, and that made him uneasy. He didn't want her to get too comfortable around him.

"Put on your shoes," he said between bites. "It's not safe to walk around in your bare feet."

"I always go barefoot at home, and you forgot to say please."

"You're not *at* home."

"My heels are sore."

Case finished his breakfast and walked to the wagon to dig out his first aid supplies. He sat down on the blanket facing her. "Give me your foot."

"That's the second order you've given me today." Eliza held out a hand. "If you'll give me the supplies, please, I'll make my own bandages."

He scowled at her for a moment, then turned over the materials. Eliza gave him a smile. "Thank you."

As Case walked away, she called, "When will the wheel be fixed?"

"The smithy didn't say. I'm going over there now to make sure he does it right."

Ye gods! Case didn't even trust the blacksmith.

At least he wasn't angry with her. It made her even more certain that he'd heard her apology last night and simply hadn't wanted to respond. That was all right with her. Seen in the clear light of day, her behavior had been shocking. She was better off putting the whole incident behind her.

But how could she look at him and not remember the tender ways he had touched her, the passion with which he had kissed her? She could pretend nothing had changed, but in her heart she knew better.

An hour later they were back on the road. Eliza pulled her shawl closer around her shoulders as she glanced up at the sky. The day had turned breezy and cool, with the smell of rain in the air and thick gray clouds blotting out the warmth of the sun.

"Looks like a storm's coming," she commented.

Case cast a wary glance upward. "I hope not. It'll slow us down."

"Yes, but look at the bright side. With the drought we've had, the farmers will be grateful."

Case shook his head and said nothing more.

Two hours later it began to pour. Eliza gratefully took Case's suggestion and sat inside the wagon, a blanket wrapped around her for warmth. She felt sorry for Case, hunched under an oilcloth slicker, the wind-driven rain pelting his face. He had on a hat, but it offered little protection.

By the time they reached Iowa City, the fierce

wind had made it nearly impossible to navigate. Case headed the wagon straight for the nearest inn.

"We're going to have to wait out the storm here," he told her, water pouring from the brim of his hat. "Take what you need from your trunks. I'll stable the horses around back and meet you inside when I'm done."

Eliza hastily pulled out her necessities and stuffed them in her traveling bag. She didn't relish another delay, but she savored the thought of a warm room and a hot meal. Before she climbed out, she checked her skirt pocket to be sure her crystal was still there, fearing a separation would break the charm's power.

The Hampstead House Inn was cozy and dry, with eight guest rooms and two baths on the second floor, and public rooms on the first floor. A charming parlor occupied the left front corner of the building, and a big dining room the right, where a midday meal was just getting started. The friendly innkeeper showed Eliza to a room so she could change into dry clothing and, if need be, spend the night.

Her room was a small but clean chamber with a high ceiling, a tall window framed in robin's-egg-blue draperies, a narrow, four-poster bed covered in a colorful log cabin quilt, a porcelain washstand and basin with a rectangular looking glass above it, and a pine armoire. Had she not been in a hurry to reach Eileen, Eliza would have loved to spend a few nights there.

She changed into a dry dress, transferred her crystal to her pocket, and checked her image in the looking glass. After closing the door behind her, she started down the hall. The wooden planks creaked as she passed the room assigned to Case. She stopped to listen and heard movement inside.

"I'm going down to the dining room," she called. "They're serving dinner now."

The dining room was as inviting as the rest of the inn. Ivy-patterned wallpaper in white, gold, and green set off the long, linen-covered oak table that dominated the room. Against one wall sat a massive golden-oak sideboard; gauze-draped windows filled the opposite wall. An ornate brass chandelier hung from the plaster ceiling, and a centerpiece of freshly cut yellow and white mums sat in a glass vase beneath it.

Eliza took a seat among the other guests and introduced herself.

"Where in Chicago do you live?" a distinguished-looking gentleman to her left asked, passing her a bowl of steaming, buttery mashed potatoes.

"On Pine Street, north of the Chicago River."

"Ah, I know that area well." He smiled at her, revealing a set of healthy teeth. Eliza smiled back. His clothing and hairstyle were a bit dreary and out-of-date, yet he seemed very pleasant.

"There are some wealthy homes in that area. Is that where you grew up?" he asked.

"No, I'm just staying with my aunt while I train to be an opera singer."

"An opera singer?" He gazed at her admiringly. "I adore opera. Will you be giving any performances? I'd love to come hear one."

Case stood in the doorway listening to their conversation with growing vexation. The man's obvious attempts to flirt with Eliza were irking him no end.

Wait a minute! Was Eliza flirting back?

A kindly lady spotted Case and invited him to sit down. He took a seat across from Eliza at the end of the table and glared at her as the bowl of potatoes and a platter of roasted pork were passed to him.

"Oh, Mr. Brogan!" Eliza said, tearing her attention away from the dandy long enough to give Case a surprised glance. "I didn't see you come in. Let me introduce you around. Case Brogan, that's Justin Hawking and his wife, Martha, at the far end; John Callen next to them; then there's Reverend Josiah Masters and his wife, Mary; and Mr. Tod Holmby to my left."

Case nodded politely as they welcomed him.

Tod. A milksop's name if he ever heard one,

especially in that dandified black suit he wore. His sideburns were too narrow, too, and his chin was weak, not to mention that he had an annoying lisp.

"Mr. Holmby is from Chicago," Eliza announced, as though that made him family.

"I understand you're with the Pinkerton agency," Holmby said, the word understand coming out as *underthtand*. His right hand bore a diamond ring—typical of a dandy.

"That's right."

"Are you after a criminal?" one of the ladies asked eagerly.

Eliza watched him intently, as though she, too, wanted to know that answer.

"I'm escorting Miss Lowe West."

"Not the sort of job the Pinkertons usually take, is it?" Holmby asked, lifting one eyebrow.

Case narrowed his eyes. "I doubt your type would understand my line of work."

Eliza's mouth fell open, and Holmby's ears turned bright red. "*My* type?" he sputtered.

"What he means," Eliza said with a conciliatory smile, "is that a refined gentleman such as yourself wouldn't have any dealings with the criminal element. Isn't that right, *Mr. Brogan*?" She gave Case a warning glance.

Case was too irritated to back down. "He knows what I mean."

Before Holmby could respond, the Reverend

Josiah Masters got to his feet, startling everyone with his booming voice: "Now that we're all gathered here, friends, let us bow our heads in prayer."

Eliza lowered her head, but her eyes were on Case. How dare he purposely instigate an argument! With a perfect stranger, no less. What had gotten into him? He'd seemed to take an instant dislike to the man, yet what did Case know about him? All the poor man had said was that he liked opera, and wanted to come hear her sing.

Eliza pursed her lips. Was it possible . . . ? No, probably not. Case didn't seem the sort, nor had he given any indication of it before. Yet she couldn't help but wonder: was he jealous?

Well, there was one way to find out.

Chapter 10

Everyone uttered an "amen" and began eating. Mary Masters engaged Tod in conversation, as did John Callen with Case, as though each were intent on preventing another argument.

"So tell me, Miss Lowe," Tod said, eventually turning away from the talkative Mrs. Masters, "what adventure takes you West?"

"How kind of you to inquire. I'm on my way to help my friend Eileen." She glanced quickly at Case, but he seemed absorbed in John's tale.

"Ah, a friend in need," Tod said, giving her his charming smile.

"Is a friend, indeed, as my aunt always says," she finished. "Eileen is expecting a child, you see, and, well . . ." Eliza paused, remembering how Case had stopped her when she'd tried to explain her mission to the sheriff. She ended her story with a sheepish shrug.

Tod clucked his tongue sympathetically. "How admirable, traveling such a great distance from home to help her. Everyone should have a loyal friend like you."

"That's kind of you to say so, but it's Eileen who's been a loyal friend. She's helped me out of more scrapes than I can remember. I've known her since I was five."

"And where was this?" Tod asked.

"Back home in Coffee Creek, Indiana," Eliza said, warming to her subject. "I had two dear friends back there—Eileen and Emeline. We were known as the Three Es."

"Charming." Tod leaned toward her and said in an intimate voice, "Please continue. I want to hear all about you."

Eliza was delighted to oblige. What a welcome change! As she recalled, Case had cut her off at exactly this point in the story.

She glanced across at Case and found him glaring at her. Perhaps he did have a jealous streak.

"Coffee Creek," Tod murmured, tapping his chin. "Where in Indiana is that?"

She drew her gaze away from Case's stony face. "Near Bloomington, down in limestone country."

"I've been down that way."

"You have? When?"

"Looks like the storm is letting up," Case suddenly announced, scraping back his chair. "Miss Lowe, we should be on our way."

All heads turned toward the window, where the wind was lashing rain against the glass.

"Son, you'd better settle in for a while," the reverend said. "That storm isn't going anywhere."

Giving the window a disgruntled glare, Case slumped against his seat back.

He endured another half hour of Tod Holmby's flirtation with Eliza. Then, when everyone headed to the parlor for songs around the piano, he pulled Eliza aside.

"Don't trust him," he warned.

Eliza gave Case a look of disbelief. "Are you referring to Mr. Holmby, by any chance?"

"You know very well I am."

"He's given me no reason not to trust him. He's given you no reason, either, for that matter."

"I know his type."

"Nonsense. He's a perfect gentleman. You'll see when you get to know him."

"I don't plan on being here that long," he called as Eliza sashayed toward the parlor. "As soon as the storm abates, we're leaving."

At the doorway, she paused to glance over her shoulder at him. "Aren't you going to join us? Tod has promised to sing with me."

Case clenched his teeth. She'd probably used that same come-hither look on Holmby. "I'd rather let my food settle. Just remember what I told you."

Case slipped out the back door, seeking the peace of the stables. The only other human around was a young stableboy who was mucking out stalls.

"Mind if I find a quiet place to rest?" he asked the boy.

"Won't bother me."

Case grabbed a hay rake and made a cozy seat against a wall at the far end, as far from the sound of the tinkling piano as he could get. He didn't like Holmby; the man was an obvious philanderer. What he did for a living Case had yet to learn, though he suspected Holmby was a cardsharp. He had that shifty-eyed look about him.

Thank goodness the reverend was there to chaperone. He didn't have to fear for Eliza's well-being with a man of the cloth nearby.

Case rested his head against the wall and closed his eyes, hoping to catch a few winks, but his mind kept going back to that dining room scene. What did Eliza see in Holmby besides his smooth, affected charm? Or was that all that mattered to her? Didn't she realize that superficial charm was what got her friend Eileen into her present difficulty?

Frank Caroni had charmed his way into the Brogans' lives, utterly beguiling his mother and father, and him, too, for a while. Even when Case had begun to understand what lay beneath that slick veneer, he still hadn't wanted to believe it. Frank had been his idol, the older brother he'd lost. Case had followed him around like an eager puppy, soaking in his words as though he'd been a prophet.

Case had also thought that Frank had adored his father and mother, treating them as though they were his real parents. So Case had kept quiet about his doubts and prayed that he was wrong.

But when the ugly truth finally came out, it was too late to save Charles Brogan.

The scene was as fresh in Case's mind as if it had happened yesterday.

He and his father had just returned from a day of fishing. His mother had been in bed, recovering from another of her ailments. A knock on the door had brought both Case and his father to see who it was.

"Hello, Charlie," one of the two police officers had said in a solemn voice. "Is Frank here?"

"Why? What did he do?" Case's father had asked.

"He's back to his old ways again, Charlie. Only this time he battered one of his victims."

Case remembered how the news had crushed his father. "Come on in, boys," he'd said grimly. "I'll see if he's here. Case, why don't you take the fishing poles to the cellar?"

Case had taken the poles around to the back of the house. He'd just started down the cellar steps when he saw someone move in the shadows below. "Frank?" he called.

"Shut up and close the doors. The cops are after me."

"They're already here, Frank. You'd better turn yourself in."

"Shit. And go to jail? No one's ever gonna lock me up again. I spent five years in a prison they called an orphanage. That was enough. Now get out of here, and don't tell anyone you saw me."

Case had stepped out of the cellar, unsure of what to do. But then his father had walked around the corner. He'd taken one look at Case's face and he'd known.

"Frank?" he'd called, walking slowly down the steps. "It's no use hiding, son. I know what you've done."

"You've got it wrong, Charlie," Caroni had said, stepping into the square of daylight at the bottom of the stairs. "They're just pinning it on me because they don't like me."

"Don't lie to me, Frank. You're in enough trouble as it is. You knew this was your last chance, and now you have to take responsibility for what you've done. It's time to act like a man."

When Case's father had held out a pair of handcuffs, Frank had backed up, crying, "Wait, Charlie, please. You can't turn me in. Would you turn in your son?"

"My son wouldn't betray my trust."

Frank had clasped his hands beseechingly. "I know you don't want me to go to jail. You care what happens to me."

"That's right; I do care. And that's why I have to take you in. Turn around, Frank."

"I'm *not* going to jail, Charlie."

That's when everything had begun to move in slow motion: a knife glinting in Caroni's hand; his arm arcing down, the blade sinking into his father's chest; his father collapsing; Case's own cry of agony, running down the stairs, stumbling, blinded by tears, cradling his father in his arms as his life's blood seeped out of him.

In the chaos, Frank Caroni had slipped away.

That event had not only destroyed Case's secure world, it had also defined his life. And now, after ten long years of waiting, the day of reckoning was almost here.

"Hey, mister, you feeling okay?"

Case opened his eyes and saw the stableboy hovering anxiously. "I'm fine."

"You're shaking. Wanna blanket?"

Case realized his teeth were chattering. "Sure."

The lad pulled a horse blanket off a low wall and handed it to Case, who wrapped it around his shoulders and drew his knees up. "Thanks."

"Why are you out here, mister, instead of inside with the others?"

"I like the quiet."

The kid hunkered down beside Case, leaned against the wall, and stuck a piece of straw in his mouth. "Me, too."

"What's your name?"

"Henry."

"How old are you, Henry?"

"Almost sixteen."

"You live around here?"

"Up there," he said, pointing to the loft.

Case glanced up in surprise, then took a closer look at the boy. He was good-looking kid, although he could have used a bath and a decent haircut. He had wide-set brown eyes, unruly brown hair, and a gap between his front teeth. His brown pants hit him too high on the leg, as though he'd grown several inches in the past few months; his shoes were worn down to the point of not having any heels; his socks were ragged at the top; and his dingy, collarless shirt had holes worn through at both elbows.

"You get room and board here?" Case asked.

"Yes, sir."

"Parents?"

"Don't have any."

"How long have you been here?"

"Since my ma died two years ago."

"Any brothers or sisters?"

"Seven."

Case stared incredulously. "Do you all live up there?"

"No. They got homes. I was too old." He looked away, but not before Case saw the stark loneliness in his eyes.

"Where's your father, Henry?"

The boy shrugged skinny shoulders. "He left when I was eight. I heard he went up north somewhere, maybe to Canada."

Who saw that the boy had decent clothes to wear? Who made sure he was warm at night and had food in his belly? Who even cared if he lived or died? Case's mother had always been sickly, but at least she'd cared about him. Yet what could he do for this kid? He couldn't provide him a home.

"What do you want to do when you grow up, Henry?"

He ducked his head shyly. "You're gonna laugh."

"No, I won't." Case nearly added, *"Trust me,"* but he bit back those words. Why should Henry trust him? He was a stranger.

He found himself wishing it anyway, and was stunned when it came true.

"I want to write stories."

"What kind of stories?"

Henry got on his knees, his eyes shimmering with excitement. "Adventure stories. I've read lots of books about jungles and deserts and mountains, and I've got all kinds of tales in my head."

"That's great, Henry. Have you ever written any of them down?"

The excitement in the boy's eyes dimmed. "I don't have anything to write on, and I can't afford to buy paper. Besides, I don't spell worth a tinker's dam anyway."

"I think I have some paper in the wagon. I'll leave it for you and you can do what you want with it."

"That's kind of you, mister."

"Name's Brogan." Case studied him a moment, then said, "Did you know there have been storytellers since the beginning of mankind, Henry?"

"There have?"

"You can be sure of it."

Henry chewed on his straw, clearly pondering Case's words. "What do *you* do, Mr. Brogan?"

"I'm a Pinkerton detective."

"What's that?"

"Kind of a cop. I look for bad guys."

"Is that what you always wanted to be?"

Case shrugged. "My father was a cop. I wanted to honor his memory after he died."

"Then why didn't you just become a cop?"

"Because I like working alone. And because I need to be able to do my work outside of Chicago."

"Why?"

"Because I have to find the man who killed my father."

The boy was all ears. "Was it a shoot-out? Did he catch someone robbing a bank?"

"Something like that."

"Are you gonna have a shoot-out when you find him?"

"No, Henry, it won't be a contest to see who's got the fastest draw. This man is going to pay for what he did."

"You're gonna kill him, aren't ya?"

Uncomfortable, Case got to his feet, put the blanket away, and looked out the window. "Looks like there's a break in the weather. Come on, Henry. We're going to get you some new clothes."

The boy looked stunned. "Why?"

Case put his arms around Henry's shoulders and walked him out the wide doors. "Because your ankles are hanging out, and no girl is going to look at a fellow whose ankles are hanging out, especially when they're as skinny as yours are. You do like girls, don't you?"

"Sure do."

Case laughed. "Then we've got to get you a courting outfit, Henry."

His eyes widened in alarm. "Courtin'? Aw, I don't know about that."

"You want to get married someday, don't you?"

"*Some*day."

"Well, Henry, let me give you a tip: it takes a long time to find the right woman. This will give you a head start."

Holding the umbrella close to her side, Eliza drew back behind one of the big stable doors as Case and the boy stepped out and headed for the street. She hadn't meant to eavesdrop; she'd come looking for Case.

But poor Henry! She couldn't believe he lived in a hayloft. Regardless of his age, someone should have given him a home. What did he do in the winter? Wasn't there a church in town? Surely a minister could've helped.

Eliza immediately thought of Reverend Masters and his wife. They were such a nice couple, and their children were grown. They lived in Des Moines, which wasn't too far away. If they took him in, Henry could still visit his siblings. The important thing was that he have a home.

Eliza opened her borrowed umbrella and started back to the inn, her thoughts turning to what she had learned about Case. His need for revenge seemed to dominate his life. She suspected the death of his father had also played a part in his cynical view of the world.

Eliza paused as a horrible thought came to mind. Could Case suspect Francis of his father's murder? What was it he had once told her? That Frank Caroni had been wanted for ten years?

Ten years ago Case would have been sixteen, the age he was when his father was killed. "Oh, please let that be a coincidence," she whispered.

Eliza hurried up the stairs and into the inn. She could only deal with one problem at a time, and the easiest one was Henry's.

Some of the guests were still gathered in the parlor, the Masterses among them. "Reverend, could I speak with you and your wife in private?" she asked.

"Of course, child," the preacher said kindly. "Our room is at the top of the stairs. Why don't we adjourn there?"

A second storm hit just moments after Case and Henry returned. The boy took his new purchases to the stable, while Case went to the inn to find Eliza. She was bound to be wondering where he'd gone.

He checked the parlor first, but only two people were there, reading quietly. He looked in the dining room and found it empty, then went upstairs to see if Eliza had decided to take a nap.

As he reached the top of the stairs, he heard the familiar, bubbly sound of her laughter, followed by a deep male voice. His fists clenched as he stood at the door. Was she in there alone with that philanderer Holmby?

Case was just reaching for the doorknob when John Callen leaned out of the next room, spotted him, and whispered, "Mr. Brogan, come here."

Case stepped cautiously into Callen's room and glanced around. "What is it?"

Callen checked the hallway, then quietly closed his door. "I knew I'd seen Holmby's face before. Take a look at this item I found in the newspaper."

Curious, Case took the paper, which was from Quincy, Illinois, a town along the Mississippi River. He skimmed the article, which said Tod Holmby was a riverboat gambler wanted for theft. During a poker game on the boat's stop at Quincy, Holmby had fleeced the mayor, who was now trying to put a halt to his game.

"I picked up the paper on my way through

Quincy the other day," Callen explained, "and just now finished reading it. You being a Pinkerton and all, I thought you'd be interested, especially since you and Holmby didn't exactly—"

Case didn't wait to hear the rest. Eliza was alone with the cur!

Chapter 11

Eliza left the reverend's room smiling victoriously. The Masterses had been just as appalled by poor Henry's situation as she had, and had agreed to meet with the lad to see what could be done.

The door across the hall opened and Tod Holmby stepped out. "Miss Lowe! I was just coming to find you. The Hawkings and I were having a little gathering in my room and—" He peered at her more closely. "What is it? You look like the proverbial cat who swallowed a canary."

"Oh, I have such wonderful, happy news."

"That sounds like a reason to celebrate. Come join us and I shall produce the means to do so. I have a wonderful bottle of red wine tucked away in my bag." Holmby hooked his arm through Eliza's and steered her into his room.

"But I should let Mr. Brogan know the news, too."

"There's plenty of time for that. Look, everyone, who I found!" he called to his guests.

Eliza really wanted to let Case know her news first, but she hated to be rude to Tod and the Hawkings.

"Now for the glasses," Tod said, heading toward the door. "I believe I saw a cabinet downstairs in the parlor."

As he stepped out the door, a fist shot out and connected with his jaw, knocking Holmby to the hallway floor.

With a cry of alarm, Eliza rushed to where Tod lay and dropped down beside him. She glanced up to see Case standing at the man's feet. "Why did you hit him?"

"Why were you in his room?"

"He invited me in."

"Alone?" Case asked, just as the Hawkings, and the Masterses from the other side, stepped out to see what the ruckus was.

"As you can see, I was *not* alone! Now, for heaven's sake, go fetch an ice pack! Mr. Holmby? Mr. Holmby, please wake up!"

"I'll get ice," John Callen said, sidestepping them.

As more of the guests gathered at the top of

the stairs, Holmby opened his eyes and looked around, dazed, until he saw Case, and then his eyes came into sharp focus. "What did you do that for?" he asked, massaging his jaw.

Case let the newspaper drop beside him. "Seems you're a wanted man, Holmby."

"I don't know what you're talking about."

"Play any poker with Quincy's mayor lately?"

Holmby snatched up the paper and read the article. Eliza leaned over to read it with him, then pulled back, staring at Holmby in surprise.

"This isn't me!" Holmby declared. "They printed the wrong name. I have a twin brother named Tad. He's the gambler. I'm a mortician."

"A twin?" Case said with obvious skepticism.

"A mortician?" Eliza asked squeamishly.

As the others whispered together behind him, Holmby pulled out a wallet, removed a faded photo, and handed it to Case. "Yes, a twin. And yes, a mortician."

Case studied the photo with a skeptical eye, then handed it back. Eliza gave Case an "I told you so" look, then helped Holmby to his feet. "You should be ashamed," she whispered to Case as she passed him.

Case bent to pick up the discarded newspaper as Callen and the two ladies hurried into Holmby's room behind Eliza to minister to the injured man. There was still no good reason for

Eliza to trust Holmby. Being a mortician didn't make him less of a philanderer.

Case glanced out the window. Damn it. Why wouldn't that storm end?

Violet Lowe passed the tray of sweets to her best friend Mabel, then removed a slice of spice cake for herself, sighing in ecstasy as she bit into it. Spice cake was her weakness—along with crumb cake, rum cake, and, well, just about any kind of cake imaginable. She settled back on the rose damask sofa with a contented smile.

"So what adventure is darling Eliza off on this time?" Mabel asked. She had come over for their weekly coffee and gossip session, an event Violet always enjoyed.

She washed her cake down with coffee, then sat forward, eager to share the news. "Eliza's on her way West to rescue her best friend from a dire predicament."

"My dear!" Mabel exclaimed, her brown eyes twinkling with excitement. "A rescue! Tell me all about it."

"Well," said Violet, snuggling up to the subject, "Eliza's dear friend Eileen and her husband, Francis, are in terrible trouble, and you know our Eliza—she had to rush to her friend's aid. The poor thing is with child, after all! One could hardly ignore her plea for help. Of course, I've hired a Pinkerton man to accompany Eliza. I wouldn't dream of letting a hair on her head come to harm."

"What is this terrible trouble?"

"Mr. Caroni—that's Eileen's husband—has been mistakenly identified in a crime, and they must prove his innocence before he's jailed."

"Caroni, you say." Mabel shook her head in disbelief. "Now there's a name from the past."

"What do you mean?"

"Surely you remember about ten years back when my neighbor, Officer Brogan, was brutally murdered by his young ward? *His* name was Caroni. Frank Caroni, I believe." Her eyes opened wide. "Did you say this man's name was Francis?"

Violet paled. "Oh, dear. You don't think this is the same man?"

"How many Francis Caronis could there be?" Mabel asked calmly.

Violet set her cup and plate on the table and rose, bustling back and forth in front of the hearth as she thought aloud. "There must be more than one Francis Caroni. But how can I be sure? Who would know?"

"The Pinkertons would certainly know."

"Yes! Of course they would. I can always count on you to keep your head in times of stress, Mabel. I must go see my friend Malcomb Riley. He's the one who told me Mr. Brogan would be perfect for the job." Violet gasped.

"Oh, dear! Do you suppose that's why Malcomb recommended Mr. Brogan?"

"There's one way to find out," Mabel said, pinning on her hat. "I'll take you there at once."

An hour later, Violet and Mabel sat in chairs across from Assistant Chief Malcomb Riley, anxiously waiting for his answer.

"Yes, ladies," he said gravely. "Francis Caroni and Frank Caroni are one in the same."

Violet's stomach gave a great shudder. To think that Eliza's best friend was married to a murderer!

"Is that why you assigned Mr. Brogan to this case?" Mabel asked.

"One of the reasons."

Violet sat forward on her seat. "Then surely Mr. Brogan has told Eliza about Francis Caroni."

Riley gave a doubtful shake of his head. "Not likely. Brogan wouldn't want her to know until after he locates Caroni. It could unduly influence your niece's behavior."

"But she needs to know for that very reason! Good heavens, Malcomb, she's meeting a *killer*." Violet grabbed her handbag and rose. "I must find a way to stop Eliza before she gets hurt—or worse."

"Don't get yourself in a dither, Violet," Riley told her. "Brogan knows how the man thinks and how he acts. If anyone can protect your niece, it's Case Brogan. Trust me, he knows what he's doing."

Violet sank into the seat and dabbed her upper lip with her handkerchief.

"Just what does Mr. Brogan intend to do when he finds Francis Caroni?" Mabel asked.

Riley leaned back in his chair, folded his hands across his stomach, and studied the women thoughtfully. "I honestly don't know."

"Mabel, I can't let Eliza go blindly into such a dangerous situation," Violet said as they proceeded down the steps to the sidewalk. "She must be forewarned."

"I agree wholeheartedly, Vi. What do you propose to do?"

"Her last telegram said she was headed to Des Moines. She always stops at the telegraph office to check for messages. I'll send a telegram there and let her know the entire truth."

Case sat grimly through a supper that seemed to drag on for hours. He'd managed to snag the seat to Eliza's left but, unfortunately, Holmby had taken the chair across from her, which put him directly in the path of her beguiling glances. Case's only consolation was the big purple bruise on Holmby's jaw.

There were five at the table that evening. Mrs. Hawking had pleaded a headache, and the Masterses had chosen to dine in their room with Henry, to get to know one another.

Case couldn't help but admire Eliza's maneuvering in that respect. He hadn't yet figured out how she'd learned of the boy's predicament. He probably wouldn't learn it anytime soon, either, since she wasn't speaking to him.

And it was still raining cats and dogs.

"Don't you agree, Mr. Brogan?"

Case stopped chewing and turned his head to glance at Eliza in surprise. She'd spoken to him! *And* she thought he'd been paying attention.

"Absolutely."

He had no idea what he had just agreed to, but receiving that enchanting smile made it worthwhile. She'd forgiven him.

Eliza held his gaze for a moment, a slight blush coloring her cheeks, then she turned back to Holmby, who had continued to rattle on as though there'd been no interruption. Case had ceased listening to him the moment he'd opened his big mouth.

From the corner of his eye, Case watched Eliza lift her fork to her lips and slide a bite of chicken inside. His groin tightened as he remembered their first meal together, at the Palmer House, when every bite she'd taken had seemed suggestively sensual. Then, as now, he'd wanted to pull her onto his lap and kiss her until her head swam.

Eliza put her fork down and lifted her napkin to her mouth. Ah, how he remembered the taste of those lips, and of the scented skin of her throat. His manhood throbbed as he recalled the velvety feel of her nipples, and the tart taste of her. Damn, he wanted to scoop her up and carry her off to his room that moment. Let Holmby turn green with envy!

He finished off his wine and glowered at the man.

With the reverend gone, Case had no choice but to stick close to Eliza after the meal was over. While she, Holmby, and the Hawkings played a game of whist at the table on one end of the parlor, Case sat at the other end and read the newspaper from front to back, then thumbed through a book without really seeing it.

"Fond of poetry?"

Case glanced up to see Mary Masters reading over his shoulder. "Is that what this is?" he muttered, looking at the cover.

She laughed and indicated a seat next to his. "May I join you? My husband is busy talking with Henry about male matters."

"Please."

Mary settled herself in one of the two blue wingbacked chairs and looked around the spacious room, which was filled with comfortable chairs, two sofas, a settee, a piano, numerous ornate lamps, and the game table.

As her gaze fell on Eliza, she said, "Your charge is quite a remarkable young woman, Mr. Brogan."

Case's glance shifted to Eliza, who was laughing at something Holmby said. "Remarkable in her naiveté."

"Naiveté can be quite an endearing quality."

"I'd say it's more detrimental than endearing."

Mary studied him intently, making him squirm inside. "You're smitten with her, aren't you?"

Case gave her a look of disbelief. "Smitten? She irritates me no end."

"She's gotten under your skin."

"Like poison ivy."

Mary smiled knowingly. "That's jealousy talking."

"Jealous? Of a mortician?"

"I didn't say of whom, but yes."

With a frown, Case leaned back in his chair. "I was hired to protect Miss Lowe. That's all there is between us."

Mary patted his hand. "I understand. That's all there *can* be between you—for now. But don't let her get away. You may not realize this yet, but she complements you."

They paused as the game ended and the four cardplayers rose.

"Will you join me in a glass of brandy?" Holmby asked Eliza.

"Is it still raining?" she replied.

Holmby strode to the window and drew back the drape. "Still raining."

"Then I suppose we'll be spending the night," Eliza said, glancing at Case for confirmation. Receiving a steely nod, she gave Holmby her wide smile. "I'd love to have a glass of brandy with you."

Case watched her hips swing enticingly as she walked over to a blue flowered sofa and sat down. He saw Holmby watching her, too.

"She's teasing you," Mary cautioned. "She's trying to discover your feelings for her."

"How do you know?"

Mary laughed. "I may be old, but I haven't forgotten what it feels like to be in love." She looked around as her husband walked into the room, and her face was transformed.

Case had a sudden image of what she'd looked like as a young woman. Clearly, she was still deeply in love with her husband. He watched enviously as the reverend strolled over, took her hand, and kissed it.

"Shall we retire, my dear?" he asked, lifting a shaggy eyebrow.

"Will you excuse us, Mr. Brogan?" Mary asked.

When they left the room, Case glanced at the book of poetry in his lap, then set it aside with a scowl. Jealous? Of a mortician? Ha! He'd prove he wasn't jealous. He'd leave Eliza alone with the man.

That idea lasted less than ten seconds. Case couldn't leave her alone with him, and it wasn't due to jealousy. He just didn't trust the miscreant.

Eliza hid a yawn, then held her hand over her glass to prevent Tod from refilling it. "I really shouldn't."

"You'll sleep better."

"I'm nearly asleep right now." She stifled another yawn. "I really must turn in. I'm sure we'll be getting an early start in the morning."

"I'll see you to your room."

Eliza rose and accepted his arm, relieved to be finally ridding herself of the man. Notwithstanding that he worked with dead bodies, she'd had enough of Tod's stories to last a lifetime. Charming though he was, his constant efforts to impress her had worn thin. She was beginning to appreciate Case's quietness.

Eliza glanced at Case as they passed by, but he was absorbed in a book. The only reason she'd endured Tod as long as she had was to spark a little more jealousy in Case. But whatever flicker she'd seen earlier had been doused.

Perhaps it hadn't been there at all. She didn't like that one bit.

No, wait. She *did* like that, because she certainly didn't want Case to fall in love with her. That would be a disaster from start to finish.

Yet hadn't he looked maddeningly handsome as he'd conversed with Mary Masters? With his thick brown hair gleaming in the lamplight, his white shirt open casually at the collar, his long legs stretched out in front of him, and his strong, capable hands folded on top of the book in his lap, he'd made it very difficult to concentrate on the game. Eliza desperately wished she could've heard what they were saying.

"Well, good night, Mr. Holmby," she said, standing at her door.

"Can I talk you into a nightcap?"

"I'm afraid you'd be talking *to* the nightcap. I'd fall fast asleep with my glass in hand."

Tod lifted her fingers to his lips, lingering over them as he said silkily, "Perhaps it will storm all day tomorrow and you'll be here another day."

Ye gods! What a dreadful thought. Eliza eased her hand from his grasp. "Yes, that would be nice. Well, thank you for your hospitality."

"If you'd like some company later . . ." He lifted an eyebrow suggestively.

Eliza leaned closer to whisper, "Mr. Brogan keeps very close tabs on me."

He winked and whispered back, "I understand." Then, as John Callen passed by, he said
in a normal voice, "I still want to come see you
in an opera."

"Oh, I haven't forgotten." She stepped back
into her room and closed the door halfway.
"Good night, then."

"Good night, Miss Lowe. It's been a pleasure." He winked again.

She shut the door and leaned against it, heaving a big sigh of relief. The man was an absolute
bore. She turned up a gas lamp, illuminating the
cozy room with a soft yellow glow, then she removed her shoes and stockings. She'd just
begun unfastening the buttons of her blouse
when a sharp rap on the door made her jump.
"Who is it?"

"Brogan."

She broke into a smile. Case was checking to
see if Tod was in her room! A sure sign of jealousy if there ever was one. "Just a minute," she
said, taking time to compose her face. She was
supposed to be angry.

She opened the door halfway. "Yes?"

His eyes narrowed as he took in her bare feet
and partially unbuttoned bodice. "Are you
alone?"

She gave him a coy glance. "If I said no,
would you be upset?"

"If you said no, I'd be right."

"Right about what?"

"About trusting Holmby."

Trust again! "Well, I *am* alone," Eliza exclaimed.

His skeptical look further exasperated her. She opened the door wide and marched over to the narrow four-poster. "Would you like to search under the bed?" she asked, lifting the hem of the quilt. Then she pivoted and strode to the window. "Or perhaps behind the drape? Ah! I know. In the armoire!"

"All right, Miss Lowe," Case ground out. "I believe you."

Eliza padded up and stared him full in the face, her hands on her hips. "Are you saying you trust me?"

His gaze traveled slowly from her bare toes to her throat, lingering for a long moment on the opened buttons, and then his voice grew husky. "I said I *believe* you."

"You *believe* that I'm alone. Isn't that the same as trust? Couldn't you also say you *trust* that I'm alone?"

Case clasped her shoulders and drew her against him for a smoldering kiss.

Eliza stiffened her mouth and pushed against his chest, infuriated by his rudeness. But as his lips gentled hers, she melted and began to kiss him back, her passion climbing at the intoxicating taste and scent of his skin, the scratch of his beard, the hardness of his muscular body.

"I've wanted to do that all evening," he whispered against her mouth, then pressed kisses down her throat.

"Me, too," she whispered back.

Case kissed her again, groping behind him to give the door a hard shove, shutting out the world. Having Eliza in his arms emptied his thoughts of everything but his pressing need for her. His blood surged through his veins, his passion inflamed to heights he'd never imagined.

He backed her to the bed and lowered her to the quilt, his hands on either side of her shoulders, his chest brushing erotically against her nipples, his legs pressing against her thighs, letting her feel his arousal. He slipped a hand between their bodies and undid the rest of her buttons, impatient to feel her naked breasts once again, relishing the silken texture of her nipples.

Case's desire surged again as Eliza moaned softly beneath him, her hips rocking against his groin. Oh, yes. He'd make her forget about Holmby, all right.

Chapter 12

No sooner had Case thought it than he heard a soft scratching on the door, then a male voice called quietly, "Miss Lowe?"

Holmby!

Case pressed his fingers against Eliza's lips, whispering in her ear, "Don't answer. I want to see what he does."

She removed his fingers and whispered back, "He won't do anything. I told you he's a gentleman."

"We'll see." Case turned off the gas lamp and pressed himself flat against the wall at the head of the bed. Nearly flat, anyway, since he was aroused and as stiff as a board.

"Miss Lowe?" The door opened quietly, revealing a man's silhouette outlined in the soft glow of the hall light. Holmby closed the door behind him, then crept across the room toward the bed. Case braced himself to spring just as Eliza spoke.

"Mr. Holmby, what are you doing here?"

"Sweet Eliza, I couldn't stay away. Your beauty has enslaved me."

"Mr. Holmby," she said indignantly, "this is quite improper. You must leave."

"Ah, now you're playing the coquette. All right, if that's what you want, I can play along."

"I'm not playing anything!" she protested.

Case quickly turned up the lamp to find Holmby leaning over her. Holmby's head jerked around, his eyes widened in shock, then he jumped away from the bed.

"Don't you dare hit me," he said, holding a hand over his bruised jaw.

Case took a threatening step toward him. "I ought to break your nose."

"This isn't what it seems, Mr. Brogan. I—I thought Miss Lowe was encouraging my attentions," Holmby stuttered, backing to the door. He glanced at Eliza guiltily. "It seems I was mistaken."

"You were mistaken, all right," Case growled.

Holmby reached behind him, found the doorknob, and opened it. Before Case could take another step, the man fled. His footsteps thundered down the steps and then a door slammed somewhere below.

Case shut the bedroom door and turned. "There goes your gentleman," he said dryly.

Eliza pushed to a sitting position and buttoned her blouse. "As Mr. Holmby said, he misunderstood my attentions."

"The way you were flirting, who wouldn't have?"

"I was only being courteous to the man," she retorted, sliding off the bed.

"Courteous my—" Case caught himself before a profanity slipped out. "You were trying to make me jealous."

"I was trying to prove a theory, which I did—admirably. Mr. Holmby simply responded as any man would, as *you* did, in fact, before he showed up."

"Yes, but—" Case began, then realized she had a point. He finished thinly, "I've known you longer."

She made a scoffing sound. "As if that mattered."

"Didn't I warn you not to trust him?"

"I could have handled the situation myself."

Case gave a sharp sigh of exasperation. "Would you just admit for once that I was right?"

Eliza clasped her hands behind her back and stared down at her bare toes peeking from beneath her hem, as though mulling over his request. Case wasn't fooled; he'd seen that stubborn look before and knew she wasn't about to admit anything.

She looked up and gave him an impish smile. "All right, I'll admit it. This once, you were right."

Case was too surprised to speak, but then he saw that devilish twinkle in her eye and he knew she had something up her sleeve. She'd made that admission just a little too quickly. However, it was best not to tempt fate. He was still aroused, and that made the situation doubly dangerous.

Eliza walked to the door and opened it. "Good night," she said a little too cheerily.

"Lock your door and don't let *anyone* in, including me." He stepped into the hall and closed the door behind him, only to have her open it again.

"You *were* jealous." She grinned. "That's why you came to check on me."

Case swung around to protest, but Eliza quickly shut her door and turned the key in its lock.

Jealous! Ha.

All right, maybe he was a little jealous, but he'd never admit it to her. And what in heaven's name had made him blurt out that he'd wanted to kiss her all evening?

Case let himself into his room and began to undress. He supposed he should thank Holmby for the interruption; he'd come alarmingly close to losing all reason.

Eliza had bewitched him. There simply wasn't any other explanation.

But at least he'd accomplished one goal: he'd finally proven to Eliza that she shouldn't be so trusting.

Eliza hummed, "O soave fanciulla," her favorite aria from *La Bohème* as she undressed and brushed out her hair. No man could have kissed her like that and not been at least a little bit jealous of another man's attentions.

How embarrassing for Tod. She'd believed the poor man when he'd said he'd been mistaken. After all, she *had* flirted with him; she just hadn't stopped to consider how it might have influenced him to pursue her. She'd been too intent on the effect it was having on Case.

No matter what Case thought, however, he hadn't changed her mind about trusting Tod. She could very easily have dissuaded Tod's attentions with one sound slap on the face that would have sent him scurrying back to his room in shame.

But Case had been so proud to be her defender that she hadn't had the heart to shatter that notion. She hadn't lied, either. After all, he *had* known her longer than Tod. He'd been right about *that*.

Eliza pulled the brush slowly through her hair, remembering the passion that had sparked between her and Case, remembering how he'd shoved that door shut and backed her to the bed, how his eyes had darkened as he'd leaned over her. It had been so very stimulating.

Auntie Vi would be appalled. She'd shake her finger and warn Eliza very sternly that she was playing with fire. But Auntie Vi didn't know Case as she did.

How was it that she felt she knew him so well, though, when they'd met only six days ago?

When Case and Eliza stepped out onto the front porch of the inn the next morning, Henry had already brought the horses and wagon around. He had on his new work pants, suspenders, shirt, sturdy boots, and even a new cap. He stood proudly as Eliza exclaimed over his clothing and gave him a hug. He accepted Case's gift of writing paper, then solemnly shook hands and thanked him for his generosity.

As they pulled away Eliza waved a final goodbye to the Masterses, who had risen early to see them off. Tod Holmby, Case noted with satisfaction, was nowhere to be seen.

Eliza had on her cream-colored calico dress,

her new hat, and, for the moment at least, her tan leather shoes. Her blue eyes seemed to sparkle beneath the hat brim, and her cheeks glowed with good health, making her the picture of a country maid. Case wished he could imprint that moment in his mind to capture it forever.

"Henry and the Masterses really seem to be taken with one another," Eliza remarked.

"How did you learn of Henry's plight?"

"I overheard you talking to him in the stables."

"I didn't see you there."

"Of course you didn't," she replied, adjusting the brim of her hat. "Henry wouldn't have wanted me to know. It would have hurt his pride."

"But he would have thanked you for what you did."

"I didn't do it to be thanked. He needed a home—and clothing. That was very generous of you to buy them. Didn't he look adorable?"

"Never call a fellow adorable."

Eliza laughed, and Case found himself grinning along with her. The sun was shining, the birds were singing, and he was alone with Eliza once again.

Alone with Eliza. When had he started looking forward to that?

* * *

"This is the flattest land I've ever seen," Eliza later remarked, as she gazed out at the endless sea of prairie grass.

"Monotonous," Case agreed.

"It certainly makes me appreciate the forests. Have you ever seen a mountain?" Eliza asked. "I'd love to see a mountain one day."

"I'd like to see one right now."

Eliza laughed. "I even miss the hustle-bustle of Chicago."

"I thought you were a country girl."

"Oh, I am. But I love Chicago, too."

"What I wouldn't give to be walking down Randolph Street right now," Case said longingly.

"Or State Street, gazing in the store windows."

"Getting splashed by passing wagons."

"Or having tea at Marshall Fields."

She sighed, wishing it were suppertime. They'd stopped midday to eat and stretch their legs, but that seemed ages ago. They hadn't come to any towns in a good while, either.

"Do you think we'll reach Des Moines by nightfall?" she asked hopefully.

"It'd be nice."

It would also be nice if Eileen was waiting for her there, Eliza thought. How dreadful it must be to have to hide from the law, always fearing capture. She couldn't help wondering why

Francis hadn't just turned himself in and explained the problem. Surely he could clear his name much quicker that way, not to mention that he could spare his pregnant wife the misery.

There was nothing to do but trust that Francis had good reasons for his decision, and that everything would work out for the best. She just wished Case hadn't put doubts in her mind about him.

Eliza patted the crystal tucked safely in her skirt pocket, only to realize it wasn't there. "Oh, no!" she cried. "My crystal is gone."

"Is it in the other pocket?"

Eliza searched both pockets again, then climbed into the back to hunt through her travel bag.

"Did you leave it at the inn?" Case called.

Eliza rubbed her temples. "I remember putting it on the bedside table beside the lamp yesterday evening. But I don't remember what I did with it this morning."

"I'll bet Holmby took it."

Eliza climbed out and settled on the bench. "For heaven's sake, why would he do that?"

"As a memento." At her look of disbelief he added, "I was right about not trusting him, wasn't I?"

"He didn't take my crystal," she scoffed.

"Who else was in your room?"

"You."

Case threw her a disgruntled look. "Besides me."

"No one that I know of. Perhaps it was inadvertently knocked off the table when you and I—" She felt herself redden.

"I still say Holmby took it."

"I'm sure it'll be found when the room is cleaned. I'll wire the inn when we get to Des Moines to let them know where to send it."

Case glanced over at her. She sounded confident, yet he could see by the furrows between her eyebrows that Eliza was worried. It seemed ridiculous to him; it was only a piece of clear rock.

"I think I'll walk for a while," she said.

Case halted the wagon so she could climb down. He decided to join her, and together they led the horses toward the setting sun.

They reached Des Moines by early evening, traveling straight through with only a few short stops to feed and water the horses. Eliza was so hungry her head pounded, but she felt an urgency to reach Eileen, an instinctive feeling that all was not well.

"Do you believe in intuition, Mr. Brogan?" she asked as they hunted for the telegraph office.

"I believe in facts."

"Well, I believe in intuition, and right now it's telling me that something is wrong with Eileen."

"Because you lost your crystal?"

"No, I just have a strong sense that something is wrong."

Once they located the Western Union office, Case let Eliza off while he went to park the wagon. She hurried to the door just as a boy of about thirteen turned the sign in the window to CLOSED.

"Hello?" she called, knocking on the glass. "Can you open up? This is an emergency."

"Come back in the morning," the boy called.

"I can't wait that long."

The door opened a crack. "Mr. VanTil went home, and I can't help you. I just clean up."

"Can't you at least check to see if I have a message? It's very important."

The boy scratched his head a moment, then said, "What's your name?"

Eliza gave him the information and waited anxiously as he went to look. She turned to glance up the street and saw the wagon parked one block away. Where had Case gone?

The boy returned a few moments later with an envelope, which Eliza instantly tore open. Her hope faded as she read the message. There wasn't a clue as to how Eileen was faring, only a question about Case and instructions for the next leg of their journey.

While she waited for Case, Eliza wrote out a message to her aunt and one to the Hampstead House Inn. "Can I leave these messages to be wired out first thing in the morning?" she asked the boy.

He shrugged. "I guess so."

Eliza gave him the slips of paper, then turned as Case walked into the office. "I was beginning to worry about you," she told him.

"Did you get your telegram?"

"We have to go to Omaha, Nebraska," she said dejectedly.

"Is that where we're meeting them?"

"It doesn't say." Eliza handed him the piece of paper. "They want to know your name."

Case scowled as he read it. "Caroni's being purposely vague," he told Eliza, handing her back the wire. "But it's easy enough to figure him out. They'll be in Omaha."

"How do you know?"

"Experience."

As Case scratched out a brief message on one of the pads of paper at the counter, the young boy said, "It's getting late. My ma's gonna fret."

"I'll make it worth your while," Case assured him. He showed the wire to Eliza.

LEAVING TODAY FOR OMAHA. SEE YOU SOON.

He hadn't given his name, which didn't surprise Eliza. Still, she felt bad withholding the information from her best friend.

Case handed the paper to the boy, along with the fee and a generous tip. "Will you make certain this is sent out tomorrow?"

The boy's eyes widened at the size of the tip. "I sure will."

"Let's go find a place to stay," Case said to Eliza.

The nearest hotel was only a few blocks from the telegraph office. Eliza packed some necessities and signed in while Case saw to the horses and wagon. It was becoming a familiar routine.

As they ate a late meal at the hotel's restaurant, Eliza mulled over the telegram. She knew it wouldn't matter to Eileen what Case's name was. Why did it matter to Francis?

"You're too quiet," Case commented.

"I was just thinking." Eliza propped her chin on her hand and studied Case as he sopped up the peppery chicken gravy with his last bite of bread. "Eileen will know something's amiss when she gets our telegram."

"Because you didn't tell her my name? Say you forgot, and explain later."

Eliza sighed morosely. "I don't like lying to her."

"What's more important, a little white lie or

her safety? If she's as good a friend as you say she is, she'll understand."

"Exactly what is it you think Francis will do if he learns your name?"

Case picked up his cup of coffee and took a sip. "Run."

"Why?"

"He knows me."

"The man called *Frank* knows you," Eliza corrected.

Case put down his cup down with a clatter and leaned forward, his eyes as hard as flint. "Do you want to help your friend?"

"You know I do."

"Then listen to me carefully. Frank Caroni and Francis Caroni are the *same man*, and you're only fooling yourself to believe otherwise. If Caroni finds out I'm with you, I promise you he'll run, and if it's in his best interests, he'll drag your friend with him. Otherwise, he'll leave her along the roadside—or worse. In her condition, is that what you want to happen?"

Eliza adamantly shook her head as that cold knot of alarm returned. What if Case was right? Could she afford to take the chance that he wasn't? Remembering what she'd overheard in the stables, she asked, "How does Francis know you?"

"We've had run-ins before."

"What kind of run-ins?"

Case stood up and put money on the table. "It's time to turn in. We need to get an early start tomorrow."

By the stony look on his face, Eliza knew he wouldn't say another word. That worried her even more.

Chapter 13

The next morning, Case was up and out before dawn. He returned to the hotel expecting to see Eliza in the adjoining restaurant, but she wasn't there. He went to her room and knocked. Hearing nothing, he knocked harder.

Where was she?

The door opened, and Eliza gazed up at him sleepily as she tied her wrapper closed at the waist. "You didn't have to pound. I was asleep, not dead."

"Don't you ask who it is before you open the door?" he chided.

"Good morning to you, too," she muttered, heading back to the bed.

"I thought you'd gone out."

"Out where? The birds aren't even awake." Eliza crawled onto the quilt and curled up. "I'll meet you in an hour."

"No, you don't. We've got to get moving. It's later than you think."

"In a few minutes."

"Now." When she didn't respond, Case walked over and shook her shoulder. "Come on, sleepyhead. Let's get going."

She smiled with her eyes closed. "My sister always called me sleepyhead. She'd say, 'The early bird catches the worm, sleepyhead, so get up!' Then I'd say, 'Let them. I don't eat worms.' That always got her goat." Giggling, Eliza snuggled deeper into the quilt.

"Do you want to get to Omaha or not?" Case asked.

Eliza yawned and stretched, then pushed herself to a sitting position. "All right. I'll be downstairs in fifteen minutes."

In the restaurant, Case ordered coffee for himself and tomato juice for Eliza. He patted the small wrapped bundle in his pocket, imagining Eliza's surprise when she opened it. By sheer luck, he'd spotted a jeweler that was still open when he'd parked the wagon last evening, and had instantly decided to look for a substitute for Eliza's lost crystal. He'd found a pendant that came close. It was smaller, and heart-shaped, and on a silver chain so she couldn't lose it.

Case didn't know exactly why he'd bought it; he certainly didn't want to give her the wrong impression about his feelings for her. But she'd been so downcast about losing her crystal that he'd wanted to cheer her. He couldn't wait to see her expression when she opened his gift.

Eliza soon appeared looking wide awake and as fresh as a daisy in her sky-blue dress. She'd pulled her long locks up into a loose knot—quite different from the disarray he'd seen earlier. Yet he'd liked that wild tumble of curls. It gave her an earthy, untamed look that set his imagination on fire.

Eliza grabbed the juice and started drinking before she'd even sat down. "Oh, thank you! That tastes so good. How did you know I liked tomato juice?"

"I guessed." Case slipped the little package out of his pocket and held it in his lap, curling his fingers around it, waiting for just the right moment to give it to her.

Eliza pulled out her chair and sat down, her eyes sparkling with excitement. "You'll never believe what happened! I was pulling my skirt over my head and this fell out." She opened her palm, revealing the missing crystal charm. "I'd checked the pockets on the other skirts, but I forgot to check *this* skirt." She beamed at him. "I told you Mr. Holmby didn't take it."

Only because he hadn't seen it, Case thought glumly. He slid Eliza's present back into his pocket, annoyed by how sharp his disappointment was. What had he been thinking? Eliza probably wouldn't have liked it, anyway. "Why don't you order some food so we can be on our way?"

Violet opened her front door that same afternoon to find a telegram delivery boy on her porch. She gave him a tip and hurriedly opened the envelope.

"Oh, dear!" she cried. It was from the Des Moines telegraph office, notifying her that the recipient of her wire, one Eliza Lowe, had failed to pick up her message. What would she like them to do with it?

Violet paced the hallway. Eliza had just wired that she was on her way to Omaha, where she would probably be meeting Eileen. There would be no way to get word to her in time.

Violet stopped before a portrait of her late husband. "Edward, what shall I do? Eliza's life is at stake."

"Mrs. Lowe, did you call me?" the hired girl said from the kitchen doorway.

"No, Mary, I didn't." Violet glanced up at the portrait once more, then turned away with a worried sigh. Almost at once, the answer came to her.

"Mary!" she called excitedly. "Pack a trunk for me. I'm going to Omaha."

Standing outside Omaha's Western Union office, Frank Caroni read Eliza's brief message, then crumpled it into a tight ball. Damn her! She hadn't given him a name. That could only mean that the Pinkerton was on to him. And the most likely Pinkerton was Case Brogan. But how in the hell had Brogan managed to hook up with Eliza?

Frank returned to the fleabag boardinghouse where they were staying, but hesitated at the bottom of the staircase. The last thing he wanted was to hear the whines of that sickly, horse-faced wife of his. He went instead to the White Gull Tavern down by the river to formulate a plan. By his estimation, Eliza would be arriving in two days.

First, he needed to know for sure if it was Brogan. If it was, he'd have to be extra clever. He'd need a way to separate Brogan from Eliza, something guaranteed to keep him occupied long enough for Frank to grab the money and get down to the docks.

Think, Frank! What was Brogan's weakness?

As Case and Eliza headed west, they left behind the flat prairie lands of eastern Iowa and moved into forest-covered hills. It was a beautiful part of the country, covered with hardwood trees of oak, maple, walnut, hickory and elm, and abloom with gentians, goldenrods, prairie asters, and sunflowers.

They stopped to eat an early lunch and rest the horses along the Raccoon River. According to the map, it would be the last river they crossed for a while.

Eliza had been quiet for most of the morning, as though pondering a weighty problem. It wasn't until they'd finished their lunch that Case learned what it was.

She had taken off her hat and removed the pins from her hair, letting the black curls fall freely around her face and down her back. Her shoes and stocking had come off, too; he could see her little toes peeping out from beneath the hem of her skirt. She was leaning against a tree trunk, her knees up, tearing bits of crust off the bread and chewing them thoughtfully.

"Do you remember what you said when I asked you how you knew Eileen would be meeting us in Omaha?" she asked.

"Yes."

"You said it was experience, but I think it was more than that."

"Don't say it was intuition," Case cautioned.

She pursed her lips. "How about a gut feeling?"

"If I say yes, then you're going to say that a gut feeling is intuition, aren't you?"

She tipped her head down to hide a smile. "Yes. I was also going to explain how your experience gave you an intuitive feeling about what was going to happen."

Case had to laugh as he leaned back on his elbows and studied her. Eliza had such strong faith in her convictions that she couldn't help but try to convert everyone to her way of thinking. He'd found it annoying at first, but now he was coming to admire her strength of character.

But the fact was that the last time he'd had a gut feeling, it had convinced him not to say anything to his father about Frank Caroni. He hadn't trusted it since.

"You really can't separate experience and intuition," Eliza continued. "It's just not possible."

"I can, and I did."

"But don't you see that—"

Case rolled over and grabbed her, taking her down beneath him, tickling her ribs. "I *can* and I *did*!" he said, as she squealed in protest, laughing and struggling to get away. "And you might as well stop trying to convince me otherwise."

"Never," she gasped, trying to tickle him back.

Case finally managed to pin her arms at her sides, then he dipped his head and gave her a long, smoldering kiss. *That* should end their discussion.

But it started something else.

Eliza's struggles ceased as her feminine instincts took over. His kisses simply intoxicated her, pushing all thoughts of trying to change his mind aside, and filling her with desire instead. She wound her arms around his neck and kissed him back, running her tongue around his lips, then slipping it inside when they parted, exploring the hot depths of his mouth. His groan of pleasure spurred her on.

She pushed against him until he rolled onto his back, taking her with him. Then she kissed him again while opening the buttons of his shirt. She sat up, straddling his thighs, her knees and calves boldly bared, as she parted the shirt all the way down to his waist. She smoothed her hands across the hard surface of his chest, familiarizing herself with the sight and feel of his muscular torso, exploring the hardness of his brown nipples and the coarseness of his curly dark hair.

Growing more adventurous, she traced a slim line down to his belly button with her index finger, feeling his skin jump at her touch, then she reached for the buttons of his pants, curious to explore further.

Case caught her hand. "That's enough."

"Is it? Are you sure?" When he didn't reply, Eliza leaned down to flick one of his nipples with her tongue. He shuddered, as though the pleasure was too intense. Excited by this new-found power, she used her tongue to trace a path down his stomach, making his muscles quiver and tense beneath her, and his breath come in short bursts.

"Miss Lowe," he groaned, "you don't know what you're doing to me."

Feeling very wicked, she raised her head and gave him a sultry glance. "I think it's time you called me Eliza."

Case dropped his head to the blanket. This was a new role for Eliza, and he could tell she was enjoying it. God knew *he* was. But she really didn't understand what torture it was for him, since it couldn't go anywhere.

She unfastened the buttons of his pants, then slipped her hand beneath the edge of his under-drawers, making his shaft pulse as blood coursed into it. His skin tingled as she ran her fingers down the smooth flesh of his abdomen, then the coarse, springy hairs on his groin. When her fingers touched his swollen member and began to explore its contours—the sensitive head, the thin ridge on the underside, the long, thick shaft—Case nearly exploded in her hand.

"Eliza!" He couldn't let her continue. It wasn't right.

"But you did it to me," she reminded him.

"That was different."

"How?"

Case couldn't think for the heavy fog of passion around his brain. "It just is."

"Nonsense. What's fair is fair." She kissed him again, a slow, deep kiss, keeping him down with her weight as she once again slid her hand inside his clothing and wrapped her fingers around his manhood. She stroked him as she kissed him, until he was powerless to do anything but let the release come.

Afterward he rolled away from her. "Damn!" he cursed, and stalked down to the riverbank.

Eliza couldn't understand why Case was so upset. When he'd pleasured her, it had been one of the most wonderful experiences of her life.

She washed, folded the blanket, and stowed everything in the wagon while he brought up the team of horses from the river. Then she stood behind him as he hitched them to the wagon. "I don't understand why you're angry, but I'll apologize anyway."

"I'm not angry with you."

"Then who *are* you angry with?"

There was a long pause, and then he said, "Me."

"Why?"

He swung to face her. "Damn it, Eliza, you're too trusting. You can't do what you did to a man and think that makes everything even, because it doesn't."

She dropped her gaze. "I'm sorry."

He sighed, then tilted her chin up. "Understand this: you are a beautiful, desirable woman, and I'd be lying if I said I didn't enjoy what just happened. But it makes me want more, and I was hired to protect you. Those two things don't go together. They have to stay separate so I can do my job." He climbed up onto the bench and picked up the reins. "So let's go, Miss Lowe."

Humbled, Eliza climbed up beside him. Case Brogan was first and foremost a Pinkerton, and she had to remember that. With him, business would always come first.

The wagon lumbered slowly through the hilly countryside, passing several sleepy villages that offered neither places to stay nor to eat, dimming Eliza's hopes of a good meal and a soft bed.

"Looks like we'll be spending the night in the wagon," she said with a sigh. "At least the weather is good. I hope we can find a general store to pick up some food."

"According to my map, we should reach a town called Adell very soon," Case assured her. "It's at a crossroads, so I expect there will be a hotel or inn nearby."

Eliza stretched her back. "Thank heavens. I

don't think I could ride another hour." *And I'm not carrying a baby.*

She worried about Eileen. Her friend had always had a weak stomach. Now she had the added burden of a pregnancy, not to mention this travail with Francis. It made Eliza wonder what kind of husband would put his wife through such an ordeal.

"What type of trouble was Francis Caroni in ten years ago?" Eliza asked.

Every muscle in Case's body tensed. "Why?" he said warily.

"You said the law has been after him for ten years. That means he's done something pretty bad."

"He killed a man."

"How?"

"Stabbed him."

"In self-defense?"

Case's chest tightened and his body was seized by a terrible chill as he saw again that flash of steel as Caroni's knife arced through air, sinking deep into his father's chest. "It was murder," he managed through clenched teeth.

"But I've met Francis," Eliza argued. "He's no more capable of killing someone than I am."

"We're all capable of killing."

"If that's what you believe, then I feel terribly sorry for you," Eliza said. "We're not animals; we have consciences."

"Some don't."

"Perhaps you don't have the whole story. Francis may have done a few things in the past that weren't—well, legal, but he's not a murderer. You didn't see him with my friend. He was kind and caring and patient, and he truly fell in love with her. No one could be that way on the outside and ugly on the inside.

"And Eileen has never been so happy. She's a sweet, loving person, and I know she wouldn't have fallen for a killer. So no matter what you say Francis Caroni did, I won't believe he's a murderer unless he tells me himself."

"I'll try to get him to oblige."

Eliza studied Case's stony expression and felt that tiny knot of alarm grow larger. "I don't think you two should meet, after all."

"Do you think I'd let you see him alone?"

"If he knows you, as you say he does, why would he meet with us at all?"

"Don't worry about that. I'll take care of it."

"How?"

He gave her a long, pointed look. "Trust me."

Eliza gazed into his eyes, wondering if he was mocking her. "All right," she said finally. "I'll trust you—if you'll trust me. Tell me what you're planning."

For a moment he held her gaze, then he looked away. "I can't do that."

"You *won't* do that. You don't trust me, even though I've never given you a reason not to."

"You will. Everyone does, sooner or later."

Poor Case, Eliza thought with a sigh. If only she could discover why he wouldn't allow himself to trust. Her only hope was to hold fast to her belief that, in the end, her trust in him would not be in vain.

Chapter 14

They rode into Adell at dusk. Like many small Midwestern towns, it owed its existence to the railroad line. Adell's main street ran directly in front of the depot, where an elderly man sat tipped back on his chair on the wooden platform, watching folks pass by. An old hound dog lay at his feet. The man nodded politely as Case and Eliza rolled past.

Across the street was the hotel, a wide yellow clapboard, two-story building with bright white trim. Farther down were the town livery stables, where Case took the horses and wagon after letting Eliza off at the hotel.

She was waiting for him on the covered front porch. "The restaurant is open," she informed him happily, leading him inside. "The cook said he'd wait for us before closing the kitchen. Wasn't that kind of him?"

Case glanced through the doorway into a rectangular room that appeared to have been tacked onto the side of the hotel like an afterthought. The room was filled with square tables covered with worn lime-green oilcloths, ladderback pine chairs, and scuffed pine floors. Faded green curtains covered the three windows along the front, and smoke-blackened oil lamps hung at odd intervals on the dingy white walls.

A group of locals clustered around a table in the front, arguing politics, but paused to study the strangers as they passed. Case steered Eliza to the farthest table from them and pulled out her chair, throwing a warning glance at the men in case they were ogling her.

A door opened in the back and the cook stuck his head out. Seeing the newcomers, he grinned and ambled toward them. He wore a long white bib apron that hit his lanky frame above the knees. His hair, mustache, and beard were long and gray, but thankfully looked clean. He smiled at Eliza, his brown eyes all but disappearing in the wrinkles, a gold tooth gleaming brightly in front.

"Howdy! What can I get you folks?"

"Do you have any beefsteak?" Eliza asked hopefully.

He shook his head. "Nope."

"How about pork chops?"

"Nope."

"Chicken?"

"Uh—nope."

"What kind of meat *do* you have?" Case said impatiently.

"Ham. Bacon. Sausage."

"Do you have eggs?" Eliza asked sweetly.

"Yep."

"Why don't you make us something with ham and eggs?" she suggested.

The cook scratched his mustache for a moment, then beamed at her. "I'll do that."

Case watched him amble back to the kitchen. "Are you sure you trust his cooking?"

"I'm hungry. If it's food, I'll eat it."

"If his appearance is any indication of his skill, I'm not sure that's wise," Case grumbled.

Eliza wagged her finger at him. "My aunt always says, 'Never judge a book by its cover.' "

Case rolled his eyes. "How many sayings does your aunt have?"

"I've never actually counted them."

Case glanced at the men at the front table, who had resumed their loud discussion. He looked around at the dingy restaurant, where his hopes of getting a good meal had vanished, then at the woman across from him, who never seemed discouraged by anything. How she maintained such good cheer puzzled him. There certainly wasn't any "gift" in their present situation that he could see.

Case wasn't in the best of moods to begin with. The closer he got to Omaha, the more he brooded over the death of his father. He didn't even try to explain his intense hatred of Caroni to Eliza; she was too naive to comprehend such a monster. She thought everyone had goodness somewhere inside them. But she'd soon discover how wrong she was.

Case had no illusions about his own nature. He wanted revenge, and he wouldn't hesitate to kill for it. But whereas before, he was determined to shatter Eliza's naiveté, now he vacillated, recognizing the likely possibility of also crushing her spirit. He reminded himself it was a necessary lesson, and eased his conscience by recalling that he'd warned her not to trust him. That she continued to do so was her own fault.

The kitchen door opened and the cook moseyed out carrying two steaming plates. He placed one in front of Eliza and another in front of Case. "Want coffee?" he asked.

"Please," Eliza said, picking up her fork.

Case stared down at his food in disbelief. Piled high on his plate were fluffy, buttery eggs topped with melted yellow cheese and accompanied by nicely browned ham slices and crisp, shredded potatoes.

"This is delicious!" Eliza said through a mouthful of eggs, as the cook returned with two cups of black coffee.

"Thank you, ma'am. Everything all right with you?" he asked Case.

All Case could do was nod. His mouth was full of the best ham and egg dinner he'd ever had in his life. He fully expected Eliza to chide him, but she only said, "I never would have thought to put cheese on eggs."

She'd proved him wrong once again, and she hadn't even said, "I told you so." How was he ever going to make his point when she kept showing him up?

"Have I ever told you about our caves?" Eliza asked.

Case swallowed a bite of potatoes. "You have caves?"

"Not me, personally," she said, with a giggle. "But there are a number of limestone caves down in my part of Indiana. Eileen and I used to explore them, pretending we were great adventurers. Our friend Emeline was always too frightened to venture inside."

"I can't say that I blame her. Caves are dangerous."

"Naturally, you have to know what you're doing. For instance, you never *ever* go into a cave without candles, matches, and a companion."

"Any rats in the caves?"

"Just bats."

"Rodents. Same thing."

"No, they're not. These cute little things wouldn't harm you. They're only as big as your thumb." Eliza paused to take a sip of coffee. "The first time I ever saw a rat was in Chicago, and I must say it was the biggest—"

Case stopped chewing. "I hate rats."

"I can't say that I'm fond of them, either, but—"

"Then change the subject—please. To anything but opera."

Eliza pondered quietly for a few moments, then her eyes widened as they did whenever she seemed particularly inspired. "Let's talk about you. Do you have any sisters or brothers?"

Case grimaced inwardly. He should have added family to that list. "I have a brother."

"That's all?"

"My mother had five children, but three were stillborn."

"Tell me about your brother," she said hopefully.

"Connor was wild. He left home when he was sixteen. Said he couldn't abide school. I was fourteen and I haven't seen him since. It broke my parents' hearts."

"I'm sorry." Eliza stared at her nearly empty plate, deflated. "I'm sure you missed him."

As she missed her own brother. Case instantly regretted his bluntness. He should have thought before he spoke. He wasn't used to anyone taking an interest in him, yet knowing Eliza as he was beginning to, he shouldn't have been surprised.

To smooth things over, he said apologetically, "It's not easy for me to talk about my family. I didn't mean to be so cold-blooded about it. But you're right, I missed my brother for a long time."

She gave him such an appreciative look that he found himself saying, "Any other topics you want to discuss?"

She drew a design in the melted butter with her fork. "Well, there is one thing I've been wanting to ask."

"Go ahead," he said magnanimously. He forked a big bite of ham and stuck it in his mouth.

"What will you do after you've found your father's murderer?"

Case studied her as he chewed his meat, suspecting there was much more behind her simple question. "What I've always done: my job."

"Will you marry?"

"I've never thought about it."

"Have you ever courted a woman?"

Her questions were beginning to nettle him. "Why don't you finish eating so we can turn in?"

"I have finished." Eliza pushed her plate away, then rested her chin on her hand and studied him. "I'll wager that the only thing you've thought about for ten years is finding the killer—not getting married, not having a family of your own, not seeing the world—just finding the killer."

Case scooped up the last of his eggs. "It's been on my mind."

"It's consumed your every thought."

He swallowed the eggs, wiped his mouth, and pushed back his chair. "Let's go. I'm tired."

"But you didn't answer my question. When you don't have the killer to hunt for anymore, what will you do with your life? And I'm not talking about your work."

Case stared at Eliza. He'd never thought that far ahead.

"Don't you see that because of your morbid preoccupation with finding this man—"

"Morbid?"

"—you have nothing in your life but your job? Is that what your father would have wanted for you?"

"It's not morbid, and I don't need anything else."

"I don't believe that."

"Believe what you will."

Eliza leaned forward, gazing at him earnestly.

"This is what I believe: you need to give up this obsession and start enjoying life before it passes you by."

So that was her purpose. Eliza wasn't interested in him; she was trying to save Caroni.

Case stood up and tossed some money onto the table. "I'll see you in the morning."

With a worried frown, Eliza watched Case stride out of the restaurant. She knew she'd struck a nerve. She only hoped it had struck deep enough to make him understand how he was ruining his life—not to mention how he would ruin Eileen's.

She only had a day or two to work on him before they reached Omaha. She had a strong feeling that it wouldn't be enough time.

"More coffee, ma'am?"

Eliza smiled kindly at the cook. "No, thank you. Everything was wonderful, though."

"Thank you, ma'am. You know, in my younger days, I was a cook in a fancy hotel in New York City."

"You were? Why did you leave?"

He pulled out a chair. "Mind if I sit?"

"Please."

"Well, it all began back in '58."

Case stood just outside the restaurant in the hotel lobby, waiting for Eliza to leave so he could make sure she made it safely to her room.

But hearing the cook start what was certain to be a mind-numbing story, Case cursed and started up the stairs. He'd be damned if he would wait around another hour. She could find her own way.

He put his key in the lock and opened the door. That was as far as he got.

"Women!" he muttered, trotting back down the stairs. He found a rickety chair in a corner of the lobby and settled in for a long wait.

Case had just brought the wagon around from the stables the next morning when Eliza emerged. She had on her straw hat and her mint-green calico dress with white collar and cuffed sleeves. Against her dress, her blue eyes stood out like sapphires.

Eliza gave him a tentative smile as he held out his hand to help her up, as though she expected him to still be angry with her. The discomfiting truth was that the sight of her gladdened his heart, when it should have had just the opposite effect.

After Eliza's little sermon, Case hadn't been able to sleep. Her words had resonated in his head all night long. "*. . . a morbid preoccupation . . . consumed your every thought . . . nothing in your life but your job.*"

He'd never thought about his life before—or about how empty it was. He'd filled his time with work and an occasional woman, and it had always seemed enough. Yet now, when he saw Eliza's sunny smile and heard her animated voice, Case felt himself yearning for more.

He tried to remember what his life had been like before his father's death, but it was as if those memories had slipped into a black mist. He lived solely for the future, for the time when he could finally get his revenge, and he felt powerless to change it. He wasn't sure he wanted to.

"Is that what your father would have wanted for you?" Eliza had asked.

His father had lost four children, had cared for a sickly wife, and had dealt with the worst humanity had to offer. Yet through it all, he'd never lost his hope or his zest for living—much like Eliza. What *would* he say about his son?

Case shoved those thoughts into a dark corner of his mind. He had to finish what he'd started. If he began to doubt himself, he'd never be able to do it.

The town was just coming awake as they left. Storekeepers rolled down their awnings and swept in front of their doors; a milkwagon rattled past; a newspaper delivery boy rode by on his bicycle, tossing papers into door wells; and the aroma of baking bread wafted from an open window. The air was refreshingly cool and the sun was shining. Eliza took a deep breath and let it out. It was a good day to be traveling.

Just outside of Adell they came to the East Nishnabatuna River. As Case slowed the wagon to cross the shallows, a young blond woman came running out of the woods, waving her arms and crying for them to stop.

Case pulled the team up short, grabbed his rifle, and jumped down.

"Please help me!" she cried breathlessly, glancing over her shoulder in the direction of the woods. "I've been kidnapped."

"Kidnapped?" Eliza hurriedly climbed down from the bench. "Who kidnapped you?"

The girl hugged a beaded black drawstring handbag against her bosom, shivering. "I don't know who they were. I escaped from them last night and hid in the woods, waiting for someone to come by." She began to sob.

Eliza immediately put her arms around her, crooning, "There, there. You're safe now," as though she were forty years the girl's senior instead of just a few.

Case studied the stranger skeptically. He figured she was between eighteen and twenty years old. She was thin and pale-complexioned, and her peach-colored dress was dirty and grass-stained, yet obviously of good quality, with expensive kid shoes to match. She was probably from a well-to-do family, a prime target for kidnappers. Yet experience, and his own deep distrust, told him to be cautious.

"Would you recognize them again?" Case asked.

"They had me blindfolded." She covered her face with her hands. "It was dreadful! They kept me locked in a room for days with only bread and water."

"Did they hurt you?" Eliza asked, looking her over.

At her shake of her head, Case asked, "How many were there?"

"Three, I think, but I can't be sure. Their voices all sounded alike."

"Where were they holding you?"

"In a house in that town back there." She pointed in the direction of Adell.

"Where are you from?" Case asked.

"Omaha."

"That's where we're headed," Eliza replied.

"They brought you all the way here from Omaha?" Case asked suspiciously.

At her adamant nod, he said, "What's your name?"

"Ivy Greene."

"How old are you?"

"Eighteen."

"Why didn't you go to the sheriff?"

"I—I just wanted to get away from them."

Case gave her a dubious glance. "You ran to

the woods, not to someone who could help you?"

Her big brown eyes teared up. "I was frightened. I don't know what I was thinking." She glanced anxiously back at the road, as though afraid her kidnappers were right behind her, then she gave Eliza an imploring look. "Please say you'll help me."

"Of course we'll help you," Eliza assured her. "Why don't you climb up on the bench? I'll be there in a moment."

She took Case aside and whispered, "You needn't be so hard on her. Can't you see she's frightened out of her wits?"

"She's making it up."

Eliza stared at him, stunned. He couldn't even trust a frightened eighteen-year-old! "She's been through a terrible ordeal. It's no wonder she wasn't thinking straight. She's fortunate something worse didn't happen to her."

"If you had been kidnapped," Case said, "and then escaped, where would you go?"

"I can't say what I'd do under those circumstances."

"You'd go to the sheriff or to the police, not to the woods—especially when you weren't familiar with the area. We're not taking her to Omaha."

Eliza bristled. "What are we going to do, leave her in the road?"

"She probably has a cohort hiding up ahead waiting to rob us."

"That's nonsense," Eliza hissed.

"It happens all the time."

"This girl is not a robber!"

A muscle in Case's jaw tensed. "You don't know anything about her. She might even be running away from home to meet a man. Whatever the case may be, we're not taking her with us."

Eliza calmly folded her arms across her chest and turned her back on him.

"If she stays, I stay."

Chapter 15

Case strode over to the wagon and stowed his rifle under the bench. Ivy was slumped at the other end, head bowed, hugging her handbag to her chest. Eliza stood where he left her, several feet in front of the wagon, her back to him, her arms folded, her foot tapping the ground.

Swearing under his breath, he stalked back over to Eliza and said through clenched teeth, "Will you please get in the wagon?"

"Only if Ivy goes with us."

"I am *not* taking the risk."

Eliza swung to face him, her eyes snapping with indignation, something he'd never seen before. "You didn't trust the Indian," she said in a low voice, "or Tod Holmby, or the sheriff in Seaton, or even the cook back in Adell—and you were wrong about every single one of them."

She paused to draw a deep breath and let it out again, as though trying to collect herself. Then, in a calmer, yet insistent, voice she said, "Please trust me about Ivy."

Case squeezed his hands into fists, waging a fierce battle with himself. He didn't believe Ivy's story, and he had a strong gut feeling that he should leave the girl where they found her. But he'd been wrong about his gut feeling before, too.

"We'll take her as far as the next town, and that's it," he finally conceded. "She can wire her family from there."

"Thank you." Eliza spun around and marched back to the wagon. Case checked the horses' harnesses, then climbed up beside the two women.

They couldn't reach the next town fast enough for his liking.

As the train chugged slowly into Burlington Station at Omaha, Nebraska, Violet Lowe lifted the window and peered out. The wooden platforms surrounding the multitude of rail lines were a beehive of activity. Porters toted luggage, conductors checked tickets, passengers searched for family members or stood in line to buy food from the various vendors, and waiting trains belched smoke and ash.

Violet sniffed the air, detecting the delicious, smoky aroma of frankfurters. It wasn't normally a food she ate, but it was past noon, her stomach was empty, and the franks were handy.

She stood up and stretched her stiff joints, then filed out with other travelers and got in line to buy the hot dog on a bun. The trip had seemed to take forever, but she was here at last. She hoped she was in time.

Holding her partially eaten frank in one gloved hand, she flagged down a porter and had the man collect her two trunks and find her a cab.

"Take me to your finest hotel," she instructed the cabby.

"That'd be the Grand Central," the driver told her. "It's the best house between Chicago and San Francisco." He flicked the reins and the horse clopped down the street. "This here," he said, as they turned onto a busy thoroughfare, "is Farnham Street. You'll find everything you need on it. The hotel is a few blocks down."

Violet finished the last of her frank and gazed at the shops lining both sides of the street. The cabby pointed out the hatter, the druggist, the fancy grocer's, the Western Union telegraph office, a millinery shop, a dry goods store, a fine furniture store, and more, as though his passenger had never seen a city before.

He pulled to a stop at the corner. "Here we are, ma'am. Isn't she a beauty?" He gestured toward the hotel.

While he unloaded her trunks, Violet gazed up at the handsomely designed brick building with delight. She'd had visions of Omaha as a rough, dusty, frontier town filled with saloons and dance halls. The Grand Central Hotel was an exceedingly pleasant surprise.

The five-story building occupied an entire corner and spread halfway down the block. There were two canopied entrances on Farnham, and through the glass windows at street level she could see the interior of a fine restaurant.

Violet gave the cabby a generous tip, thanked him for his helpful discourse, then turned to find a doorman. She waited for five minutes but none appeared. Surely a hotel as fine as the Grand Central had doormen.

Not wanting to appear foolish, Violet decided to take matters into her own hands. But then she eyed her trunks in dismay. How was she going to get them inside without help?

Out of desperation, she began to tug them toward the doors, using the bottom trunk's leather handle. She had no idea how she would hold the doors open and drag them through at the same time.

She spotted a boy of about eleven years of age coming up the street and quickly dug a nickel out of her coin purse. "Young man, I'll give you this shiny nickel if you'll hold the door for me," she said, waving the coin.

"A nickel? Sure, lady," he said with a toothy grin. He held out his hand, and she put the coin in it. "Thanks!" he called, and sped away.

"Well, I never!" she huffed. "The youth these days!"

At that moment a dapper-looking, older gentleman in a smart navy three-piece suit came toward her from the other direction. Violet fluttered her handkerchief at him. "Yoo hoo! Excuse me, sir. Would you mind holding the doors open for me?"

As soon as he saw what she was trying to do, he said, "Please, allow me." He squatted before the trunks and wrapped his arms as far as they would reach around the lower one. His face turned bright red and the veins in his temples stood out as he attempted to lift them both at once. Another gentleman, witnessing his struggles, volunteered his help, and soon several passersby had stopped to watch the fun.

"Oh, dear," Violet moaned, glancing at the curious faces around her. What a scene she'd caused! She wanted to die of mortification.

* * *

Eileen Caroni sagged against the brick front of a real estate broker's office, fighting a wave of nausea. Closing her eyes, she took deep breaths until the feeling passed. When she opened them again, the first thing she noticed was a commotion in front of the hotel across the street.

Her curiosity whetted, she started across, but then hesitated. She wasn't supposed to be out; Francis had given her strict orders not to leave the boardinghouse. But she was so tired of staring at the walls of their tiny room that she'd decided he wouldn't mind overly if she took a short walk down to the grocer's to buy an apple. She could tolerate apples.

Suddenly Eileen spotted a short, plump, familiar-looking lady in an expensive plum and black traveling costume, wearing a stylish black hat perched on her white hair. Could it be—but surely it wasn't—Eliza's aunt?

Eileen blinked twice, not trusting her vision, then she wended her way through the buggies and wagons jamming the street. "Mrs. Lowe?"

Violet was so distraught that when a young woman called her by name, she didn't pay her any mind. But finally a doorman arrived, apologizing effusively, and called for help. Within moments, the trunks were whisked into the hotel.

"Mrs. Lowe?" she heard again.

Violet turned to the girl. "Yes?"

"Mrs. Lowe, it's me, Eileen Caroni."

"Eileen? Oh, good heavens!" Violet threw her arms around the girl's shoulders, then remembered her delicate condition and patted her gently on the back instead. "How are you, dear?"

Eileen managed a weak smile. "As well as can be expected."

Violet glanced around furtively and whispered, "Where's your husband?"

"He went out somewhere. Did Eliza come with you? I thought she said that she was traveling with a Pinkerton."

"She is, but I came separately. She should arrive soon."

"Why did you come separately?"

Violet glanced toward the hotel. "It's a long story, dear. Why don't you come inside with me, and we'll have tea just as soon as I see to my luggage."

Eileen nibbled her lower lip and glanced around, as though afraid someone would see her. "I really should get back. I only stepped out to buy an apple."

"Where are you staying?"

Eileen looked down ashamedly. "A boardinghouse near the railroad yard."

Violet took a long, hard look at her. Despite her pregnancy, Eileen had grown thin and pasty-complexioned, all due to that monster of a husband, no doubt. She hooked her arm through Eileen's. "A good cup of tea will do you wonders, and while we're there, we'll see what other fare we can tempt ourselves with."

Ignoring the girl's feeble protests, Violet led Eileen inside.

The hotel was quite satisfactory, Violet decided, after being shown to her room. The blue, green, and gold patterned carpeting was tasteful, the mahogany trim was well polished, and the cherry furniture suited to the formal decor.

"This is so beautiful!" Eileen said, gazing around the room. She sat on the bed, tested the springs, and declared the room the nicest one she'd seen since leaving Coffee Creek. "Much better than the places I've stayed in lately."

At her wistful expression, Violet pursed her lips. Nicest room, indeed. She'd have to do something about that! She unpinned her hat, placed it on her trunk, and marched to the door. "Let's go have our tea."

Seated at a small table in a quiet corner of the hotel's fancy restaurant, Violet poured steaming tea from a silver teapot into two china cups. "Sugar, dear?"

Eileen smiled weakly. "I don't dare. My stomach doesn't react well to sweets."

Violet couldn't think of anything worse than that.

It being well after the noon hour, the restaurant was nearly deserted, affording them privacy. Violet thought the place was divine. Not only did they serve marvelous little petit fours, they also had a wonderful selection of finger sandwiches. She'd even managed to convince Eileen to try the egg salad sandwich, which would be gentle on her stomach.

Violet studied Eileen as she stirred her tea, wondering if she should tell the girl right out that her husband was a murderer, or break it to her gently. Time was, after all, of the essence.

"Eileen," she began, "how is Mr. Caroni treating you?"

Eileen looked down, as though embarrassed. "He gets very impatient with me, but I can't blame him for it. I'm not a very good wife, I'm afraid. I've been continuously ill since I learned I was with child. I have little strength and can't do much but read and sew."

"How does he—er—*show* his impatience?" Violet asked, trying to be tactful.

Eileen's eyes mirrored her sadness as she said, "He stays away a lot. I suppose I would, too, if I were married to me."

Violet simmered inwardly at the man's insensitivity. "Have you seen a doctor?"

Keeping her gaze on her plate, Eileen shook her head. "Francis didn't think it would be wise. He doesn't want anyone to learn of our whereabouts."

"You wouldn't have to give your real name."

"I'm fine, really. It will pass."

Violet took a delicate bite out of a cream-filled cake. "Eileen, what do you know of Francis's background?"

"I know he came from California and that he tried his luck at panning for gold in Colorado before becoming a traveling salesman."

"Did he tell you he lived in Chicago?"

Eileen stared at her in surprise. "No."

"Eat your egg salad, dear. I have quite a story to tell you."

When Case stopped beside a creek to feed and rest the horses, Eliza was more than ready for lunch. It was past noon, and her limbs needed a stretch. While Ivy slept soundly on a bedroll in the back of the wagon, and Case led the team to the water, Eliza prepared their meal, spreading a blanket beneath a shady elm and setting out the food.

She returned to the wagon to wake the girl, who slept with her knees curled up and her pale hair fanned out around her. She seemed uncommonly thin and her skin had a waxy appearance, as though she suffered from some illness.

"Ivy, it's time to eat." Eliza shook her gently, but she didn't respond. She tried twice more, until finally the girl opened her eyes and looked at her blankly.

"Where am I?"

"You're in our wagon. We're stopping for lunch."

Ivy sat up slowly, wincing as though her joints ached. "I'm not very hungry."

"Nonsense. You probably haven't had any food since yesterday, have you? You need to get something in your stomach. Come on. I'll take you to our picnic site."

"A picnic?" Ivy rubbed her eyes. "All right. I'll be there in a moment."

Case was standing beneath the elm when Eliza returned. Even before he spoke, Eliza could sense the tightly coiled tension inside him. He was still on his guard, behaving as if the girl could do him harm.

"Is she coming?" he asked tersely.

Eliza glanced around to check just as Ivy climbed down from the wagon. She wandered over and sank onto the blanket as though she had no energy. Eliza knelt beside her and passed her a basket of bread, cheese, and jerky.

"I hope you don't mind our limited menu," she joked.

As though she hadn't heard Eliza's comment, Ivy selected a piece of bread and began to nibble on it, keeping her focus on the blanket. Eliza glanced at Case, who was eyeing the girl distrustfully.

"When we reach the next town," he said to Ivy, "I'm going to stop so you can wire your family."

That seemed to get her attention. She looked up with wide, alarmed eyes. "Oh, no, please don't stop now. I want to get as far away as possible." She held out her tin cup with hands that trembled. "May I have water, please?"

"You need to let your family know you're safe," Case remarked, as Eliza filled her cup.

Ivy gulped thirstily, then held the cup out for more. "I don't have any money for a wire."

Eliza gave her more water. "Don't worry about that; I'll pay for it."

"We're going to stop to see the sheriff, too, so you can make a report," Case added.

With her head bent over her cup, her pale hair falling around her face, Ivy gave a nod of agreement. She drank the water, then excused herself and went up a hill into some bushes, her handbag clutched to her bosom as though she was afraid to leave it.

"I still don't believe her," Case groused, and strode off to take care of the horses.

Eliza huffed as she packed up the food. For heaven's sake, couldn't he see that Ivy was still suffering? Just wait till she recovered. Then Case would see how wrong he was.

By the time the horses had been hitched, Ivy still hadn't returned, and Case was growing impatient.

"I'll go get her," Eliza volunteered. She followed the path Ivy had taken and finally found her sitting alongside the creek, trailing her fingers through the water, her handbag in her lap.

"Ivy, we're ready to go."

"The water is so pretty," she said dreamily. "I just hate to leave."

"You want to get home, don't you?"

Sighing wistfully, she rose and followed Eliza to the wagon.

Ivy slept all afternoon and was still asleep at dusk, when they reached the little town of Crawford. Case located the Western Union office on one of the cross streets, and Eliza accompanied the girl into the building.

"Here's money for your telegram," Eliza said, handing her some coins.

Ivy gazed at the change in her palm, then raised frightened eyes to Eliza's face. "Are you going to leave me in this town?"

She looked so young and vulnerable that Eliza's heart ached for her. How could she abandon her? "Why don't you wire your family and see when they can come for you? I'll wait outside."

She left Ivy and went straight to the wagon. "We can't leave her yet," she told Case. "We must wait until she hears from her parents."

She heard him muttering angrily as he jumped down. "Two days ago," he said tersely, "you had a strong feeling that your friend was in trouble, and you couldn't wait to reach her. Now you're willing to give up a day for someone you don't even know."

"We can't just ride away and leave Ivy in a strange town. Where will she go?"

"We can leave her with the sheriff."

"To stay where? In the jail?"

"She's not your problem."

"I can't just abandon her. At least Eileen has Francis to lean on. Ivy has no one."

"She's not a child; she doesn't need a nurse-maid."

Eliza checked the watch pinned to her bodice and saw with dismay that she'd forgotten to wind it. "It's getting late anyway," she told Case, after a quick glance at the setting sun, "and the horses need a rest. We can get rooms at a hotel and Ivy can stay with me. Hopefully, she'll receive a reply tomorrow morning, then we can be on our way."

At Case's continued scowl, Eliza put her hand

on the front of his shirt. "My intuition is very strong on this. Please trust me."

If the pleading look in those big blue eyes hadn't softened him, the touch of her hand would have. But as Case saw it, he didn't really have a choice. If Eliza stayed, he stayed.

Chapter 16

ⲉEileen Caroni stared hollow-eyed at her reflection in the looking glass above the washstand. A jagged crack in the glass gave her face an unreal appearance. It seemed fitting.

Her life had become unreal—a nightmare of cheap, shabby rooms, constant nausea, an absent husband, and now the shocking story Violet had told her.

Of course, Eileen hadn't believed it.

But now the doubts were creeping in, fueled by Francis's eccentric and often suspect behavior. And then there was his insistence to know the Pinkerton man's name. Why would that matter unless he had something to hide?

More than once, Francis had come home with

a strange coin purse and no explanation. After the first incident Eileen had stopped questioning him, deciding it was better not to know.

But if he was indeed a murderer, was it still better not to know? She had no idea how Francis would react if she asked him. He had never hurt her, but the look in his eyes when he got angry frightened her. She tried not to provoke him.

Eileen took down her hair and began to brush it, the mere act of running the boar bristles across her scalp soothing her nerves. Her wavy auburn hair lay thick and glossy on her shoulders. Francis had always professed to like her hair; it was her one shining glory.

When the door opened suddenly, Eileen dropped the brush and turned guiltily. "Francis!"

He paused, his questioning gaze sliding from the brush on the floor to her face. "That's the most enthusiasm I've seen in a long time," he commented dryly, sauntering toward her. "Did I startle you, sweetheart?"

"Y-yes. I didn't hear you coming up the stairs."

He picked up the brush and handed it to her, studying her as though he knew she was hiding something. "You must have been lost in thought, then, if you missed all that creaking." He ran his palm down the side of her face, then cupped her chin, breathing hot, alcohol-laden breath on her. "You look a bit flushed, sweetheart. Something you want to tell me?"

Eileen shook her head and tried to smile as she replied, "No. Nothing." She turned back to the looking glass and pinned up her hair, watching as he moved about the room, picking up the book on the table, glancing out the single narrow window, as if hunting for a clue to her jumpiness.

Stay calm, Eileen told herself. She had promised Violet she would say nothing to Francis about their meeting until after she'd talked to her again tomorrow. Putting down her brush, Eileen turned. "There. All done. Shall we go out to eat?"

"Sure, sweetheart, anything you want. I got lucky in a card game today."

"I—I thought you were working down at the wharf."

He shrugged casually. "No jobs today. Are you sure you feel like eating? You seem awfully edgy."

"Some soup would be nice."

"Soup it is. Anything for my pretty baby." He flashed his charming smile at her, but it never reached his eyes.

Eileen took his arm, suppressing a shudder. She had conceived a child with this man, and suddenly she didn't even know who he was.

* * *

A slight shaking of the bed woke Eliza in the middle of the night. She lay still, wondering what it was, until she realized it was Ivy scratching her arms and chest. She fell back to sleep only to be awakened later by the same shaking motion. Then the bed dipped, and then the floor creaked somewhere in the room. Eliza patted the bed next to her and found it empty.

"Ivy?" she said, sitting up.

"I have to use the lavatory." The girl's words came out in a shaky, hurried voice.

"Are you ill?"

"It's just nerves. I'll be fine."

Eliza heard the door open as Ivy stepped into the hall. The single bathroom was one door down from their second-floor room. Case's room was at the end in the opposite direction.

Eliza supposed that nerves could cause a severe itching of the skin, and that a frightening experience could cause a loss of appetite and a need for sleep, yet something about those symptoms nagged at her. She tried to fall asleep again, but found herself counting the minutes instead, wondering what was taking Ivy so long.

She was just about to get up and put on her wrapper when she heard the door open, and then the floor creaked again as Ivy crossed to the bed. She heard a thunk as the girl placed her handbag on the bedside table, then slid under the covers.

How odd that Ivy took her bag with her to the lavatory in the middle of the night.

As soon as the sun came up, Eliza got dressed and put up her hair, then poured water from a pitcher into the wash basin and washed her face and neck. When she was done she woke Ivy, who had fallen into one of her deep sleeps.

When the two women entered the hotel restaurant, Case was nowhere to be found. Eliza guessed that he'd eaten early and had gone to the livery stables to ready the team. She ordered two hearty breakfasts, but Ivy ate very little and seemed inordinately jumpy, scratching her arms, shifting in her seat, and glancing over her shoulder as if she expected the kidnappers to show up at any minute.

"Do you want me to accompany you to the telegraph office to check for a message?" Eliza offered, when they'd finished.

"What for?" Ivy asked irritably.

"Just for the company."

"I can go myself," she snapped.

Startled by the change in her demeanor, Eliza only said, "I'll wait here at the hotel for you, then."

As soon as Ivy left, Eliza returned to the room to pack her bag, pondering the girl's odd behavior. She had just finished when someone rapped on her door. She opened it and found Case outside, his face stormy.

"What happened?" she asked in alarm.

"Ivy stole something from my bag."

"That's impossible. She's been with me."

"She could have taken it when she was in the wagon."

"What did she take?"

Case's jaw worked, as though debating something. Finally he said, "A pendant."

"A pendant?"

"A crystal pendant," he said grudgingly. "I bought it for you when you lost your charm."

Eliza stared at him in amazement. Case Brogan had bought her a gift! She was stunned, and very, very touched.

"I had it in the bottom of my bag, and now it's gone," he said. "The only time that bag wasn't with me was when it was in the wagon with Ivy."

"Why would she steal from you?"

"For money. She's probably planning to pawn it."

Eliza sat down on the bed and stared at him. "I just don't believe Ivy would do that. We rescued her!"

"Where is she now?"

"She went to see if she had a reply to her telegram."

Or did she?

Eliza met Case's skeptical gaze, and saw at once that their thoughts were the same. "We'd better go find her."

"I'll bet she's not there," Case muttered.

Eliza prayed he was wrong, yet she had to admit that there was something odd about the girl's behavior.

As they headed for the Western Union office, Eliza related Ivy's middle-of-the-night activities and her testiness at breakfast. "There's something familiar about her behavior, but I haven't figured it out."

"Sounds like she's an opium eater to me," Case said.

Eliza came to an abrupt halt. "Her handbag!"

"What about it?"

"She keeps it with her all the time. She even took it to the bathroom last night."

"You think she has opium in it?"

"Laudanum. Doctors prescribe it for nervous conditions. That's why those symptoms seemed familiar: my father used to treat people for laudanum addiction. I'll wager Ivy took the pendant to buy more."

They stopped at the telegraph office first, but, as they'd suspected, Ivy wasn't there. Case asked for directions to the nearest doctor's office, and there they found the waiting room in disarray and the sheriff talking to the doctor and his assistant.

After Case identified himself, the sheriff told him that a young woman had come to the doctor to buy laudanum with a piece of jewelry. When the doctor had refused to give it to her, she had thrown a fit, tipping over a table and struggling with him. When the doctor's assistant went outside to call for help, the girl fled.

"She matches the description of a young woman I received by wire yesterday," the sheriff told them.

"Had she been kidnapped?" Eliza asked, still hoping that Ivy hadn't lied to them.

"No, ma'am. She ran away from home."

"Where is home?" Case asked.

"Next town east—Adell."

Case shook his head in disgust. "She told us she was from Omaha."

Disheartened, Eliza left the office. Ivy *had* lied to them, and she had gullibly believed every word of the girl's story. The worst part was that after Eliza had insisted that Case trust her, he had been proven right. What chance did she have of changing his thinking now?

Case discussed the situation with the sheriff, then walked outside, where he found Eliza pacing back and forth, her forehead furrowed. "We think Ivy will probably try to get the laudanum from the druggist's shop," he told her. "The sheriff is headed there now. Do you want to go along or do you just want to leave?"

"Perhaps there's some truth to Ivy's story," Eliza said, as though trying to convince herself. "Perhaps she was being held against her will by her family to try to cure her addiction, and she couldn't stand it."

Case pitied Eliza. He'd warned her this would happen: she had trusted and been betrayed. And now she was trying to justify what had happened.

For reasons Case didn't want to examine, he didn't have the heart to lecture her. Instead he found himself saying, "She told a pretty convincing story."

"You didn't believe it." Eliza sighed deeply, then squared her shoulders, her face set determinedly. "Let's go find Ivy. She has something of yours."

They followed the sheriff to the druggist's shop, only to discover that she'd been chased away after trying to pawn the pendant. They searched in the other shops on the street and finally in the livery stable at the end of the block, thinking she might have tried to take a horse.

"I'll send some men out to hunt for her in case she's trying to hitch a ride out of town," the sheriff suggested.

Case turned his head, listening intently. "I hear something."

Eliza, listened, too, and heard the unmistakable sound of a girl crying.

Behind the stables, they found Ivy kneeling on a blanket in their wagon, sobbing as she clawed wildly at her face and arms. Seeing Eliza, she cried in desperation, "Spiders! Get them off! Please, get them off!"

Case jumped in the wagon, grabbed a blanket, and wrapped it around her, holding her so she couldn't move. "It's all right, Ivy," he said with surprising tenderness. "There aren't any spiders on you."

Ivy struggled to break free, but she was no match for Case's strength. Finally she sagged against him, sobbing. "They were all over me—biting and stinging and crawling in my eyes. I couldn't stand it. I just couldn't stand it."

Case picked her up and carried her out of the wagon. As soon as he set her down, she started struggling again. "My bag," she cried, trying to free her arms. "I need my bag."

While Case restrained Ivy, Eliza found her handbag in the wagon, loosened the strings, and removed a brown bottle. She removed the cap and sniffed, wrinkling her nose at the sickly sweet smell. "It's laudanum."

"It's for my nerves!" Ivy cried, reaching out a hand. "My doctor said I need it. Give it to me!"

Eliza turned the bottle upside down. "It's empty, Ivy."

At that, the fight drained out of the girl. She didn't move when Case removed the blanket, and she barely noticed when the sheriff took her arm.

"Come with me," he said kindly. "We'll take you somewhere to rest, and then I'll let your parents know you're safe."

Ivy jerked her arm from his grasp and would have fled but for the sheriff's quick reaction. "I won't go back!" she said, struggling with him. "They'll just lock me in my room again."

"I'm going to take you to Mrs. Bakewell's house," he assured her. "She'll take good care of you. You'll like her."

To Eliza and Case he said, "Reverend Bakewell's wife takes in wayward girls. Ivy will be in good hands there until her parents can collect her."

"May I have a word with her?" Eliza asked.

She took Ivy aside, standing her against a wall to ensure that she wouldn't run. Then she handed Ivy her handbag and showed her the pendant she had removed from it. "You stole this from Case."

"I needed my medicine," the girl replied sullenly.

Eliza lifted her chin, forcing Ivy to look at her. "Your medicine is a dangerous drug that affects the mind. Look what it's done to you. It's turned you into a liar and a thief. I'll wager you made your family miserable with your behavior, and they locked you in your room to wean you from the drug. You should be ashamed of yourself, Ivy. Imagine how worried your parents are."

At Ivy's blank expression, Eliza gave up and turned to signal to the sheriff that she was done. As he led the girl away, Eliza could hear her whimpering pathetically, "I need more medicine. It's for my nerves, don't you under-stand?"

Eliza watched sadly, wondering if Ivy would ever rid herself of her addiction, then she turned to Case. "This is yours," she said, and put the crystal pendant in his palm. "It was in her bag. I'm ready to go now."

Chapter 17

Case stared at the pendant in his palm as Eliza headed for the stables. He pocketed it and followed her, gathering up the harnesses as she led the horses around to the front of the wagon. She worked silently, then walked with him as he led the wagon to the road.

He glanced at Eliza as they left the town behind, wondering what was going through her mind. He wanted to say, "I told you not to trust her," but he figured she had suffered enough.

"I should have suspected laudanum," Eliza finally said. "I once saw a young woman with those same symptoms. She had just moved to town and came to my father to get more of the drug, but he saw what it was doing to her mind and refused to give it to her." Eliza shook her head sadly. "Some doctors prescribe it just to keep women quiet."

She turned to look at Case. "You were correct not to trust her. It wasn't that she's not a good person; she just couldn't make the right choices because of what the drug did to her mind.

"And I was correct to trust my intuition," Eliza continued. "Ivy needed our help. Who knows what would have happened to her if we hadn't come along?"

Case frowned as he guided the team around a bend. Had he won, or not? Had Eliza learned her lesson, or was she trying to teach him one?

"Next time I tell you not to trust someone," he said sternly, "I hope you'll listen. You're too kind to people, and most don't deserve it."

"It's the only way I can be."

He was coming to realize how true that was. Still, he had to try. "You'll get hurt that way."

Eliza shocked him by scooting over and resting her head against his shoulder. "Do you know what my aunt says about that? She says you can't smell the roses without encountering a few thorns."

Case smiled inwardly, imagining plump little Violet Lowe fluttering about her parlor, spouting her pearls of wisdom.

"Do you know what one of those roses was,

for me?" Eliza asked, glancing up at him. "You trusted me."

And we both paid for it, he wanted to say. But then his gaze met hers, and she smiled, a warm smile of appreciation that filled him with a contentment he'd never known. Case put his arm around her and she snuggled closer, sighing happily.

When had his happiness come to depend on Eliza's presence in his life? Case gazed down at the top of her head, suddenly realizing how dangerous his thinking had become.

Eliza would never be a steady presence in his life. She was a shooting star, blazing a brilliant trail across his life, in and out in the blink of an eye. When she was gone, she'd leave nothing but the blackness of night in her wake. If he wasn't careful, she'd take his heart with her.

Eileen's heart pounded against her ribs as she crept down the boardinghouse's creaky stairs and peered around the corner. The manager sat on a stool behind a wooden counter as ancient as he was, reading a newspaper through glasses perched on the end of his red veined nose. Quickly Eileen stole across the short space to the door and slipped outside. The effort exhausted her.

She moved away from the building, pressing one hand over her mouth to fight back the nausea. Francis had said he wouldn't be home until suppertime, but just in case he returned early, she didn't want the manager to know what time she'd left. She felt guilty about sneaking out, but she had promised Eliza's aunt that she'd see her again, and she just couldn't hurt the dear, sweet lady's feelings. Neither did she want to anger Francis.

When she arrived at the hotel, she found that Violet had already secured a table in the dining room for them and was contentedly sipping a cup of tea. Eileen paused outside the door to smooth back her hair, tucking stray wisps beneath the brim of her straw hat. She'd once had a closet full of nice hats; now she had one. She'd been forced to abandon the others when they'd fled their home.

"Hello, Mrs. Lowe," she said with forced cheer.

"Oh, here you are, dear!" Violet beamed as Eileen slid into a chair across from hers. "I've ordered more of those delicious egg salad sandwiches for you."

Eileen's mouth watered. It was amazing what good food did for one's appetite.

"Did you have any problem coming here?" Violet asked in a whisper.

"No. Francis leaves early each morning."

"Where does he go?"

Eileen glanced down guiltily. "He takes odd

jobs down at the wharf. At least that's what he says."

"What do you think he does?"

Eileen bit her lip. "He plays poker sometimes."

Violet clucked her tongue. "We've got to get you away from him, dear. He's no good for you. I want you to pack your things and come stay with me."

Eileen stared at her, aghast. "I can't leave my husband. I took a vow. I'm going to have his child! What would I do on my own?"

"Listen to me, dear: your husband is a criminal. He's been lying to you all along. You can have your marriage annulled. I know a very competent attorney in Chicago who will handle it discreetly. Then you can go back to Coffee Creek and live a quiet life."

"But what will people back home say? What will they think of me if I return with a child?" Eileen shook her head, her eyes swimming with tears. "I love Francis; I can't leave him. I just can't."

"Then you'll be putting your child *and* yourself *and* your best friend in danger."

"How?"

"Eliza will be here in another day or two, bringing with her a man who will probably want to take your husband back to Chicago to stand trial. What do you think Francis will do when he finds out?"

Eileen dropped her head into her hands, moaning, "I don't know. I can't think."

"Yes, you can, dear," Violet argued. "You must do the right thing. I came all the way to Omaha to save my niece, and you're going to help me."

At the corner across the street from the hotel, Frank Caroni leaned casually against the lightpost, puffing on a cigar as if he hadn't a care in the world. Inside, however, his mind had never been keener, his nerves never more tightly coiled and ready for action.

By his calculations, Brogan should be arriving today. To that end, he'd paid a clerk in the Western Union office to notify him immediately.

What Frank hadn't foreseen—and who would have?—was that his mousy, good-for-nothing wife would have the courage to sneak out and meet someone. He'd had a strong hunch yesterday that Eileen was lying to him.

He couldn't wait to find out who she was seeing.

"If we keep going, we should reach Council Bluffs by nightfall," Case told Eliza as he studied his map. "It's the last stop before Omaha, which is just on the other side of the Missouri River."

"Let's keep going."

They had stopped late in the afternoon to feed and rest the horses, and to eat. Now Eliza sat with her back against a cottonwood tree, her hair loose, her feet bare, picking blades of grass and tearing them into pieces.

Case put down the map and studied her. Those little worry lines were back. A week ago he wouldn't have noticed, and even if he had, he wouldn't have cared. He didn't particularly like what that change represented, but he found himself asking anyway, "What's troubling you?"

She sighed. "I was just thinking how terribly lonely it would be to have a new baby and no husband around to help care for it."

Case's good mood vanished. Eliza was on a campaign to save Caroni again. "It's better than being on the lam with a new baby and a husband who's a felon," he said grimly.

Eliza plucked another blade of grass. "What if there's not enough evidence? He could be set free, couldn't he?"

Case pressed his lips together, his insides churning at the thought of Caroni going free again. Case wasn't about to take that chance; he'd already decided Frank's fate. He just couldn't tell Eliza that. "There's enough evidence."

He felt her eyes on him, but his were too full of bitterness to meet her gaze.

"Eileen deserves to have her baby safe in the knowledge that she has a husband to support her," Eliza argued. "And Francis deserves an opportunity to start fresh. He's going to be a father, Case, and nothing changes a man more than that."

When Case didn't reply, she said, "Why do you hate Francis so much?"

"I'm just doing my job."

She crawled over to him and took his hand, his reward—and punishment—for allowing her to get close to him before. "I know you well enough now to realize that's not the whole truth. It goes beyond doing your job. It's personal."

When he again said nothing, she squeezed his hand. "You think Francis Caroni killed your father, don't you?"

Case lifted his head and met her gaze, letting her see the hatred that filled his soul. "If I say yes, will you lecture me on forgiveness? Will you heap guilt on my shoulders for harboring such animosity, hoping I'll confess my sins and repent?" He took his hand from hers and turned his head away. "Save your breath. I've waited too long for this day."

He waited for her admonishment, but none came. She was silent for a long moment, then she said evenly, "I understand."

Case glanced at her in disbelief, as Eliza continued. "I've seen your sorrow when you talk about missing your father, and I've seen your loathing when you hear the name Caroni. I can only guess at the depth of your suffering."

He waited for her to finish. He knew what was coming: *"But Francis has changed his ways. He loves Eileen and she's carrying his child. Please spare him."*

Yet Eliza didn't argue. Instead, she modestly turned her back and began to pull on her stockings. Despite his dark mood, Case found himself imagining her sliding them up over slender ankles and shapely calves, up to those beautiful ivory thighs, and he felt his tension ease as tiny embers of desire nudged into its place.

Perhaps that was her plan: to seduce him into surrendering.

But again Eliza surprised him. She tied her shoes and stood up, brushing off her skirt. "You're a good man, Case Brogan, even though you don't believe it."

He watched mutely as she gathered up the food and returned to the wagon. Eliza was a remarkable woman. She was naive, yet wise beyond her years, coquettish beyond her experience—and she saw goodness where there was none.

Eliza's mind raced as she put away their supplies and joined Case on the wagon bench. It was just as she'd feared: he blamed Francis for his father's death. But her mind refused to accept it as truth. She'd only met Francis on three occasions, to be sure, yet her impression of him had been of a man who radiated charm and confidence, and who could fault him for the lavish attention he'd heaped on Eileen?

But to be an actual cold-blooded murderer?

Eliza rejected it. Case's father's death could have been an accident.

She wanted to ask Case what the actual circumstances of his father's death were, but she sensed that he had been pushed as far as he was going to go on the subject. She didn't like it when he sat as stiff and silent as a rock, because she knew he was suffering inside. She wondered how much of it was self-inflicted.

"... *will you lecture me on forgiveness? Will you heap guilt on my shoulders for harboring such animosity, hoping I'll confess my sins and repent?*" he'd asked. In her mind, those were the words of a man torn between right and wrong. He knew what he should do—but would he?

* * *

Eileen snuck past the manager and hurried up the stairs, breathing a sigh of relief when she reached the door of her room. It was only two o'clock; she had plenty of time to compose herself before Francis came home.

Her conversation with Violet had been upsetting. She didn't want her best friend hurt, but she had her baby to think of, and a baby needed its father. At that moment her stomach roiled, reminding her of her tremendous obligation to the life inside her.

"Where have you been, sweetheart?"

Eileen gasped and swung around as Francis came up the hallway behind her. "I went to the grocer's to get an apple."

"I don't see the apple."

"I—I ate it. It tasted so good I couldn't wait until I got home to finish it."

He opened the door and waited until she walked inside, then he followed her in and shut it firmly. Eileen sat down on the bed, twisting her fingers in her lap, as he came toward her.

"Where else did you go?"

"Nowhere."

He cupped her chin. "I don't like it when you lie to me, sweetheart. I saw you go into the Grand Central Hotel today."

Eileen swallowed bile that had risen to her throat. "Oh, silly me!" she said, forcing a laugh.

"I almost forgot. I ran into an old friend from Chicago."

You shouldn't have said Chicago, her frantic brain screamed. *Francis is from Chicago.*

Francis pulled the rickety chair away from the table and turned it backward, straddling it as he faced her. "And who is this old friend?"

"Violet," Eileen said quickly. "Her name is Violet."

"Does Violet have a last name?" he asked, treating her as though she were a slow child.

Eileen began to quake inside, knowing what was coming. First Francis would talk to her with unsettling calmness, then he would lose patience and his features would distort, his tone becoming more sarcastic, then he'd hurl cruel insults, until she'd break down in tears.

There was nothing to do but come out with it. He'd find out eventually anyway; he always did. He was so much smarter than she. "Violet L-Lowe," Eileen stammered. "Eliza's aunt."

Francis's eyebrows shot up. "Eliza's aunt is in Omaha? My, my. And you just happened to run into her?"

"Yes, Francis, that's the God's honest truth. I went to the grocer's to get an apple and there she was, across the street in front of the hotel."

"So naturally you had to go across and speak to her, even though I told you not to talk to anyone, or leave the room." He stood up suddenly, shoved the chair aside, and began to walk back and forth in front of the bed, his hands behind his back, as though pondering what to do with her.

"You went inside the hotel with Violet Lowe."

"Yes, we went to the restaurant for tea. She insisted, Francis, and it did taste good." At his cold glare, Eileen dropped her gaze.

"So you and Violet had tea. And conversation, too, I assume. What did you talk about?"

"Lots of things: h-her health, and the baby— our baby, Francis, and her trip, and—"

"And me?"

"She did ask how you were."

Suddenly Frank was looming over her, his mouth twisted into a cruel slant. "And you said I was fine, and *then what*, Eileen? Did she mention at all where her niece was with the *money*?"

Eileen cringed away from him. "She said Eliza would be here in a day or two."

"A day or two?" He straightened with a jerk. "Shit! They should have been here today."

"She wasn't sure," Eileen offered meekly.

"Did she happen to tell you the Pinkerton's name?"

Eileen nodded hastily, then swallowed hard. "It's C-Case Brogan."

She saw his eyes widen, then turn as black as

coal. Francis strode to the window and braced his hands against the trim, staring through the dirty pane. "I knew it was Brogan."

"What are you going to do, Francis?" she ventured timidly.

He stared outside for a long moment, then finally turned to face her. Eileen breathed a sigh of relief. He was smiling again.

"Don't you worry, sweetheart. I'll take care of everything."

It took all afternoon and part of the evening to traverse the low, rolling hills and the towering bluffs of western Iowa. Case had to stop the wagon several times to rest the horses. Each time, Eliza wandered a short distance off, sometimes plucking idly at plants that grew in the mountainous area, as though deep in thought, sometimes just quietly studying him from afar. Each time, he had to stop himself from asking her what was on her mind. He already knew, and he didn't want to discuss it.

At their last rest stop, Case sat on a grassy hillock, watching the horses nibble contentedly nearby. Eliza had gone exploring, so he was alone with his thoughts. He felt a mixture of building tension and regret. Everything he had planned for was about to happen, but he was that much closer to losing Eliza.

He'd simply grown accustomed to her odd little ways, that was all—and of course, he couldn't deny the desire she aroused in him.

But it would all end in Omaha. And Eliza couldn't say he hadn't warned her.

"Ouch!" he heard Eliza say. He glanced over his shoulder and saw her limping toward the back of the wagon, her shoes and stockings in hand.

Case immediately jumped up and strode toward her. "You've stubbed your toe again, I'll bet."

"Then you'd lose the bet." She climbed inside and began digging through his supplies. "It's just a little splinter in my heel."

"Here," he said, crawling in behind her, "let me get the iodine."

"I can find it."

"Yes, but in what century?" Case retorted dryly.

Giving him a disgruntled look, Eliza moved back, and he took over, removing a small bottle, gauze and tape, and a packet of needles in less than a minute. "Let me see your heel."

"You've seen my heel," she said, stretching her hand toward the bottle. "I can take care of it myself."

Case held the iodine out of reach. "You always have to have your way, don't you?"

"Not always," she said with mock petulance.

"Name one time since we left Chicago when you haven't."

She thought a moment, then gave him a slow, seductive smile, her eyes sparkling impishly. "Well . . ."

He saw the challenge in her gaze and his body responded instantly, those embers of desire sparking brightly to life. Case tried to smother them with reason. "You're wasting valuable time. Now give me your heel."

She sighed resignedly. "All right."

He narrowed his eyes at her. When Eliza conceded that quickly, she was up to something.

She stretched out her right leg, lifted the skirt to mid-calf, and leaned back on her hands. "Go ahead."

Case picked up her foot to examine her heel, causing her skirt to slide further back, exposing a bare knee. His manhood began to stiffen.

"Be careful," Eliza said, wincing as he probed for the splinter.

She didn't know how pertinent that advice was. Case carefully kept his eyes away from her leg, and finally spotted the point of a brown sliver sticking from her foot. He doused the area with iodine, then used the tip of a needle to loosen it, managing to pull it free with his fingernails.

"Here it is," he said proudly, displaying the splinter.

"Good. Thank you," she said, and tried to remove her foot, but he held tight to her ankle.

"We're not finished yet," he said. Case knew he was flirting with danger, but he was enjoying keeping her captive.

Eliza seemed to sense it, and played along. "Oh, really? Then what are you going to do to me next?"

"First," he said, holding up the gauze, "I'm going to bandage your wound."

"And then?"

Case cut a strip of gauze and two strips of tape and fastened them around her heel. "And then I'm going to put on your stocking."

"That should be interesting—I didn't think you wore my size," she quipped.

He grinned at her as he took one of the cotton stockings from her hand and bunched it up on his fingers. He slipped it over her toes, up the arch, over her heel and slowly up over her calf to her knee.

"And then what will you do?" she asked breathlessly.

"The other stocking." He repeated the same movements on her left leg, his fingers moving steadily up her naked flesh, ever closer to those luscious thighs. He glanced up at Eliza and found her watching through heavy-lidded eyes, her mouth parted slightly as tiny gasps of pleasure slipped through her lips.

Dear God, how he wanted to taste those lips. They looked so soft and inviting that his resolve began to weaken. And when the tip of her pink tongue darted out to wet them, he surged with desire, wanting nothing more than to surrender to his lustful urges.

Gazing deep into Eliza's sultry eyes, Case leaned over her, bracing his hands on either side of her shoulders, lowering his head until his lips met hers. He kissed her gently, still fighting the passion that raged through his loins. But when she wound her arms around his neck and arched her body up against his, Case knew he had lost the battle.

By God, if only for today, Eliza would be his.

Chapter 18

When Case lowered his weight onto her and began to kiss her fiercely, needily, Eliza welcomed him with open arms. Before, she'd been intent on satisfying her curiosity about all those delicious cravings Case aroused in her; now she also felt an overwhelming fondness for him.

But was it love?

No, she immediately assured herself. She couldn't be in love with Case Brogan—not only because of her singing aspirations, but also because of his job. She didn't want a husband who was involved in dangerous work, especially if she were to have children. What would happen if he were killed?

She could be fond of him, though. Very fond, she thought tenderly, running her hands down the sides of his face.

Case had changed over the past nine days; he was no longer the cold, unfeeling detective she'd first met. Just in the past two days alone, he'd shown a gentleness and caring that he'd never revealed before. Most important, Eliza knew that he had come to trust her.

It filled her with an overwhelming joy. She wanted to sing out her happiness, to share it with the world. Case Brogan trusted her!

She wove her fingers through his hair and thought no one in the world had such thick, handsome hair as Case did. And his smooth, square jaw—was there a man in creation who had such a fine, manly jaw? Case was a man among men. She had been right to trust her intuition.

Case immediately sensed a change in Eliza's responses. Her hands stroked his face tenderly and her kisses became gentler. He lifted his head and gazed at her questioningly, and was stunned by the love that shone from her blue eyes.

More than stunned, he quaked with fear.

His desire evaporated as the burden of that love pressed down on him. He didn't want Eliza's love, because he sure as hell couldn't give her his. There wasn't any to give her. He shouldn't even have started kissing her, but he'd ignored his common sense once again. What was he supposed to do now?

His instincts told him to run.

Case eased himself off, avoiding her gaze, and began to put away the supplies. "How does your foot feel?"

"Much better." She sat up and wrapped her arms around him, laying her head on his shoulder. "Thank you."

Case closed his eyes and dropped his head back as his heart constricted. She was so trusting, so damned trusting, that he hated himself for not being the kind of man she thought he was.

"We'd better get going if we want to make Council Bluffs by nightfall," he said, his voice tight with emotion.

She gave him a final hug and began to put on her shoes, humming happily. Case hopped down from the wagon and went to hitch up the horses. His insides knotted as he fought off unfamiliar emotions bubbling up from some hidden well. Damn it, he didn't want to feel anything. He'd kept his distance from people for expressly that reason. Now Eliza had changed everything.

Somehow he had to change it back.

Council Bluffs was a prosperous river town that benefited from both the trade on the Missouri River and the multitude of railroad lines that ran though it, the biggest being the transcontinental railroad.

Eliza gazed at the many shops in delight as they rode down the main street. There was even a goodly number of hotels from which to choose.

Eliza knew that if Case had been traveling alone, he probably would have kept going, crossing the river into Omaha; she could sense how keyed up he was. But he'd also pushed the horses hard that day, and he knew that she was tired.

It was just one of the many little ways Case had proved how much he cared for her, but this afternoon was most telling. She knew he'd seen the warmth and caring in her eyes, but she wondered if he knew he had reflected it back. Eliza had seen it. She'd also felt his fear.

Yet that fear encouraged her. Case had opened himself enough to let her see inside his soul; now all things seemed possible. Eliza was sure she'd convinced him not to take action against Francis, to wait and find out the truth.

Case let her off in front of a hotel near the river while he took the horses to the closest livery stable. Eliza took her bag to her room, then went downstairs to wait for him.

The hotel's restaurant was actually a cozy tavern. Dark wood beams crossed the ceiling; the same dark wood had been used for the bar stools and the heavy benches and trestle tables. The walls were painted a mustard-yellow, and the floors were wooden. A polished walnut bar with brass foot rail occupied one side of the room, with long tables filling the rest of the space.

Eliza settled herself at a table opposite the door so she could watch for Case. A barmaid brought a short, hand-printed menu, and asked to take her order.

"It'll be a few minutes; I'm waiting for some-one," Eliza told her. She glanced at the door and smiled, her heart overflowing with happiness. "There he is now."

Despite the jumble of emotions running wild in his head, Case felt a sense of comfort as he headed for the restaurant. Their nightly meals had become a pleasurable routine, as he and Eliza had suffered good weather and bad, deli-cious food and hard jerky, and questionable companions.

It was astounding, when he thought about it. Case had never worked with a partner for more than a day, and had never had a relationship with a woman for more than a night, and even those had been infrequent and unfulfilling.

Now, as Eliza looked up from her menu and smiled from across the room, Case's heart felt as though it were tripling in size, warming him all the way to his heels.

But that brought a chill to his soul. He couldn't fall in love with Eliza, and he didn't want her to be in love with him. When this assignment was over, they would both go back to their separate lives. That's the way it had to be.

He sat across from Eliza as a comely barmaid stepped up to their table. "What can I bring you?" she asked, giving him a slanting glance that in the past would have started his juices flowing. Now it fell flat.

"I'll have a beefsteak sandwich," he told her, then added, "Bring a pitcher of ale, too." He ignored Eliza's raised eyebrows. Tonight he felt like soaking his brain in alcohol.

"Isn't this a charming place?" Eliza asked with her usual exuberance. "Just look at the beautiful frosted glass in the windows. I usually don't frequent taverns, but this is quite homey. And the menu looks good, too."

Case glanced around. Had Eliza not made a point of it, he wouldn't have noticed a thing about the tavern. But now he saw it through her eyes and decided it was charming, after all. Just like her.

He patted the crystal pendant in his pants pocket. He'd decided to give it to her tonight, while she was still speaking to him.

Eliza's eyes widened as the waitress brought

her a huge, steaming bowl of beef stew. She picked up her spoon and dug in, pausing after her first bite to exclaim over it.

"Did I ever tell you about Annie Applegate?" she said between bites. "Annie lived next door to us in Coffee Creek and took care of us after my mother died. She made the best beef stew in the whole world—and still does. I saw Annie just this past summer when I returned for my friend Emeline's wedding. She hasn't changed a bit; still as feisty as ever."

Case watched her as he ate his sandwich and worked on his mug of ale, but he wasn't thinking about beef stew or her Annie. And he most definitely wasn't thinking about the love he'd seen in Eliza's eyes that afternoon. He was purposely thinking about anything *but* that.

What he *was* thinking about was that kiss in the wagon. And those bare legs. And remembering the feel of her thighs as his hands and tongue slid along her silken flesh.

Sweet Jesse, how he wanted to experience that again. How he'd love to open those thighs and bury himself deep inside her, spending himself until he'd sated his desire for her forever.

Could he ever sate his desire for Eliza?

She loves you, his reason whispered. *If you seduce her, she'll only believe you love her, too.*

"Case?"

He lifted his head, not realizing until that moment that he'd been staring down into his mug.

She reached out and covered his hand. "What's wrong?"

Case stared at that capable, feminine hand and had the strongest urge to lift it to his lips, to press kisses in her palm. Instead he turned it over and pressed the crystal pendant into it.

At her look of surprise he said, "It's yours. I bought it for you."

Eliza gazed at it for a long moment, running the fine gold chain through her fingers, then she looked at him with eyes brimming with tears. He braced himself for a long, sentimental speech about how much she appreciated his thoughtfulness and how she'd wear it forever. Instead, she stood up and came around the table.

"Will you fasten it for me?" she asked, presenting her back.

Case rose and took the tiny gold clasp in his big, clumsy fingers, fumbling with it until it finally latched into place, fighting the urge to lean down and kiss the tender nape of her neck.

Eliza turned, fingering the simple pendant, and smiled at him. "I like it."

Case sat down and started to laugh, whether from nerves or surprise or relief, he didn't know. He only knew that Eliza never ceased to amaze him. And that he would be lost without her.

And that he would have to get over her.

* * *

Eliza found herself laughing with him. "What's so funny?" she asked, settling on her bench.

Case wiped his eyes with the heels of his hand, suddenly somber. "I had expected a different reaction." He finished his ale, then signaled for the barmaid to settle their account.

Eliza stroked the crystal at her throat and studied him thoughtfully. What had he expected? Had he thought she'd refuse the pendant? Or perhaps he'd expected a kiss in return.

She smiled to herself. That would be easy to remedy.

Frank Caroni gave the doorman a nod as he stepped outside the Grand Central Hotel. At the curb he flagged a hackney cab, gave the cabby a hefty tip and a few instructions, and told him to wait. Smiling jauntily, Frank nodded to the doorman once again as he sauntered inside, adjusting the brim of his gray felt hat. He looked good and he knew it. New suit, new hat, new shoes, even new stockings, all thanks to a twenty-dollar gold coin he'd nabbed from some tottering dowager's handbag earlier that afternoon. What a windfall that had been.

Train stations were exceptionally lucrative places for a clever fellow like him. He'd learned how to pick pockets in busy train stations when he was ten years old. Sure, he'd gotten caught a few times, but with his wide smile and a big dose of charm, he'd always finagled his way out of trouble—and kept himself out of the orphanage.

The thought of that place still gave him nightmares. Once he'd escaped, he'd vowed never to be kept anywhere against his will again. He'd rather starve on the streets than be locked up like an animal. And he'd kill anyone who tried to do it to him.

Frank began to whistle. That coin he'd nipped had even allowed him to sit in on a few hands of poker down at the wharf. Could life get any better than that?

Yes, it could—once he'd picked up the one thousand dollars and rid himself of that deadweight wife of his. Ah, the things he'd be able to do with that kind of money, and his freedom to boot.

Frank flipped open the cover of his pocket watch—another one of his quick-fingered gains—and checked the time. Seven twenty-five in the evening. In five minutes, Violet Lowe would step off the elevator and hurry over to the reception desk to pick up a message.

And Frank would be waiting to give it to her.

He settled down on one of the plush, wine-colored chairs in the lobby to wait. He'd been there for an hour, quietly observing the moneybags coming and going, passing the time while

Violet ate at the restaurant. Five minutes ago, she'd come through the lobby and taken the elevator to her room, where Frank had left a note under her door that said, "There is an urgent message for you at the reception desk." He'd signed it, "The Management."

At exactly seven-thirty, the elevator's metal accordion door opened and a short, dumpy, overdressed matron scurried out, looking very flustered. Frank rose, removed his hat, smoothed back his well-greased hair, adjusted his vest and necktie, and strode confidently toward her, cutting her off a few yards in front of the reception desk.

"Mrs. Lowe?"

"Yes?" she said, giving him a quick once-over.

Frank smiled placidly, knowing exactly what she would see: a handsome gentleman in a gray suit, the same suit that all hotel management wore. "We have a message for you."

"Yes?"

"If you'll come with me, please."

"Yes, thank you."

He nearly laughed out loud as he led her to one of the exits. It was just too easy.

But then she surprised him by pulling her arm away, halting just before the door. "Why are we going outside?"

"I'm sorry, I should have delivered the mes-

sage first. I was asked to escort you to a hired
cab and instruct the driver to take you to the library." He looked up as a doorman on the outside opened the door for them.

"The library?" Violet asked, giving him a
speculative glance as she followed him to the
street.

"Omaha has quite a fine public library," Frank
continued smoothly. "I think you'll be very im-
pressed with the architecture."

"But why am I to go there?"

He shrugged his shoulders. "I'm sorry. The
young lady—Eileen was her name—only said to
tell you she'd be waiting there for you. She was
in something of a rush so I didn't press her for
more details."

She pondered it for several moments, making
Frank wonder if he'd have to resort to force.

"Would you like me to have someone accompany you?" he asked. "Although I can assure
you, the library is perfectly safe."

"No, no," she said, "I can go alone. But I must
leave word at the desk for my niece in case she
arrives while I'm gone."

"I'd be happy to leave a message for you,"
Frank offered, smiling gallantly.

"Then please tell her where I've gone. Her
name is Eliza Lowe."

"I'll deliver the message in person," he said.

He escorted her to the buggy and helped her inside. "On second thought," he said, stepping into the buggy, "perhaps I should escort you myself."

Violet's eyes widened in surprise as the hotel manager climbed in beside her. "What are you doing?"

"I can't send you off to a strange building alone," he said, removing his hat.

Violet suddenly had an uneasy feeling about him. "As I've already told you, that's quite unnecessary."

"Consider it a hotel courtesy."

Violet turned to look out the window, her mind working furiously. She'd never heard of a hotel manager accompanying a guest anywhere. Why was he being so courteous to her? And what of the message he had promised to give Eliza?

"I've changed my mind," she told him. "I'd like to go back to the hotel."

"And leave your friend waiting?" the man asked with condescending charm. "Would that be polite?"

Violet nibbled her lower lip. She didn't want to leave Eileen waiting, but she also couldn't ignore her strong feeling that something was wrong. "I'll send her a message. Please take me back at once."

"Now, now. Calm yourself," he said, patting her knee.

Violet pushed his hand away. "Watch your manners, young man."

He laughed, a horrible sound that made her skin crawl.

"Stop this vehicle at once!" she cried, rapping on the roof, but the driver paid no attention. Violet tried to open her door, but the man beside her grabbed her arm.

"Don't try it," he sneered.

Violet tried to yank her arm free, but he held tight. "Who are you?"

"Haven't you guessed?"

Violet peered at him in the dim light. He was very handsome, but his eyes were odd—one blue and one green. She gulped. "Francis Caroni!"

"At your service."

Violet's palms began to sweat in her gloves. "We're not going to the library. Where are you taking me?"

"To meet my wife."

When the buggy came to a halt, Francis got out and offered her his hand. Violet ignored him, looking up instead at an enormous warehouse facing the river. She had a very strong suspicion that Eileen was in trouble. She shoved his hand aside and stepped down, straightening her jacket.

"This way," he said, taking her elbow.

"I don't need your help," Violet retorted, lifting her chin.

He pushed open a huge metal door at the end of the long building and took her inside. Violet stopped and gazed around in growing alarm. By the moonlight streaming through the high windows, she could see row upon row of wooden crates. Why would Eileen be here?

"Why did you bring me to this place?"

"My wife said you wanted to see her privately."

"Yes, but she wasn't—"

"—supposed to tell me?" Frank finished. "You don't know Eileen very well. She tells me everything. Now if you'll come with me, I'll show you that she's perfectly fine and waiting eagerly to see you."

They walked past the rows of storage and stopped before a closed door at the far end of the building. Frank opened it and Violet blinked hard, trying to see inside, but it was pitch black and she couldn't see a thing.

"Eileen?" he called. "Shame on you for playing games."

"She isn't in there!" Violet cried. She turned to run past him, but Francis shoved her into the room, knocking her on her seat. He laughed as he shut the door. A moment later she heard something being shoved against the door from the outside.

Violet rose and brushed off her skirt and jacket. By the thin light from one window high up on the wall, she could just make out shapes in the room. She felt her way to the door and tried to open it, but as she'd feared, Francis had braced it.

Tiny threads of fear tightened in her chest as she felt her way around the room, looking for another way out. There seemed to be a rickety table against one wall, and several bales of what felt like straw, but nothing else other than the high slit of a window. She felt her way around to the door and pounded on it, but doubted anyone would be around at that time of night.

"Don't panic now, Violet," she said aloud, sinking to the floor as she fanned her face with her hand. "Panic won't help you save Eliza." But oh, dear, how frightened she was.

Clearly Francis had wanted her out of the way so she couldn't warn Eliza. All she could hope for now was that someone at the hotel would tell her niece she had arrived.

A steaming bath awaited Eliza when she returned to her hotel room. She had paid for it in advance, and had also ordered one for Case as a surprise. Now, as she sank down into the tub, she closed her eyes, leaned her head against the high back, and sighed in ecstasy, imagining Case doing the same.

She had another surprise in store for him.

Giggling, Eliza scrubbed herself clean and dried off, then sprinkled on some rose water, tied her hair back in a white ribbon, put on her nightdress, wrapper, and her pendant. Then she padded barefoot to his room one door down, a bottle of wine and two glasses in hand.

Eliza waited excitedly as Case opened the door for her. He had bathed, too, and had put on a clean white shirt and brown pants. He hadn't quite finished buttoning the shirt—she had obviously caught him in the act of dressing—leaving his tanned throat and the top of his chest bared.

"Surprise," she said, holding up the bottle.

"What's that for?" he asked suspiciously.

"It's my intention to poison you. Will you shut the door, please? I wouldn't want any witnesses."

Giving her a wary glance, Case shut the door, but didn't lock it. He watched Eliza struggle with the cork for a moment, then held out his hand. "Allow me.

"Champagne?" he asked. The cork popped and the wine overflowed the top.

"Note the tiny bubbles that indicate freshness," Eliza said with an impish grin. She caught some of the froth with her finger and stuck the tip in her mouth.

Case dragged his gaze away from her lush mouth to pour the wine. "What are we celebrating?"

"Your birthday."

"My birthday? But it isn't until—"

"Tomorrow."

He looked at her askance as he handed her a glass. "Are you sure?"

"Of course. When we started out you said your birthday was on the twentieth, and that's tomorrow. And since tomorrow may be a bit hectic, I thought we should celebrate tonight. So here's a toast to many more healthy years. May they also be happy ones." She touched the rim of her glass to his, then took a sip and immediately rubbed her nose. "It still tickles."

Case tried it, swirling it in his mouth. "Decent wine. When did you buy it?"

"While you were taking care of the horses."

"And the bath? Was that your idea, too?"

Eliza gave him a flirtatious smile. "You see? You're not the only one who can carry off a surprise." She put down her glass and moved up close to him, her breasts nearly touching his chest. "Did you enjoy your bath?"

Eliza's eyes held that mischievous glimmer that always led to Case getting aroused, and ultimately frustrated. The danger was greater now, because he'd been semi-aroused ever since he'd kissed her earlier.

She reached up to caress the crystal heart at her neck. "Do you know how much this pendant means to me?"

"I'll take your word for it."

Eliza raised on tiptoe, wrapped her arms around his neck, and pressed her mouth to his. "This much," she whispered, nibbling at his lips, teasing him with her tongue, until he groaned and tried to send her away.

"Miss Lowe, don't start this."

She gave him a frown of displeasure. "Case, we've known each other long enough for you to call me Eliza."

He unwrapped her arms. "I know what you're up to."

"I don't think you do." She held his face between her hands. "I don't think you understand how much your gift means to me. It means you care."

"You've already thanked me."

"That was with words." Eliza pulled his face down to hers and kissed him slowly, tenderly, devouring him with painstaking thoroughness, until he groaned in sweet agony.

Case forced himself to keep his hands at his sides. If he started kissing her now, he wouldn't stop until he'd sated himself with her.

Then Eliza ran her tongue across the seam of

his lips, causing a deep shudder of pleasure to ripple through his body.

He gripped her around the waist. "Stop!"

Eliza met his lips again, her tiny nibbles driving him insane, her breasts pressed against his chest, letting him feel the soft curves and hard buds through the silky material. "Say my name," she whispered.

Case tensed his whole body, battling the rampant lust sweeping through him. But as she slipped her tongue inside his mouth, his manhood pulsed and thickened against her belly, demanding surrender, driving out the last sane thought in his head. He gave up the fight.

Chapter 19

Case cupped Eliza's head in his hands and kissed her deeply, entwining his tongue with hers, feeling his manhood respond with a hard throb. She tasted as good as she felt, soft and sweet and desirable. His fingers sought the ribbon holding back her hair. He tugged it, letting the heavy locks fall free, then ran his hands over it and through it, enjoying the luxurious silkiness of her curls, pushing them off her face as he kissed her forehead, temple, earlobe, jaw and chin. He pressed kisses on her eyelids, making her giggle, then dropped his mouth to hers once again.

Eliza was everything he wanted in a woman. And he wanted her so much he ached.

His hands rested briefly on her shoulders while he nibbled her lips, then he ran his hands down her arms and back up to her breasts, fitting his palms over them, molding them. He had to see them naked. Case untied the sash of her wrapper and pushed the garment off her shoulders. He felt Eliza's trusting gaze on him as her wrapper slid to the floor and pooled around her bare feet.

God, how he wanted to kiss those feet.

Case removed the pendant, then worked the buttons down the front of her nightdress, his fingers fumbling impatiently. At last the material parted and he eagerly tugged it down, baring ivory shoulders, creamy breasts, rose-hued nipples, a slender waist, shapely hips, and finally those luscious silken thighs with that triangle of ebony hair at their center.

His eyes darkened as Eliza stepped free of the nightgown, lifting her arms to him in a gesture of welcome. With a lusty growl, Case swept her in his arms and carried her to the bed, gazing down at her hungrily. Laying her on the coverlet, he hurriedly tossed his shirt aside, unfastened his pants, and kicked them out of his way.

He wanted to dive on top of her, to part her thighs and drive himself into her until he had spent himself. But he refused to give in to those baser instincts. He wanted Eliza to share the pleasure with him.

He knelt at her feet and lifted one slender heel to his mouth, nibbling lightly at her arch, causing her to giggle and try to pull her foot away. He kissed her toes, then took the biggest in his mouth, making her gasp in shock.

Case smiled to himself, glad he had resisted the urge to take her quickly. This was much more rewarding. He kissed her ankle, then slid his tongue along her calf to her knee. Moving between her legs, he drew a circle on the tender flesh along the side of her knee, watching her eyes close in ecstasy. He licked a path up her thigh, drawing closer to that irresistible center until his lips brushed over it.

Eliza's anticipation had grown to such a height that when he reached the junction of her thighs, she drew in a sharp breath, anticipating what was to come. She watched expectantly as he started down the other leg, never imagining such delights.

His tongue on the inside of her thigh nearly drove her mad, then he followed it by lightly stroking down her calf to her sensitive arch, which made her giggle again. He put her foot down and gazed at her voraciously as he knelt between her spread legs, his beautiful erection jutting out from the mat of dark hair on his groin.

It was the most erotic, most stimulating sight Eliza had ever seen.

"Turn over," he said in a voice husky with desire.

Eliza's eyes widened. What in the world was he planning now? She rolled onto her stomach, her muscles tightening in anticipation. She felt his tongue on the back of her ankle, sliding up her leg, lingering on the ticklish underside of her knee, grazing her thigh and then, ye gods, he nipped her bottom!

She gasped in surprise and would have rolled over, but he was already working down the other leg, letting his tongue glide all the way to her ankle. Eliza held her breath, eagerly waiting to see what his next move would be.

Case straddled her legs, his knees on either side of hers. He cupped her bottom with his hands, then let his palms slide up over her hips, up the curve of her waist, up her back, gently massaging the muscles along her spine and in her shoulders, making Eliza sigh with pleasure.

Her eyes opened wide when she felt his erection glide between her legs, but as it rubbed back and forth, pressing deeper into that sensitive valley, she felt a delicious throbbing, a throbbing that grew stronger with each stroke until she thought she'd lose her mind.

Case grasped her hips and lifted them up, spreading her legs at the same time. She felt his fingers touch where his erection had been, stroking to and fro, and then sliding inside, until she was so painfully aroused that she felt like she would explode.

"Case," she panted.

"What is it?" he whispered. "What do you need?"

"I need *you*; I want to feel you—inside me."

She expected him to ask her to turn over. Instead, Case braced his hands on either side of her and pushed his manhood against her opening until it was just inside.

"It'll be easier this way for your first time," he assured her, and gently probed further, until Eliza felt a sharp stabbing pain and gasped aloud.

Case immediately withdrew, then used a deft touch to bring her back to arousal, until all Eliza could do was moan from the intense pleasure. Then he again pushed inside her, farther this time, but without as much pain. He was so big and she was so tight, yet the feel of him inside her was intoxicating.

As her passion grew, Case moved faster, but just as she felt the momentum building, he withdrew and turned her over. His manhood gleamed with her wetness as his gaze slid down her body and up again, causing her to shiver with excitement. Now what was he going to do?

He leaned down and flicked one nipple with his tongue, then covered it with his hot mouth and sucked, drawing it deeper, sending shock waves of electricity down to her toes. He moved to the other breast, and as he sucked, his finger stroked between her thighs, driving her to even greater heights of pleasure, until Eliza felt as though she were about to soar through the air.

At that moment Case covered her with his body, penetrating her deeply, then moving in and out, faster and faster. Gasping for breath, Eliza clasped her hands around his back and held on to him as she arched her hips, seeking release from her delightful torment.

Then she was soaring and dipping on waves of bliss, each one so pleasurable that she cried out again and again. And only when she had floated back to earth did she hear Case's long groan of relief and feel him shudder as he collapsed beside her.

Eliza wrapped her arms tightly around him and held him as close as she could to her heart. They had joined body and soul. Case and she had become one. She had never thought to feel such deep emotion. She had never been happier.

Case lay panting against her, his thoughts drifting lazily, drunk on spent passion. He felt sated as he'd never been sated before. Eliza had been everything that he'd expected. She was as exuberant, as accepting, as trusting in making love as she was in everything else she did.

She lay her head on his chest, saying nothing,

seeming content just to be close to him. Case stroked her hair, overcome with the longing to never let go. He cradled her in his arms, wishing he could hold back the day, knowing he had only this night.

Case turned his head to the window, which he'd opened to catch the cool evening breeze. He inhaled deeply, feeling refreshed, reborn, and infused with energy. Eliza had shaken his bleak world down to the center of his being. She had invaded that cold dark space inside and filled it with warmth and light. He never wanted to go back to the darkness.

Floating in a cloud of euphoria, Eliza slid off the bed, padded over to the table where they'd set their glasses, and padded back. She sat on the bed and held out a glass to him, unashamed of her nakedness. This man was in her heart, a part of her soul. There could be no shame with him.

He rolled to a sitting position and took the glass.

"To the future," she said.

She thought she saw his eyes cloud for an instant, but then he touched his glass to hers and drank the champagne straight down. Eliza sipped hers, watching him with adoring eyes.

Unable to resist, she reached out with her free hand and ran her fingers across one smooth, muscular shoulder, down his arm and over his chest. She smoothed her palm against the hair there, stirred by the coarse, masculine feel of it. Her gaze dropped lower, following his flat stomach down to his groin where she was amazed to see that he was growing hard again.

Feeling her body throb with rekindled passion, Eliza moved her hand lower, covering the head of his organ, tracing the ridge around it with a light touch, making him groan in ecstasy. Urged on by his enjoyment, she stroked her palm down further, fascinated by the rougher, pebbly texture of that skin.

"Curious, are you?" Case asked huskily, placing his glass on the table.

She smiled up at him. "Always."

He took her wine from her hand and eased her back on the bed. "Doesn't your aunt have a saying about curiosity?"

"Yes, but since I'm not a cat, it doesn't apply."

"I'll bet I can make you purr."

Eliza giggled as he nuzzled her neck. Oh, yes, he could make her purr. Especially when he touched her right there. She arched her back as his mouth found a nipple and his fingers found the dampness between her legs.

When Eliza was fully aroused and gasping for relief, Case sat up and placed her over his lap, her knees on either side of his hips, letting her settle herself on his engorged erection and rock against him as he cupped her breasts and kissed her mouth. His body pulsed with energy; he felt as though he could make love to Eliza all night and never get enough of her.

Case tipped his head back to gaze at her as she strained against him. Her eyes were half shut and glazed with passion, her black hair curled in wild abandon around her face and shoulders, and her hands gripped his shoulders as she sought completion.

Eliza's release came moments before his. Case emptied himself inside her again, feeling as though he could both laugh and cry from the enormity of the emotions washing through him. He held her tenderly, breathing in the fresh scent of her hair as she laid her cheek on his shoulder. After a long while, she lifted her head to smile up at him. She kissed him lightly on the mouth, then rose and went to the bathroom to cleanse herself.

Case lay back on the bed with a new understanding of contentment. He couldn't believe the passion she had unleashed in him, not to mention the depth of emotion. He'd never had such feelings for a woman, and he eagerly awaited Eliza's return. He shut his mind to the little voice inside that warned him not to fall in love with her.

Much later, after a long, lingering kiss, Eliza slipped from his bed, put on her nightdress and wrapper, scooped up the pendant, and returned to her own room. Case fell at once into a deep sleep, something he hadn't done in a decade.

The morning light woke Eliza. She yawned and stretched luxuriously, going over every moment of their glorious night of lovemaking. She ran her hands over her breasts, reliving the feel of Case's touch, and she felt a quickening between her thighs at the memory of their lusty coupling.

Throwing back the cover, Eliza hopped out of bed. She couldn't wait to see him; she felt as if her whole life had changed overnight.

She dressed and put on the pendant, then spied her crystal charm lying on the bedside table. She picked it up and closed her hand around it, remembering the Indian's prophetic words: *"Take this and keep it close to you. It will help you find the one you seek."*

Eliza's heart began to pound as she suddenly realized what he'd meant. He hadn't been speaking of Eileen at all. What she'd really been seeking was her true love. And that love was—

Eliza sat down hard on a chair. It couldn't be Case Brogan! The charm had obviously failed. There had to be someone else who was meant for her, because loving Case would be a terrible mistake. He was devoted to his job; there was no room in his life for a wife and family. And even if he made room, would she want a husband who could be killed at any time?

Eliza opened her fingers and gazed at the charm with a mixture of longing and regret, then, with a sigh, she slid it into her pocket, determined to put it out of her mind. She had to focus on Eileen.

She had just finished putting up her hair when Case knocked on her door and called, "Eliza?"

Despite her resolve, just hearing him say her name sent a rush of exhilaration through her. "Coming," she said, trying to tamp it down. But when she opened the door and saw him, her breath caught in her throat.

Case's eyes radiated such warmth and affection that her heart ached anew. He'd never looked more handsome. Or more rested.

"Ready for breakfast?" he asked.

"I'm always ready for breakfast." She smiled as she linked her arm through his and walked beside him down to the lobby. She'd never felt closer to anyone in her life. She was lucky to have him—for a friend.

The afterglow of their lovemaking basked Eliza in newfound contentment, and though Case didn't say so in words, she could tell he felt the same. It wasn't until they got back on the road that her thoughts began to shift away from Case and to her upcoming meeting with Eileen.

Case had felt confident that Eileen would be waiting for them in Omaha. Eliza hoped he was right. She hated the thought of her friend moving from city to city, always fearful of her husband being caught and hauled off to jail. That was no way for anyone to live.

What Eileen and Francis needed was the opportunity to start anew. With Eliza's money, they'd have that opportunity. After all, Francis had a wife to think of now, and a baby on the way. If any event could change a man's life, it was becoming a father. Eliza was certain that once Case met them and saw how much they loved each other, he'd allow them that opportunity, no matter how he felt about Francis.

Although it was still early, the traffic crossing the bridge into Nebraska was heavy. Coming off the bridge, they saw barges being unloaded along the docks and cargo being transported to the huge warehouses and meat-packing houses facing the Missouri River. Just beyond that lay Omaha's busy industrial district, composed of factories, workshops, smelting and refining works, breweries, brickyards, and stockyards.

Case glanced at Eliza, who sat tensely beside him, her fingers gripping the bench, her gaze sweeping the faces on the sidewalks, as though hoping she could conjure up her friend. Case knew her thoughts were on Eileen, but his thoughts were still on Eliza.

He hadn't yet absorbed how profoundly she had touched him. What he felt for her now shattered everything he knew about himself. The complex, powerful emotions that filled his soul couldn't be explained or shoved aside. Yet those same profound feelings created a terrible dilemma.

For ten years he'd had one burning desire. Now he was caught between his need for that final revenge and his deep feelings for Eliza. Dear God, why couldn't he have both?

He already knew the answer: because Eliza was counting on him to be merciful, and Case had no mercy for Caroni. The bastard had escaped the law time after time and had lived freely for a decade, while Case's father lay buried in the cold earth. Justice had to be done, even at the cost of losing Eliza.

Bleak emptiness filled his soul at that thought. It was a horrible pain, one he'd vowed never to feel again. Now there was no escaping it. His deepest regret was that Eliza would suffer, too.

He stopped to ask directions to the Western Union station, then they proceeded to Farnham Street, where it took a good quarter of an hour to find a place to park the wagon. They waited in line to pick up their telegram, then moved to a quiet corner to read it. The message was short and terse:

ELIZA, PLEASE MEET ME AT BURLINGTON STA-TION AT 2:00 P.M. THURSDAY. STOP. EILEEN

As Case read it over her shoulder, his body surged with vengeful power. Caroni was here, and he had timed their arrival to the day.

"Eileen's here! You were right," Eliza said, her relief evident in the sparkle of her eyes. "But I wonder how they knew we'd get here today."

Case barely heard her. A primitive force was at work inside him, controlling his thoughts, driving out all other considerations. He glanced up at the clock on the wall. "We have three and a half hours before the meeting. Let's go find a hotel. Then I have some business to attend to."

"I'd better send a telegram to my aunt to let her know I've made it safely," Eliza told him. "She'll worry if she doesn't hear from me soon."

She sent her wire, then they left the office and headed up Farnham Street. "There's a nice hotel," Eliza said, pointing to a large, five-story building on the next corner. "The Grand Central."

While Case signed in, Eliza wandered around admiring the paintings, the fresh flower centerpieces, and the charming accent tables placed among the burgundy chairs in the lobby. She turned to find Case striding toward her.

"We're signed in, and I've put the money in the hotel safe under both of our names. Here's your room key. I'll meet you back here at half past eleven for lunch."

"Where are you going?" she asked.

"To pay a courtesy call on the police chief."

At her alarmed look he said, "Don't worry. It's just standard business practice."

A young boy pushed open one of the swinging doors of the White Gull Tavern and looked around. "Message for Mr. Smith," he called loudly. "Mr. Frank C. Smith."

Frank Caroni folded his cards and pushed back his chair. "I'll be right back," he said to the four fellows sitting with him.

He strode over to the lad, gave him a coin, and opened the scrap of paper. It said, "Telegram picked up at ten-thirty this morning." There was no signature on the message, only the initials "LS," a clerk at the telegraph office who'd been only too happy to earn a half dollar for passing on the information.

Frank's gut tightened with nervous excitement. Eliza had finally arrived with his money. He was on the road to freedom at last.

He crumpled the paper and tossed it over his

shoulder. Striding back to the poker table, he sat down, picked up his cards, and smiled. "Whatever the bet is, I'm raising it. Today is my lucky day."

Chapter 20

⟨⟨◦◦⟩⟩

Sitting in the office of the chief of police, Case glanced at his watch for the tenth time that hour, wishing he could make the minute hand move faster by sheer force of will. His thoughts were completely focused on that two o'clock meeting. He knew Caroni wouldn't brazenly show himself. He'd hide in the shadows and wait for his opportunity to separate Case from Eliza so he could get her money without interference.

Case's best bet was to go early, without Eliza, to catch Caroni off guard. He hadn't decided yet how to tell Eliza.

"Afternoon," a voice boomed from the doorway.

Case swiveled as a big, ruddy-complexioned man in a dark suit strode toward him. He rose and shook the offered hand. "Case Brogan."

"Robert O'Malley. Have a seat, son."

Case sat down again as the chief eased his bulky frame into his chair behind the desk and lit up a cigar. As Case had told Eliza, paying a courtesy call on the chief of police was good business, since the local constabulary sometimes got touchy about an outsider working in their territory.

"So you're a Pinkerton man," O'Malley said, puffing on his cigar. "I have a lot of respect for you fellows." He blew smoke into the air. "What can I do for you?"

Case handed him the envelope given to him by his boss. "I have a warrant for Frank Caroni's arrest. I have reason to believe he's here in Omaha."

O'Malley took out the warrant and examined it, then handed it back. "I didn't know he was in our area, but I did get notice that he's wanted by the authorities in Wyoming for fraud. Murder, too, eh?"

Case smiled grimly. "I hope I can count on your help if I need it."

"You just let me know and we'll do whatever we can."

Case rose and shook his hand once again. "Thank you, Chief."

"Good luck."

Case left the station and headed back to the hotel. He didn't actually want police assistance—this was a matter he had to take care of alone—but it never hurt to have backup.

He met Eliza right on schedule outside the hotel's café.

"How was your meeting?" she asked, as they found a vacant table.

"It went well."

"Did you tell the police chief why you've come here?"

"I mentioned it. Do you want to order?" He nodded at the waitress standing beside their table.

"I'll have the soup, please," she told the girl.

"Ham sandwich and coffee," Case added.

Eliza spread her napkin on her lap. "I suppose we should leave for the train station around one-thirty."

Case pressed his lips into a resolute line. There was nothing to do but tell her right out. "I'm going alone."

Eliza's mouth opened in surprise. "You can't go alone! I have to meet Eileen."

"You can meet her afterward." He paused as the waitress brought his coffee.

"Case, you don't understand."

"I'm going alone, Eliza," he repeated firmly.

She reached across the table to grip his hand. "I gave my word to Eileen. If I don't show up, it will be a betrayal of our friendship; she'll be devastated."

"I was hired to protect you," he said tersely. "That's what I intend to do."

Eliza shook her head, denying his words. "That's not why you want to go alone. If you simply wanted to protect me, you'd come with me; you wouldn't try to stop me from helping them."

"Eliza, you've known my intent for several days."

"And you've known mine." Eliza waited until the waitress had delivered their food, then she leaned forward to say quietly, "I know you were hired to protect me, Case, but after last night, I thought we understood each other."

"Apparently we don't."

"But surely after experiencing such closeness, you can understand how Eileen and Francis feel about being torn apart, and how they deserve a chance to have a life together."

He gazed steadily at her for a long moment, raising her hopes that he understood at last. Then he said evenly, dispassionately, "My feelings about Caroni haven't changed, Eliza."

All the noise in the restaurant seemed to stop, and Eliza's heart with it. She sat back, dazed and wounded. How could he be so callous? How could she accept that what had been such a beautiful and powerful experience for her hadn't changed Case at all? Lying in his arms last night, she'd seen his feelings reflected in his eyes and felt it in his touch. Why was he denying it now?

She pushed away her bowl of soup. "I refuse to believe it."

"Believe what you want. But don't expect me to see the world through rose-colored glasses just because you do. I've waited too long for this day."

"What *did* last night mean to you?" she challenged.

Case rubbed his eyes, as though weary of the conversation. "Eliza, this won't do any good."

"Do you care about me?"

"Of course I care," he retorted harshly, as though offended by her question.

"Then help me convince Francis to turn himself in, Case. Let the courts decide his fate."

"He's evaded the courts for ten years, Eliza, and you can bet he'll do it again if he has half a chance. I'm not giving him that chance."

"So you're going to take the law into your own hands? What do you plan to do, shoot him in the back, or will you have him face you, so you can watch him die?"

"Enough!"

"No," Eliza shot back. "Think about what you're saying. You're playing God."

"He took my father's life, Eliza. An eye for an eye."

"What about 'Judge not lest ye be judged'?"

"He's wanted *dead* or alive."

"Then take him back alive. It's the right thing to do, Case."

He drew a deep breath and let it out slowly. "With all your talk about trust, Eliza, why don't you trust *me* to do the right thing?"

Eliza clasped her fingers tightly together beneath the table, battling her fears. She'd hoped that their intimacy would open Case's eyes to what life could be like with an unburdened soul. She'd hoped that entrusting him with her most prized possessions—her body and her heart—would vanquish his cynicism and make forgiveness possible. Were those hopes futile? Had ten years of harboring such bitterness left scars too deep to heal?

Now he was asking for her trust. Now was the time to prove to him what trust meant. Could she do it?

"I do trust you, Case. You know in your heart what you should do. Just let me go with you to make sure Eileen is all right. I won't interfere with Caroni."

Case studied her for a long moment. She'd never before referred to Eileen's husband as Caroni, and he took it as a sign that what he'd told her was finally sinking in. But he knew better than to believe she wouldn't interfere.

He reached across the table for her hand. Lifting it to his lips, he kissed her knuckles and gazed deep into her eyes, wishing everything could be different. "All right," he said, desperately regretting that he had to betray her.

She turned his hand over, palm up, and placed her crystal charm in it. "Maybe this will help you."

"It's your charm, Eliza. You keep it."

She touched the pendant at her throat. "I have my charm right here."

Case stared at the crystal in his hand for a long moment, his heart twisting, then he slowly closed his fingers around it. A charm couldn't help him now, but it would serve as his reminder of Eliza.

They finished their meal in silence, then left the café at half past twelve. Case walked Eliza to her room and opened the door for her, quietly pocketing her key.

"We have over an hour yet," he told her, unable to keep himself from running his palm along her face. "I'm going to catch a few winks to make up for the sleep I lost last night."

"I think I'll have a bath," she announced. "Have you seen the bathroom yet? It's wonderful." She rose on tiptoe and kissed him lightly on the mouth. "I'll see you soon."

Case had never felt so torn as when he left Eliza standing there, gazing at him trustingly.

After he'd gone, Eliza undressed, laid her clothing on the bed, then padded into the luxurious, green-tiled bathroom and turned the water on to fill the big, claw-footed porcelain tub. When it had filled halfway, she closed the bathroom door and stepped into the soothing water. For a moment she lay against the back of the tub, reveling in the memories of Case and their night of love, but then her thoughts turned to the upcoming meeting.

Had he really given up his plan for revenge? All Eliza had to go on was her trust in him to do what was right. What she didn't know was how Caroni would react to seeing Case. Would he run, as Case had predicted?

She sat up and reached for the soap, working up a lather on her palms. As she soaped her arms, she heard someone come into her room. "Case, is that you?"

A key turned in the bathroom door.

"Who's there?" she called, but no one answered.

Eliza listened carefully, sure she heard someone on the other side of the door. Suddenly she heard another click that sounded like her hotel room door closing. Quickly she rinsed off, wrapped herself in a bath towel, and padded to the door, leaving a trail of water. She turned the knob, but the door wouldn't open. Had someone locked her in the bathroom?

Eliza gasped as the truth hit her. "Case!" She pounded on the door. "Let me out at once! You won't get away with this." She paused to press her ear to the door, but didn't hear a thing. That other door sound she'd heard had probably been him letting himself out.

She paced back and forth, stunned by his deception. Case—the man to whom she had given her absolute trust—had lied to her. He had purposely misled her into believing he had changed his mind. He couldn't have found a more powerful way to wound her.

Case had to know how terribly hurt and angry she'd be, but obviously that didn't matter. All that mattered was his hunger for vengeance. It just proved she couldn't ever share her life with a man who would betray her trust. As he'd told her many times, she'd been incredibly naive.

But she had no time now to dwell on her anguish. She had to get to the station and stop Case from killing her friend's husband.

Eliza tied the towel more tightly around her and glanced around the room, looking for something she could use to open the lock. There was an ivory pedestal sink, a stack of towels, and a cake of soap, but nothing that would slip into the keyhole.

She felt above the door frame in case some thoughtful person had stowed an extra key there, then had a flash of inspiration and pulled a pin from her hair. She knelt down in front of the doorknob, squinted one eye, and inserted the pin in the hole, trying to jimmy the lock. But after what seemed like hours of frustrated attempts, she gave up.

"How am I going get out?" she said to her reflection in the looking glass above the basin. She paced to the window and back, her arms folded across her bosom, thinking hard.

Suddenly she swung around. "The window!"

She ran to the small window on the end wall, stood on tiptoe, and looked down—way down. Five floors down. Hmm . . . Perhaps she could attract someone's attention.

Eliza tried the latch on the side of the window, but it wouldn't budge. "Move, darn you!" she said through gritted teeth, using her thumbs to push the tiny handle up. She stopped to rub the indentations in her thumbs, then pushed again. Slowly the latch began to turn, until finally it cleared the window and she swung it out.

"Help!" she called, standing on tiptoe. Unable to see the street below, Eliza looked for something on which to stand, and ended up climbing onto the slippery edge of the tub two feet away, and bracing her hands against the wall.

"Help!" she called again. She saw the top of a man's hat and watched as he paused to look around. "Up here!" she cried. "Look up!"

But then she saw a woman walk up to him, link her arm through his, and off they went. Sighing sharply, Eliza waited until she saw another man, then called again.

This time the man looked up. Eliza struck her bare arm through the window and waved. "I'm locked in a bathroom!" she called.

He removed his hat and cupped one hand around his ear. "What was that?"

"I'm locked in a bathroom! Please ask someone in the hotel to come up to room five-oh-six."

"You're locked in a bathroom?" he called back, as several curious passersby stopped to gawk up at her.

"Yes!" Eliza huffed in frustration. "Will you please send help?"

She watched until he'd moved out of her view, then she shut the window and waited.

"Oh, good heavens! My clothes!" Realizing she had nothing on but a skimpy white bath towel, Eliza grabbed another towel and draped it around her shoulders, fastening it down the front with hairpins. She took the last towel and tied it around her hips, covering her legs to the ankles.

She waited five minutes, toes tapping against the tile floor, then she opened the window again and peered out.

"There she is!" someone below cried, and a crowd of people cheered.

Eliza ducked back inside, waited a moment, then carefully peered out. The crowd had gone.

She heard someone come into her room, and then a key was inserted in the lock, and the bathroom door opened. A maid peered in. Behind her stood a man in a gray suit, no doubt the hotel manager, and behind him, two more curious maids.

"Are you all right, ma'am?" the maid asked.

"Yes. Thank you." Mustering her dignity, she swept past them in her strange costume. A dozen more gawkers stood in the hall outside her room.

"Look! There she is!" one of them called.

The manager quickly shoved them back, shutting the door in their faces.

"I'm so sorry to have caused all this trouble," Eliza said, "You see, my. . . ." She paused as her glance fell on the empty bed. "My clothes are gone! I've been robbed!"

Chapter 21

"**W**ould you like me to call the police, madam?" the manager asked Eliza.

Eliza pursed her lips in concentration. "Not just yet. I think I know who the culprit is. Do you have a key to the next room?"

"I have one," the first maid said, taking out a heavy ring of keys.

"Would you open the door for me? I believe I'll find my clothing inside."

They paraded down the hall—the maid, the manager, Eliza holding on to her towels, the other two maids, and the curious onlookers. The first maid opened the door and stepped back as Eliza and the hotel manager walked inside and looked around.

"There's my dress!" Eliza said, pointing to her green calico lying over the back of a chair. "And that's my bag, too."

"Would you describe something inside the bag, madam?" the man asked, opening the clasp and peering inside.

"Well, there are my unmentionables, of course. Did you want me to mention them?"

"No, madam," he said instantly. "But surely there's something else you can identify."

Eliza tapped her chin. "At the bottom you should find a crystal pendant in the shape of a heart."

The manager pulled out her pendant, then returned it to the bag and handed it to Eliza. "Do you want me to notify the police?"

"That's not necessary." Eliza glanced down at her towel ensemble. "Would you mind if I changed into my dress here?"

"You'll come right out, won't you?"

Did the man think she would retaliate by stealing something of Case's? "Of course I will."

As soon as the manager and the maids had gone, Eliza unfastened the towels and began to dress, her fingers fumbling with all the ties and buttons in her rush. Stopping to pick up her handbag, Eliza hurried downstairs to the reception desk in the lobby, where she spotted the helpful manager.

"Is everything all right, now, madam?"

"Yes, thank you. I'd like to take my money out of the safe, please."

"You'll have to sign for it," he said, sliding a receipt book toward her.

Eliza quickly wrote her name and pushed it back. The manager turned it around and read it. "You're not related to Mrs. Edward Lowe, are you?"

"Why, yes, I am. She's my aunt."

"I assume you know that she's staying with us."

"She's here? In Omaha?" Eliza asked incredulously. "What room is she in?"

He turned the registration book around and ran his finger down the list of names. Then he flipped back a page and scanned that list. "Here it is. Mrs. Edward Lowe. She checked in two days ago. She's staying in room three-oh-nine. Third floor."

Eliza was stunned. If Auntie Vi had come all the way to Omaha, it must have been for a very important reason. But she could only think of one reason that important—her niece's safety. What could Auntie Vi have possibly learned that would make her fearful? Was it something about Case—or Caroni? And why hadn't she tried to contact Eliza?

"I'll be right back with your money, Miss Lowe."

"Never mind," she said, and dashed for the elevator. Case had accused her of being too trusting, and perhaps he was right. If she couldn't trust him, how could she be certain she could trust Caroni? Wouldn't it be wiser to meet with him first, and then if all seemed well, to give him the money?

Eliza tapped her toe impatiently as she waited for the elevator to slowly descend to the main floor. A man in a red coat sitting on a stool inside nodded politely as she entered.

"Third floor, please."

As the elevator's cables jerked into motion, Eliza nibbled her lower lip. She'd just speak briefly with her aunt and then be on her way. There was no time to spare.

The metal accordion door folded back on three and Eliza dashed out. She stopped at number three-oh-nine and rapped sharply. "Auntie Vi? It's me, Eliza." *Oh, please be there.*

She waited, then knocked again. Where could her aunt have gone?

Down in the lobby, Eliza again approached the hotel manager. "My aunt wasn't in her room," she said breathlessly. "You didn't see her leave, by any chance, did you?"

"No, I didn't," he said. "Let me check with another manager."

Eliza drummed her fingers rapidly against the marble counter while she waited. It was five minutes before two o'clock. She had to get to the station quickly, before Case met up with Caroni.

"No one has seen her today," the manager reported, "however, one of the clerks remembers seeing her leave yesterday evening with a gentleman."

"How odd—I didn't know she knew anyone in Omaha. If my aunt should return, would you please tell her not to leave again, but to wait for me here? It's very important."

"I'd be happy to."

Eliza thanked him and hurried outside to hail a cab. "Burlington Station, please," she said, settling against the back.

Wearing borrowed workman's overalls and cap, Case pushed a broom around the perimeter of the huge depot, surveying the people passing by. He had arrived half an hour early, paid a workman to let him use a pair of overalls and a broom, and started sweeping.

As he worked, he studied the men sitting on the wooden pews inside the depot, men lined up to buy tickets and waiting on the platform outside, and most especially, the men who appeared to be doing nothing more than loitering. Eventually, he'd spot Caroni among them.

He pushed the broom through the wide arches in the rear and out onto the big wooden platform in the back, where a train had just arrived from the East. He moved slowly through the disembarking travelers, and when the area had emptied, he worked his way back inside, casually glancing at the big clock on the wall. It was nearly two o'clock. Caroni would have to show up soon.

At ten minutes past two, Frank Caroni watched from his hiding place across the street from Burlington Station as a black buggy pulled up and an attractive young lady stepped out. He was certain it was Eliza, but just to be on the safe side, he waited until he saw his wife wave to her from her cab. Then he gave a sharp whistle to an older woman—an acquaintance of his from the White Gull Tavern—who was standing inside the doorway of the train station. She lifted her hand in response and disappeared inside.

Frank smiled as he headed for the boardinghouse. Everything was going just as he'd planned. He'd had to spend his last fifty cents to pay for the woman's help, but it had been well worth it. An hour from now he'd be swimming in money.

Case stood near the ticket window and glanced at his watch. Ten minutes after two. Where the hell was Caroni? He'd been all over the place four times without a sign of the bastard.

Just then, he heard a scream and swung around to see an elderly woman fall to her knees on the platform just outside the rear doorway.

"Help! Police!" she cried. "I've been robbed!"

For a second Case hesitated, his instinct telling him it was a trap. But when no one made a move to help her, he stood the broom against the wall and ran.

As the cab pulled up to the station, Eliza glanced down to check the time, only to discover she'd forgotten her watch. She hoped she wasn't too late.

She had no sooner stepped out of the cab when she heard her friend call, "Eliza! Over here!"

She swung around and spotted Eileen waving from a hackney cab parked on the other side of the street. Eliza eagerly waved back. She wasn't too late! Lifting her skirts, she hurried across the brick-paved street, stopping midway to let a carriage pass.

"Eileen!" Eliza cried, climbing into the cab and enveloping her friend in a big hug. "I've missed you so!"

"I've missed you, too, Liza. Oh, it's so good to see you again!"

"Where's your husband?" Eliza asked curiously.

Before Eileen could reply, the buggy jerked

into motion. Eliza looked out the window in surprise. "Where are we going?"

Eileen gave Eliza's hands a squeeze. "I hope you're not angry, but Francis is in a hurry and he thought it best that we don't delay. He also thought you and I should meet alone—without your escort. So if you don't mind, I'll just ride with you back to your hotel."

Eliza agreed wholeheartedly that it was best to meet without Case present. Yet the fact that Caroni didn't want a Pinkerton man there gave her an uneasy feeling.

She turned to take a closer look at her friend and was dismayed by what she saw. Eileen was ashen and gaunt and so sad-eyed Eliza wanted to weep for her. Even her clothing looked haggard. What had happened to her cheerful, robust childhood chum? "How are you feeling, Eileen?"

Eileen laughed nervously. "It seems like I've been sick for ages. I guess I'm not meant to carry babies."

"Nonsense. You're just not meant to be dragged all over creation. I don't understand what your husband could have been thinking."

Eileen looked down. "I couldn't stay behind. I need Francis, Liza. He's so much smarter than I am. I wouldn't be able to survive on my own."

"Of course you could survive. Where did you ever get such an idea? You ran your father's farm for nearly a year after he took ill, didn't you?"

The cab pulled up across the street from the Grand Central Hotel. Eliza turned back to her friend. "This is too quick, Eileen. At least come inside and have tea with me."

Eileen sighed forlornly. "Perhaps some other time."

"You're going to Mexico! I haven't seen you in ages and I don't know when I shall see you again. Surely your husband won't mind if you spend a few more minutes with me. There's a nice tea room in the hotel."

Eileen twisted her fingers together. "This is very difficult for me, Liza, I just want you to know that. And someday we'll repay you, I promise. But I have to leave now."

Eliza was taken aback. Was her friend expecting her to simply hand over the one thousand dollars and walk away? Her intuition began to flash strong warning signals, but she tried to ignore them. She had never doubted Eileen before.

But Eileen has never behaved this way before, her intuition whispered. *Don't be naive.*

"I'll give you the money, Eileen," she said, and saw the instant look of relief in her friend's eyes, "but I want to speak to your husband first."

Eileen's eyes widened in alarm. "Why do you need to talk to Francis?"

"To reassure myself that he'll take care of you."

"Oh, he will!" she answered too eagerly. "Francis takes very good care of me."

"You don't look well cared for, Eileen. Now, where can we find Francis?"

Her friend stayed silent for a long moment, as though struggling to decide what to do. Finally she sighed wearily. "I'll take you to the boardinghouse. He should be there soon. But bear in mind that it's an old building in a run-down part of the city. You won't find it much to your liking."

Eliza sat back grim-faced. There was little about the whole situation she was finding to her liking.

Case reached the elderly woman just as she picked herself up off the ground.

"My handbag!" she cried in a panic, pointing down one of the boarding platforms, where at least a dozen men waited to board a westbound train. "That man stole my handbag!"

"Which man?" Case asked.

"He's wearing a gray fedora. Hurry!" she pleaded. "My life savings are in that bag."

Case scanned the group in dismay. At least half of the men had on gray fedoras. He saw one man moving away from the waiting passengers at a fast pace, carrying something in his hand.

Case gave chase, nearly knocking his suspect to the ground. But the item in the man's hand turned out to be his own traveling bag.

Case questioned the others, but none proved to be the thief. Frustrated, he went back to where he'd left the old woman, only to find that she had disappeared.

Damn it! His instinct had proved right.

Chapter 22

Gnashing his teeth in fury, Case quickly checked the station for signs of either Caroni or Eliza, knowing even as he did that he wouldn't find them. He grabbed a cab back to the hotel, took the stairs to the fifth floor, and used his skeleton key to enter Eliza's room, praying she was still locked in the bath.

Even before he stepped inside, Case sensed that she was gone. Had she taken the money with her? As trusting as Eliza was, he feared she'd done exactly that.

He hurried down to the front desk. "I need to get my money out of the safe."

A clerk had him sign a receipt book, then went into a back room. He returned in a moment carrying the small leather case. "Here you are, sir."

Case's shoulders sagged in relief. She hadn't taken it! He still had a chance to catch Caroni. "Did Miss Lowe happen to leave a message for me?"

A man standing nearby looked up curiously. "Pardon me, sir. Did you say Miss Lowe, or *Mrs.* Lowe?"

Case eyed the man skeptically. "Miss Lowe. Why do you ask?"

He hesitated, as though he wasn't sure if he should say more. "We have two ladies by that name staying here."

Case rubbed his jaw. Lowe was a fairly common name. It seemed odd that the manager would even mention it. Surely there was more he wasn't saying. "What is Mrs. Lowe's first name?"

"I'm sorry, sir. I'm not at liberty to give out that information."

Case took out his wallet and showed him the Pinkerton badge. "Now are you at liberty?"

The manager's eyebrows lifted. "I beg your pardon, Mr.—er—Brogan," he said, peering closer to read the name on the ID. "We have a Miss Eliza Lowe and a Mrs. Edward Lowe registered."

Mrs. Edward Lowe? What the hell was Violet doing in Omaha?

"What is your room number, sir? I'll check for that message for you."

"Five-oh-eight."

The manager checked the cubbyholes behind him. "I'm sorry. Miss Lowe didn't leave any message for you. But she did seem quite anxious when she learned her aunt was here."

"What room is Mrs. Lowe in?"

"Three-oh-nine, but she's not there at present. We've been watching for her at Miss Lowe's request. In fact, she hasn't been here since yesterday evening, when she was seen leaving with a gentleman."

"Can you tell me what he looked like?"

"I wasn't here, sir. Perhaps the doormen can help you."

Case found two doormen standing outside and described Violet to them. One of the men said, "I remember a lady matching that description. She left with a good-looking fellow, an employee at the hotel, I believe, although I haven't seen him here before. Odd, too, that he got into the cab with her."

It had to be Caroni. But how the hell did he find out Eliza's aunt was in town? Had Violet wired Eileen? "Did you happen to hear where they were going?"

"No, I didn't. Sorry, sir."

Now Case had two missing women. He suspected that wherever Caroni was holding Violet, he'd find Eliza. "Do you know the driver of the cab?"

"I know what he looks like, but I don't know his name." The doorman blew his whistle and waved a cab over. "You might ask this fellow. I've seen the two of them standing around talking."

Case checked the time and cursed silently. Almost three o'clock. His chances of catching Caroni were growing slimmer with each passing minute.

The cab carrying Eliza and Eileen halted before a shabby two-story, gray frame building. Eliza paid the driver, then followed Eileen up the sagging wooden steps, past peeling paint and rotting trim, to the front entrance. Eileen opened the door onto a long, narrow hall and walked straight to the staircase on the left.

As Eliza followed, she noticed an old man sitting behind a counter in a small parlor off to the right, peering at them curiously. Eliza smiled, and the man scowled back.

At the rear end of the hallway, she caught a glimpse of rats scurrying along the baseboard. With a shudder of disgust, she lifted her skirts and hurried up the steps behind Eileen.

On the second floor, Eileen stopped at the last door on the right and inserted her key. Eliza followed her inside and glanced around, appalled by the dingy, musty-smelling room. It contained only a lumpy bed; two white wooden chairs with most of the paint worn off; a small, scarred, pine table; a chest of drawers with someone's initial carved into its lime-green paint; a metal washstand and basin; and a cracked looking glass. Eileen had attempted to make the room more homey by placing a framed photograph of her father on the table.

"This is it," her friend said with an unhappy shrug. "Do you want to sit down?"

"You should sit, too, Eileen. You look tired."

Her friend placed her hands over her stomach, which was starting to bulge slightly beneath her narrow skirt. "I guess that's what having a baby does to you." She broke into tears, sinking weakly onto the bed.

Eliza sat beside her and wrapped her arms around Eileen's shoulders, shocked at how frail she'd become. "Take heart, Eileen. Things will get better."

"I hope so. I'm so tired of living in dismal rooms, and always moving, and being alone, and feeling sick all the time. I don't know what we'd do without your help, Eliza. Once Francis clears up this terrible error, I hope we can live a normal life again."

"I don't understand why you must go to Mexico. Why can't your husband just turn himself in and explain the misunderstanding?"

"He says they won't believe him because he has a record."

"He surely didn't have a record in Wyoming. You were only there a few weeks."

Eileen pulled out a frayed handkerchief and wiped her eyes. "Francis says this is the only way."

"I don't believe that, Eileen. Where is he, by the way?"

"He should be here soon."

Eliza unpinned her hat and set it on the bed. "Good. I have some questions for him."

"He may not take kindly to your questions, Eliza."

"He'll have to take kindly to them if he wants the money." Eliza peered closer at her. "Are you afraid of him?"

Eileen shook her head, refusing to meet her gaze.

"Look me in the eye, Eileen. Are you afraid of him?"

"No!" she replied, shaking her head adamantly. "I love Francis. And he loves me."

"Then why is he keeping you in places like this?" Eliza said, sweeping her hand around.

"Once he clears his name—"

"What if he can't clear his name, Eileen? What if he *has* committed those crimes?"

Eileen's brown eyes opened wide. "Oh, Liza, please don't say that!"

"All I'm saying is that you must consider the possibility of his guilt."

"You don't understand, Liza. I don't care what he's done—I love him. Francis is the first man who's ever paid any attention to me."

"That's not a good enough reason to stay with him."

"It's enough reason for me. Besides, I'm carrying his baby. I couldn't abandon him even if I wanted to."

"Eileen, listen."

"No, Liza. You'll never know how deeply it hurts to be ignored by the boys at school when all your friends are being courted, or how it feels to pretend to understand when other girls discuss their beaus. But how could you know? You're beautiful. The boys always fell over their feet trying to please you. I was never even asked to a dance.

"But Francis thinks I'm pretty. Me, Liza! Ol' horse-faced Neeley. For that reason alone, I'll follow him to the ends of the earth."

Eliza's heart ached for her friend. "I'm so sorry, Eileen. I wish I had known."

"I don't want pity. I just want you to understand why I love Francis, and why I have to stay with him."

Suddenly Eileen turned her head toward the door. "He's coming."

Eliza's stomach clenched nervously as she

heard the creaking of stairs and a man whistling a carefree tune. The door opened and Caroni walked in, his eyes instantly registering his surprise at seeing Eliza there. He looked around quickly, as if to make sure no one else was in the room.

Then he smiled broadly, exhibiting the charisma she remembered so well. "Miss Lowe! What a delight to see you again."

He seemed exceedingly fit and cheery, looking quite the gentleman in his clean-lined gray suit and striped tie. When Eliza contrasted that with her friend's pitiful condition, she couldn't help but feel that something was way out of kilter.

"How are you, Mr. Caroni?" Eliza responded politely, offering her gloved hand.

He clasped it warmly in his. "I'm always well in the company of beautiful ladies." He left Eliza and strode over to his wife. "Hello, sweetheart," he said, leaning down to give her a loud smack on the lips. "How's my pretty baby?"

Eliza watched Eileen's pinched face magically transform. Her love for her husband radiated from her eyes, making Eliza feel guilty for doubting Caroni.

But then a shadow of concern crossed her friend's face. "Eliza wants to speak with you personally, Francis, before she gives us the money."

"I see." He pulled out the other chair and sat in it, facing Eliza. "I'll wager I know exactly why you want to see me. You're concerned about my wife's situation, am I right?"

"Partially, yes."

"Believe me," he said, leaning forward to gaze earnestly at her, "I detest keeping my wife in this squalor, especially in her delicate condition."

"Then why are you doing it?"

Caroni heaved an exaggerated sigh. "Unfortunately, as I'm sure my wife explained in her letter, the Wyoming police have identified me as a suspect in some kind of phony bond scheme." He shrugged. "I have no idea why. Whatever the reason, I had to leave quickly or be thrown in jail."

He turned to smile at Eileen. "And I didn't want to leave my wife all alone. Who would take care of her? She has no one but me. I'm sure you've heard that her father is ailing."

Case's words suddenly sprang to mind: *In all instances, the young women were the sole beneficiaries, and their fathers were on their deathbeds . . . Before that, he ran a bogus railroad bond scheme, targeting widows' life savings.*

Eliza had defended Caroni then, refusing to believe him capable of such deceit. But seeing Eileen now, she could believe it. If Caroni truly loved his wife, he wouldn't run away from his troubles to hide in Mexico. He'd stay and prove his innocence, sparing Eileen, and the new life inside her, such an ordeal.

It made Eliza wonder if Caroni was actually guilty of Case's father's murder.

"If I had a wife and a babe on the way," Eliza said, "I would have hired an attorney to straighten out the misunderstanding."

Caroni laughed. "You're very naive, Miss Lowe. The Wyoming police would have loved nothing better than to send me to prison. It would have saved them the bother of finding the real crook."

"Correct me if I'm wrong, but don't they need evidence first?" Eliza asked. "If you're innocent, Mr. Caroni, they'd have no evidence to convict you."

Caroni laced his fingers behind his head and leaned back, regarding her through sly eyes. "Eileen, didn't you tell me Miss Lowe was traveling with a Pinkerton?"

Catching the swift flash of panic in her friend's eyes, Eliza quickly replied for her. "I'm sure Eileen *did* tell you. However, it doesn't matter who I traveled here with, because we've recently parted ways. I only needed an escort to get to Omaha."

"It sounds like your *escort* also managed to sway your opinion against me."

Before Eliza could frame an acceptable reply,

Caroni checked the time on his pocket watch and then rose. "I hate to rush you, Miss Lowe, but I was hoping that Eileen and I could get started on our journey today. We have a long trip ahead of us."

"Just one more question," Eliza said. "When you reach Mexico, how will you clear your name?"

"I suppose I'll hire a lawyer."

"You could do that here."

She could hear the underlying anger in Caroni's voice as he answered tautly, "I know what I'm doing, Miss Lowe. Now you can either help us or go back home and lead your prissy, privileged life while your dearest friend suffers."

"Francis!" Eileen whispered in shock.

"You needn't try to blame me for your wife's suffering, Mr. Caroni," Eliza stated evenly. "I'm not the one forcing her and your unborn babe on this unnecessary journey. But I promised Eileen I would help, and I intend to keep my promise." She turned and started for the door.

"Where are you going?" Caroni asked sharply.

"Back to my hotel. I didn't bring the money with me."

"You're lying!" Without warning, Caroni grabbed Eliza's handbag from off her wrist and yanked it open, dumping the contents on the floor.

"Francis!" Eileen cried in horror, rising from the bed.

"How dare you!" Eliza said, kneeling to retrieve her belongings.

"Where's the money?" Caroni demanded, his upper lip curling menacingly as he stood above her.

"I told you where it is."

Caroni grabbed Eliza's upper arm and hauled her to her feet. "You're setting me up, aren't you?"

"Don't be absurd."

"Francis, please don't hurt her!" Eileen whimpered.

"Release me at once," Eliza commanded. "You won't gain my cooperation by intimidation."

She glared at him until he finally complied, then she straightened her bodice with a huff. "I never go back on my word. The money is in the hotel safe. If you don't believe me, you may accompany me there."

Caroni suddenly calmed. "All right, Miss Lowe, I'll do just that. After all, you gave your word." He cupped her chin and stared into her eyes. "And besides, you want to see your auntie again, don't you?"

Chapter 23

Eliza pushed Caroni's hand away. "What does my aunt have to do with this?"

"Let's just say she's my insurance that all goes well."

At her friend's horrified gasp, Eliza's stomach twisted in dread. Caroni must have been the gentleman the hotel manager had seen leaving with Violet. "Where is my aunt?" she demanded.

"If I told you that, I wouldn't be very smart, would I?"

"Eileen," Eliza said, swinging to face her friend, "please tell me where Auntie Vi is."

Eileen stared at her with wide, frightened eyes. "I truly don't know, Liza."

Eliza turned back to glare at Caroni. "I said

I'd give you the money. There's no need to hold my aunt for ransom."

"Sure there is. I want to be sure Brogan doesn't try to stop me."

Eliza cringed inside. Caroni knew Case had come with her; Auntie Vi must have let it slip. "Brogan won't stop you; I'll see to that."

"Then as soon as I get the money, I'll tell you where she is." Caroni turned to admire himself in the cracked looking glass, placing his hat at just the right angle on his head. "Shall we go?"

Violet rose with a groan from her bed of straw. Every joint in her body ached and her stomach growled from hunger. She glanced up at the window and saw the sun shining brightly. She guessed it to be midafternoon.

She'd heard faint noises in the warehouse earlier, and had pounded on the door and called for help until her hands were black and blue and her throat was raw, but it had done no good. Her little prison was so far back from the entrance that she began to fear she'd die before anyone found her.

Luckily she'd found a little sack of peanuts in her handbag and had been trying to ration them out, but it never quite stopped the gnawing hunger pangs, and it only aggravated her thirst.

But worse than her discomfort was the fear

that Eliza would be harmed. Violet wanted to give in to the urge to cry, but her eyes were too dry to tear, and she knew it would only made her throat ache more.

"Edward," she whispered raggedly, "I've failed Eliza, and you know how I love that child. She's the daughter I could never have. What if I lose her now?"

She could think of nothing to do except get down on her knees and pray.

Case sat on the edge of his seat in the hired cab, watching anxiously out the window as they rode along the wharf. He had only two thoughts: find Eliza, and kill Caroni, in that order. Nothing else mattered.

The trip from the hotel had seemed endless, although it had taken no more than fifteen minutes to reach the river. The docks swarmed with ship hands, horse-drawn wagons, and dock-workers shouting to one another as they un-loaded cargo from the barges, all eager to finish and go home for the day.

The buggy passed three large warehouses and finally came to a stop in front of a fourth, a huge brick building half a city block in length and at least two stories tall.

"This is the one," the cabby said.

"Did you see the man take the lady inside?" Case asked.

"No, sir. After he paid me I left. He was very direct in his instructions."

"You didn't realize the lady was in danger?"

"Why would I? He'd told me beforehand that she was dotty, not to pay her any mind."

Case took a fifty-cent piece from his pocket and gave it to the cabby. "Wait here for half an hour. If I don't come back, go to the police."

He found the main entrance on the far end of the building, where huge crates were being unloaded near the door. Case stopped to question the dockworkers, but none had noticed or heard anything unusual.

"Mind if I look around inside?" he asked, showing his badge.

"Suit yourself," one of the men said.

"Any small storage rooms in the building?"

"There's one all the way at the other end."

The warehouse was a hollow brick shell with big windows encircling the structure near the high ceiling, and long rows of crates stacked over ten feet high. Case wove his way through the rows until he reached the far side, where he spotted a door with a thick piece of wood propped beneath it.

Tossing the wood aside, he yanked open the door and looked in, only to find the room empty. Case's heart sank. Where had Caroni taken them? And why had the door been secured from the outside?

Suddenly he heard a slight rustling sound, like silk might make. "Show yourself," he commanded.

"Mr. Brogan?" a woman's voice rasped faintly, "Is that you?"

"Mrs. Lowe?"

There was a sob of relief, then Violet rushed out from behind the door and threw her arms around him. "Thank goodness you've come. I thought I would die in here. Is Eliza all right?"

"I was hoping she'd be here with you."

Violet pulled back to stare at him in alarm. "You've lost her?"

"Misplaced might be a better word. Caroni separated us. Come on; let's get out of here."

"Mr. Brogan, I don't know if I can make it. If I don't have some water to drink soon, I'll faint."

"I'm sorry," he said guiltily. "Let me help you."

He put his arm around her back, and Violet leaned weakly against him. However, she was strong enough to chatter, dry throat and all.

"Thank goodness I had some peanuts in my handbag to tide me over. But they made me thirsty, and I haven't had anything to drink since yesterday at supper. Goodness, was it yesterday or the day before? Surely not two days. No one can last two days without water, can they?"

"You'll be fine, Mrs. Lowe. We'll get you back

to the hotel and you can have something to drink there."

"Thank you, Mr. Brogan. To think that the miscreant left me to die, and now he has my Eliza. Oh! I just had a thought. He might have taken her back to his room at that dreadful boardinghouse."

Case's heart began to race in anticipation. "Do you know where the boardinghouse is?"

"Eileen showed it to me. It's a horrid place, full of rats and spiders and rotten wood and—"

Rats. Case shuddered inwardly. "Would you be able to recognize it again?"

"Oh, my, yes! It's not something I'll soon forget."

"Here's the cab," he said, directing her to the waiting buggy. "Can you hold off awhile longer on something to drink?"

"If it means finding Eliza, I certainly can."

"What's the name of the boardinghouse?"

"The Wilton Arms."

Case repeated it to the driver, who asked for the address.

"I don't remember," Violet said, her face puckering in distress. She leaned out the window to talk to the driver. "Just look for a dilapidated old boardinghouse on a crowded, narrow street."

"Lady, we've got lots of streets that fit that description," the cabby called back.

"It's not far from the railroad yards," she added.

"All right. I'll do my best."

Violet studied each building as the driver steered the buggy down one narrow street after another.

"Oh, I see it!" she called at last. "There! At the corner!"

"Pull around to the alley in back," Case told the cabby.

"Why are we going in that way?" Violet asked, as Case helped her down.

"I don't want to alert Caroni." He stopped in front of a weather-beaten wooden door and rattled the handle. When the door wouldn't open, he threw his weight against it, breaking it in on the third attempt, sending rats scurrying up the hallway.

"They live upstairs," Violet told him in a whisper. "Last door on the right."

"Wait here," he instructed quietly.

"But the rats!" she whispered, glancing around in fear.

Case couldn't blame her. "Wait on the landing then," he told her, "but don't come all the way up unless I tell you to. Caroni may have a weapon."

Violet nodded, her eyes wide with concern. "You'll take care of Eliza, won't you, Mr. Brogan?"

"You can be sure I will."

Case moved quietly up the hall to the front of the building, then peered around the corner to make sure the way was clear. He saw an old man asleep behind a battered wooden counter, snoring loudly. Motioning for Violet to follow, he took out his revolver, crept up the stairs, and moved cautiously down the second-floor hallway. He stopped at the last door and listened, but heard no voices.

Kneeling down to peer through the keyhole, he caught a glimpse of a young woman curled up on a bed, but his view went no further. He stood, rapped twice on the door and stepped back.

"Who is it?" he heard a woman call fearfully.

"Mrs. Caroni?"

"Yes?"

Case stood up and held the gun behind him. "I'm a friend from back home."

"From Coffee Creek?" A moment later he heard a shuffling sound as she moved toward the door. She opened it and stared at him in bewilderment.

"Are you Eileen Caroni?" he asked.

"Yes, but I don't know you."

"Where's your husband?"

"He's not here. Who are you?"

"I'm a Pinkerton detective," he said, showing

her his badge. "I'm looking for Eliza. I have her aunt here with me."

"Mrs. Lowe is here?" Eileen cried in obvious relief. "Is she all right?"

Case called to Violet from the doorway. As soon as the elderly woman stepped into the room, Eileen burst into tears.

"I was afraid Francis had done something terrible to you," she sobbed as the elderly woman wrapped plump arms around her.

"There, there, now," Violet cooed, sitting the young woman on the bed and stroking her hair. "I'm just fine, thanks to Mr. Brogan."

"I didn't believe all those things you said about Francis," Eileen wept, "but they're true. How could I have been so blind?"

"It happens to the best of us, dear. But you must help us now. Do you know where Eliza is?"

Eileen sniffled tearfully and turned to gazed at Case through swollen, lifeless eyes. "She went to the hotel with Francis to get the money."

"Stay here with her, Mrs. Lowe," Case said quietly. "I'm going after Caroni."

Chapter 24

～◯◯～

"I demand to know where my aunt is," Eliza said firmly as she rode back to the Grand Central Hotel with Caroni.

"You'll find out when I get the money."

"You don't seem to understand that when I give my word, I mean it. What you've done is horribly shameful and underhanded. My aunt is an elderly woman with delicate nerves. If she comes to any harm—"

"It'll be your fault for bringing Brogan with you."

"Don't try to blame me for your criminal acts," Eliza scolded. "To think that all along I've defended you, when you didn't care one whit about Eileen. She's just another one of your victims. How many wives do you have now? Five? Six? Can you even keep them straight? And how many elderly widows have you hood-winked out of their savings? I'll wager you'd bamboozle your own mother, too, wouldn't you, Mr. Caroni?"

"Is the money in your room?" he asked irritably.

"The hotel safe," she said reluctantly.

Caroni sat forward. "All right, here's what you're going to do. There's a railroad ticket office inside the hotel lobby. I'll wait there while you go to the desk and get the money. If you see Brogan, don't let him know what you're doing or you won't see your aunt alive. Understand?"

"And what am I supposed to tell him if I have the money in my hand?"

"You'll think of something."

Eliza sank into worried silence.

"What if everything I told you about him was true?" Case had once asked her.

"If it were true, I wouldn't give him the money. I'd help Eileen leave him instead."

If only she had believed Case. Her supreme gullibility appalled her. How could she have been so duped by Caroni's false charm?

"You always think the best of people." Case had said. *"You're blind to their faults."*

How true that had turned out to be. She knew

Case would be furious with her, and rightly so. If she had only listened to him.

Now Eliza had the unpleasant job of convincing her dearest friend to abandon her husband. If Caroni went to Mexico and never returned, Eileen would be much better off. She could go back to Coffee Creek and raise her child there, where everyone knew and loved her.

But perhaps Eliza wouldn't have to convince her friend. Perhaps Caroni had no intention of taking her with him. It would be just the sort of thing a scoundrel would do.

"I have one request to make," Eliza announced. "Leave Eileen here with me. Just take the money and go."

Caroni smiled smoothly. "Only too happy to oblige."

As they approached the hotel, he called to the cabby, "Let us off in the back."

Eliza clasped her handbag nervously. All she wanted to do now was get her aunt back safe and sound.

Pulling his hat down to shade his eyes, Caroni stepped out of the buggy and waited for Eliza. "I'll be watching you from the ticket office," he warned.

"You'll get your money," she retorted icily. "The sooner we're rid of you, the better."

They parted at the door and Eliza quickly

wove her way through the crowded lobby. As she approached the registration desk, she glanced over her shoulder toward the railroad ticket office across the big, high-ceilinged room. Through a glass window Caroni stood watching her.

Squaring her shoulders, Eliza marched up to the counter, waiting with a tapping toe while the clerk registered a gentleman in front of her. When he'd finished, she stepped up to the counter and smiled. "I'd like to take my money out of the safe, please."

"Sign here," he said, sliding a receipt book toward her.

Eliza signed her name and room number, then glanced around the lobby apprehensively as the clerk left to go to the back. She didn't know what she'd do if Case appeared. Caroni would spot him instantly and flee. And then what would happen to Auntie Vi?

Just then, the manager spotted her and hurried over. "Miss Lowe! Mr. Brogan was looking for you."

She felt heat color her cheeks. "Yes, I know. Thank you."

He peered at her curiously. "Is everything all right?"

Eliza hesitated, debating whether she should have him call the police. But she didn't dare do anything that could put Auntie Vi's life in danger. "Yes, of course. Everything's fine." She smiled at him until he went back to his work.

A moment later the clerk returned. "I'm sorry, miss, but the money isn't there. Mr. Brogan signed it out earlier."

Eliza's breath caught in her chest. Case had taken the money! What was she to do now?

Think, Eliza. What would Case have done with it?

As mistrustful as Case was, he would probably have stowed it in his room to keep her from getting it. He wouldn't carry it on him; he was too cautious.

"Is there a problem?" the clerk asked, as though sensing her distress.

Eliza glanced at him speculatively, wondering if her acting was good enough to convince him to give her Case's room key. She tried to imagine how Madame LaToux would play the role.

"This is quite embarrassing," she said, batting her eyelashes at him, "but earlier today I left a few of my—er—belongings in Mr. Brogan's room." She gave him a sheepish smile, letting him think the worst.

"As it turns out," she continued, giving him her most beguiling glance, "I need them now. I hate to ask such a huge favor of you, when I'm sure you have much more important matters to attend to, but could you lend me the room key for just five minutes? I'd be ever so grateful."

She dipped her head down slightly and watched him through her lashes.

For a long moment the young clerk studied her, clearly debating the wisdom of such an act, until Eliza began to fear he'd turn her down. But then he lifted one eyebrow and gave her what he probably thought was a debonair smile. "I'd be happy to help."

He swaggered over to a cherry board behind him, removed a key, and swaggered back. "Here you are," he said, trying to be very suave about it.

"You are much too kind," she said in a breathy voice. Giving him one last flirtatious smile, Eliza gripped the key in her sweaty palm and walked over to the ticket office. Madame LaToux would have been proud.

"It took you long enough," Caroni snarled. "Did you get the money?"

"It wasn't there."

His face turned an ugly shade of purple. "You're lying."

"You didn't let me finish. The money is in Mr. Brogan's room."

Caroni swore softly until she held the key up under his nose. "You're a lucky lady, Miss Lowe. All right, you go up to his room and make sure he's gone. I'll be right behind you. Don't try to pull anything funny on me, either."

Eliza twisted the strings of her handbag as the

elevator made its way slowly up to the fifth floor.

"Third floor," the elevator man announced, stopping to let someone off. Eliza was the only passenger left; Caroni had taken the stairs.

Her mind worked at lightning speed, tossing out one worry after another: What if the money wasn't there? What if Case was? What would happen to Auntie Vi if something happened to Caroni?

"Fifth floor."

With her heart pounding like a kettle drum, Eliza stepped out of the elevator and walked down the hallway, trying to be as casual as possible. She nodded politely to two hotel guests passing by, then stopped at Case's door and tapped.

"Case?" she called. A moment later she tapped again, then pressed her ear against the wood. Her shoulders sagged in relief. He wasn't there.

As she slid the key into the lock and opened the door, she saw Caroni step out of the stairway and head toward her. She went straight to the cherry armoire and pulled open the upper doors as Caroni came in and closed the door.

She found Case's traveling bag and set it on the bed, praying the money would be inside. Just as she opened it, Caroni grabbed the bag from her, turned it upside down, and shook it, sending Case's clothing tumbling to the floor.

"There's no money in here!" Enraged, he kicked the pile of clothes high into the air.

"You needn't make a mess of his things," Eliza chided, and began to collect the scattered items. "I'm sure it's here somewhere."

Caroni grabbed her upper arm and yanked her around to face him, his face a mask of malice, his teeth bared. "You bitch! You've tricked me. You knew the money wasn't here. This is Brogan's trap, isn't it?"

For the first time, Eliza began to fear for her own safety. "I didn't trick you," she said quickly, trying not to betray her trepidation.

Caroni squeezed her arm so tightly she gasped. "Then where's the damn money?" he thundered, giving her a hard shake.

Eliza winced at the loudness of his voice. "Perhaps it's under the bed. If you'll kindly release me—"

"It's not under the bed, and you know it," he raged, shoving her away. "Brogan has it. He planned this all out."

"How could he have planned this? I didn't know I'd be bringing you back here now."

"Do I look stupid to you?" He kicked Case's bag across the room. "Ever since I hooked up with that horse-faced nag I've had nothing but bad luck. Now I've got Brogan on my trail, too. Shit! Where am I going to get money fast?"

Eliza panicked when Caroni headed for the door. "Where are you going?"

"You think I'm going to stick around here and wait for Brogan to come get me?"

She started after him. "You can't leave without telling me where my aunt is!"

"You lost your chance, sweetheart. The next time you see her will be at her funeral."

Blind fury descended on Eliza. She threw herself at Caroni, grabbing his hair with both hands and pulling his head down, twisting his neck around. "Tell me where she is!"

With a bellow of rage, Caroni wrenched her away and shoved her to the floor, then kicked her in the ribs. Crying out in pain, Eliza curled inward to protect herself, only to feel his hard kicks to her kidneys, causing her nearly to black out.

"Bitch!" he ranted, "you'll pay for that!"

The door burst open and hit the wall with a thunderous crash, bringing Caroni around with a gasp. Dazed with pain, Eliza lifted her head and saw Case standing in the open doorway, his gun pointed straight at his enemy.

"No, Frank," Case said with deadly calm, "it's your turn to pay."

Chapter 25

Case's mouth hardened in bitter hatred, and a red haze of fury colored his gaze as he stared at his foe. All the waiting and planning, all the desolation and rancor of the past ten years swirled around him like a turbulent vortex of destruction, with the man standing before him at its eye.

Retribution throbbed in Case's veins and reverberated through his head, obliterating every other sound in the room. In his mind's eye he saw once more his father's collapse and heard his mother's agonized cries of grief. Case rubbed his chest to ease the constriction around his heart, feeling the unbearable loss as sharply as if it had just happened.

Caroni had destroyed Case's trust and innocence, turning his dreams to nightmares, and changing his hopes for the future to schemes of revenge. Now Caroni had caused even more damage, injuring the only other person for whom Case had ever cared.

As the roar of anger inside him ebbed, Case slowly became aware of Eliza calling his name. He glanced down at her, but seeing her doubled over in agony, her beautiful features twisted in a grimace of pain, he nearly killed Caroni on the spot. It was only by sheer force of will that he stopped himself from pulling the trigger. The bastard was going to suffer before he died.

"Move away from her, *coward*," he said through gritted teeth. "It's easy to pick on someone who's defenseless, isn't it, Caroni? You want to kick someone? Here I am. Come get me. Try being a man for a change."

Eliza fought back a crushing wave of pain in her ribs as she attempted to stand, only to sink back weakly. She knew what Case was doing: he was baiting Caroni, hoping he would give Case a reason to shoot.

Caroni carefully stepped back, holding his hands up, palms facing Case.

"I didn't mean to hurt her," he said. "She attacked me. She nearly broke my neck."

"It's never your fault, is it, Caroni?" Case shoved the door closed and took a step closer.

"Case, please don't shoot him!" Eliza beseeched, gasping as she struggled again to push herself to a sitting position. She leaned against the end of the bed, holding her ribs, gazing at him imploringly.

But he only looked at Caroni as though her words meant nothing.

"Case, please listen!" she cried. "He has my aunt. He's holding her hostage!"

"That's right, Brogan," Caroni said smugly. "You don't want to cause an old lady's death, do you?"

"Violet is safe, Eliza," Case replied without taking his gaze from Caroni's stunned face. "She's with your friend right now."

Eliza sagged weakly against the bed. Auntie Vi was safe! Thank heavens!

As he realized his peril, a strangled sound came from Caroni's lips and beads of sweat broke out on his forehead. His Adam's apple bobbed wildly as he tried to swallow. "You're lying!" he cried in a hoarse voice.

"I tracked down the cabdriver," Case said grimly. "He took me to the warehouse on the river. It's all over, Caroni."

Caroni backed up another step, sweat running down his temples. His gaze darted around the room as though he were seeking an escape route.

By the murderous glint in Case's eye, Eliza

knew he was about to pull the trigger. She couldn't let him do it. No matter how much Caroni deserved justice, it couldn't come by Case's hand. She knew he'd live to regret it.

"Case," Eliza pleaded, fighting the pain, "you told me that you'd do the right thing. Shooting him isn't right. You can't play God."

Caroni wiped the sweat off his forehead with his coat sleeve. "What would you do, Brogan, claim it was self-defense?" He pulled out his pockets, then opened his coat. "I don't have a weapon."

"Doesn't matter," Case replied in a steely voice. "You're wanted dead or alive. Guess which it's going to be?"

"You don't want my death on your conscience, Brogan. Come on! We were friends once."

"I don't have a conscience anymore. You saw to that. Back up against the armoire."

"Case," Eliza began, struggling to her feet, "please don't!"

"Stay back, Eliza."

Shaking, Caroni dropped to his knees. "I didn't murder your father. It was an accident. I never meant to kill him."

"Tell me how the knife accidentally came out of your pocket," Case ground out. "Tell me how it accidentally sank into my father's chest."

Caroni wiped the sweat that had dripped into

his eyes. "It was an accident, I swear it! I only wanted to get away."

"My father trusted you," Case sneered.

"Trust? Charlie turned me in!"

"The police were already at our door when we came home that day. My father hadn't called them. He didn't want to believe what they'd claimed you did."

Caroni blinked, as though stunned by the news. "Then why did Charlie come around to the cellar to get me? Why did he try to handcuff me?"

"He was trying to protect you—he didn't want them to rough you up." Case's lip pulled back. "And you killed him for it."

"I swear," Caroni said through chattering teeth, "I was only trying to get away. I didn't want to kill Charlie. He was the only man who ever treated me kindly."

"I watched you pull out that knife and stab him," Case whispered hoarsely, his voice shaking with emotion. "I held him while he took his last breath. He died with your name on his lips, and now you'll die with mine."

Eliza listened, horrified, imagining Case as a sixteen-year-old, witnessing the brutal stabbing, watching helplessly as his father died in his arms.

But what if Caroni was telling the truth?

She took a step toward Case, wincing from

the pain. "Perhaps he *didn't* mean to kill your father, Case. He might have been frightened. He was only a kid himself."

Case's hand shook as he aimed the gun. "You didn't see him, Eliza. You didn't see the ruthless look on his face as he sank that blade into my father's heart. You didn't see the blood spurt as he pulled it out. You didn't see him shove my father away and run, letting him collapse onto the dirt floor."

"Oh, God help me, please don't kill me!" Caroni begged, clasping his hands together.

Eliza choked back tears. "Let the courts handle this, Case. Justice will be done this time, I promise."

"The only promise is right here in my hand."

"No!" she cried, moving between him and Caroni. "You're a good man, Case, and this isn't the right way to avenge your father's death. He wouldn't have taken the law into his hands. Don't dishonor his name by taking a man's life."

Case tried to block out her words, but they hit home as surely as that knife had hit its target. When he looked at Caroni he was filled with bitter loathing, remembering the agony on his father's face as he lay dying. But when he looked at Eliza and saw the love and trust in her eyes, he saw life and hope, and he saw himself reflected in her admiration.

Case blinked to clear his vision. He had loved his father, and he loved Eliza. If he pulled the trigger, not only would he dishonor his father's good name, but he'd also lose the woman of his heart.

He dropped the gun to his side.

Eliza gave a sob of relief as he put an arm around her.

Suddenly Caroni launched himself at them, knocking them both to the floor. Before Case could scramble up, Caroni had opened the door and fled. Case helped Eliza to her feet, then ran after him, ordering her to wait there.

He caught a glimpse of Caroni just as the bastard flung open a door and darted into the stairwell. Case dashed after him, reaching the door as it closed. He yanked it open and ran onto the landing, and heard the heavy clump of shoes hitting the steps below. Tucking the gun in his belt, he started after Caroni, reaching the fourth-floor landing just as the door one floor below banged shut.

Case ran down, pulled the door open, and stepped out, stopping short in the deserted hallway. Guessing that Caroni had ducked inside a room, he began checking each door until he found one that was unlocked. He opened it cautiously and looked around, then crossed the room and stopped outside the bathroom, where he could hear someone moving around inside. He kicked open the door and burst in, startling a maid cleaning the bathtub.

"Sorry," he said, and backed out, his heart racing. He checked under the bed and in the armoire, then stepped back into the hall. Hearing the whirr of the elevator as it descended, he dashed for the stairs and raced the lift three flights down to the lobby. But when it opened, only the operator was inside.

Case thought hard. Where had Caroni gone? He stepped into the elevator and looked up at the trap door. It was knocked ajar.

"Did a man just climb through that opening?"

"Yes, sir, he did," the operator said. "Told me he had to check the cable."

"Wearing a three-piece suit?"

The operator shrugged. "I thought he was a manager."

"Is there a way to climb out of the elevator shaft through the roof?"

"No, sir. It's closed at the top."

"Give me your stool. How do you keep this elevator from moving?"

"This is all highly irregular, sir," the elderly man said.

"I'm a Pinkerton," Case said, displaying his badge, "and that man up there is wanted for murder."

The operator quickly threw a switch and vacated the elevator. Case pulled the stool to the center and stepped onto it, raising the door in the ceiling.

"Caroni?" he called. "Give yourself up. There's no way out."

"I'm not going to prison, Brogan," Caroni called back. "You'll have to kill me first."

Eliza winced in pain as she made her way to the elevator. She had to get down to the lobby and call the police. With Caroni on the loose, there was no telling what would happen. She couldn't stand the thought of Case being in danger.

Out of habit, she reached for the crystal charm in her pocket, only to remember she had given it to Case. *Please, let it help him now. I love him too much to lose him.*

Eliza paused. It was true: she truly loved him! She couldn't deny her feelings any longer. She loved him, and that knowledge was both profoundly freeing and terribly frightening. But she had no time to worry about the implications: Case's life was in jeopardy.

Eliza pushed the button and waited anxiously for the elevator, but heard no noisy grinding of the cables. In a panic, she pushed the button again, then headed for the stairs, making her way as quickly as she could down to the main floor.

"Call the police," she gasped, holding her sides, as the manager and two clerks rushed to her aid. "Tell the chief that Case Brogan needs help at once."

As a clerk ran to sound the alarm at a call box on the street, the manager peered at Eliza in concern. "Do you need a doctor, Miss Lowe?"

"I'll be all right. Just please get help quickly."

She eased herself down onto one of the lobby chairs and began to pray for Case's safety.

Case grabbed the rim of the opening in the ceiling and hauled himself up, the muscles in his arms straining with the effort. The elevator shaft smelled of grease and hot, musty air, and was lit only by a square skylight six stories above. Sturdy cables ran from the elevator to a giant pulley at the top of the building, and an iron ladder had been built into one wall, running beside the heavy, steel elevator doors on each floor.

Case glanced up and saw Caroni on the ladder moving toward the second floor. Case quickly shrugged off his coat and tossed it through the trap door, then stepped to the edge of the elevator and looked down. The elevator shaft appeared to go at least two levels below ground.

Fighting a momentary wave of dizziness, Case reached across the gap to grab hold of a rung, then stretched one foot across until he had a toehold, following with the other foot. He looked up as he began to climb. Caroni was one floor above him, grunting as he tried to pry open the heavy steel doors.

As Case climbed, Caroni cursed viciously, abandoning the doors in order to move higher. "Stay away from me, Brogan!" he yelled.

Case climbed steadily after him, forcing Caroni to go higher and higher, until he'd reached the last floor. All that was above him was the closed skylight.

"Damn you to hell, I said stay away from me!" Caroni cried, his voice rising in panic. "You'll kill us both."

"You said you'd rather die than go to prison," Case called back.

Reaching the third floor, Case stopped to wipe one sweating hand and then the other on his pants leg, fearing his grip would slip and send him tumbling to the basement. As he passed the fourth-floor opening, Case could hear Caroni struggling to pry apart the heavy doors above him, his panic-filled grunts and curses echoing down the shaft. Case saw with dismay that Caroni had managed to edge one side open an inch, then two.

Case climbed faster, nearly falling as his hand slipped from the rung. He caught himself, took a shaky breath, and looked up to see Caroni's foot just a few feet above his head.

But before he could grab it, Caroni hoisted himself halfway into the narrow opening he'd created. "You'll never catch me, Brogan!"

Case moved a step higher and stretched his arm up, grabbing Caroni's pants leg as he attempted to pull himself through the opening. Caroni kicked out at Case, trying to free his leg, but the effort caused him to lose his balance. He slipped back through the opening, his feet missing the rung beneath him. He clawed the floor as he slid, trying to stop himself.

"Help me!" he cried as his fingers slipped closer and closer to the edge.

As Case watched, everything suddenly began to move in slow motion, just as it had the day his father had died. How easy it would be to let the bastard fall to his death, to end his miserable life so he'd never hurt anyone again. Justice, sweet and quick—the way Case had dreamed of it for ten long years—would come at last.

But Eliza's words suddenly ran through his mind, echoing in his soul. *"You're a good man, Case Brogan, even though you don't believe it."*

He shook his head, trying to drive out her words.

"I trust you, Case. You know in your heart what you should do."

God help him, it *wasn't* what he wanted to do. He wrapped his arms around the ladder and leaned his head against a rung, battling the darkness inside him. He felt a hard lump over his heart, where a lower rung pressed into his chest. Carefully he let go with one hand and eased it into his pocket. His fingers closed over Eliza's crystal.

"Maybe it will help you."

Case shut his eyes, wrestling with his conscience. All he had to do was let Caroni fall, and vengeance would be his. Why, then, when it was finally within his grasp, did that victory suddenly seem hollow?

Because in gaining his goal, he'd lose that one bright light in his heart.

He couldn't lose Eliza.

Chapter 26

～∽○○∽～

Case's hands were slippery with sweat as he moved up another rung.

"Help me, please!" Caroni begged.

Bracing his knees against the wall, Case released one hand just as Caroni's fingers slipped off the edge. Case made a grab and caught Caroni's arm as he fell past, the heavy drag of his body nearly costing Case his grip.

Caroni used his free hand to grasp the ladder, then found purchase with his feet. He held on tightly, shaking so hard Case could hear his teeth chattering.

At that moment, voices called up the shaft. "Brogan? It's O'Malley. Are you all right?"

"I'm coming down," he called tiredly. "Caroni is with me."

Eliza waited anxiously outside the elevator with Chief O'Malley. Minutes after the alarm from the call box had been set off, two policemen had arrived. The chief had come rushing in moments ago, bringing a troop of officers with him. A curious crowd had gathered in the lobby to watch, but the hotel staff kept them back.

"You'll make sure that Frank Caroni doesn't escape, won't you?" Eliza fretted. "He's very good at escaping."

"He won't escape this time," the chief replied. "I promise you that."

"There's no chance he'll be set free, is there?"

"No, ma'am. After what you've told me, we'll get him on kidnapping charges here, on top of what he's facing in Wyoming and Chicago. He won't even get bail."

The chief stepped forward as Caroni came through the elevator ceiling and was immediately cuffed. As he was led past Eliza, Caroni sneered, "I'll be out of jail in no time. You just watch and see if I'm not."

"I won't hold my breath," Eliza replied.

She turned with a quickening pulse as Case jumped down from the opening. As he picked up his suit coat and shrugged it on over his shirt, her heart overflowed with relief to see that he was unhurt. The only evidence of his struggles was a smudge of dirt across his forehead and a smear of grease on one pant leg.

Case glanced at her briefly, but his face looked as though it had been carved from stone, and his eyes were like flint.

Eliza nibbled her lower lip as he paused to speak with the police chief. Surely he wasn't angry with her. After all, if it hadn't been for her, he wouldn't have found Caroni.

Perhaps he was still upset that she'd left him waiting at the train station. But that hadn't been her fault, either. He was the one who'd locked her in the bathroom. Indeed, she should be angry with him!

Eliza's breath caught in her throat as Case left the chief and walked straight toward her, his compelling gaze holding her uncertain one. She straightened her shoulders and curled her fingers into her palms, bracing herself for whatever he might say.

But he didn't say a word. He only enveloped her in his strong embrace, running his hands up and down her back as though to reassure himself that she was real. She gasped at a sharp, stabbing pain in her ribs, and Case pulled back in alarm.

"Are you all right?"

"A little bruised, but I'll be fine."

Case put his arms gently about her and held

her for several precious, blissful moments, then pressed kisses on her forehead and temple and eyelids before hugging her gently to him once more. Eliza meant more to him than he could ever express. There was no doubt in his mind now: he loved her, and he wasn't going to lose her.

Eliza wrapped her arms around his waist and held him, cherishing the steadfast beat of his heart beneath her ear, her own heart singing with joy. Case had triumphed. He had done what was right.

"It's over," he said in a strained and exhausted voice. "It's finally over."

Eliza hugged him reassuringly, then pulled back to gaze up at him. Her heart swelled with love and admiration, and her eyes filled with tears of gladness. "Your father would be very proud of you."

She saw moisture pool in his own eyes as he wiped away her tears with his thumb. "Yes, he would be. And I have you to thank for that."

"You would have done the right thing anyway."

"Thank God I'll never have to find out." He cupped her face in his big hands and dipped his head to kiss her.

Suddenly a familiar voice rang out, "Eliza! Oh, dear, thank heavens you're safe!"

Eliza turned as Auntie Vi came huffing across the lobby, her plump arms outstretched, the bright flower on her hat bobbing. She held Eliza's face between her soft hands and pressed kisses on her cheek. "My dear, sweet Eliza! I was so worried about you."

"I'm all right, Auntie. How are you?"

"A little worse for the wear, but surprisingly well. I'm much stronger than I thought I was. After a hearty meal and a sound sleep, I'll be fit as a fiddle."

Eliza glanced over her aunt's shoulder and saw Eileen standing timidly behind her. She left her aunt and went to her friend, putting her arms around Eileen's shoulders.

"I'm so sorry, Liza," Eileen whispered tearfully. "I'm so dreadfully sorry. I didn't want to believe that Francis could have committed those crimes. I should have known he wouldn't have genuinely fallen in love with me."

Eliza leaned back to gaze at her. "Someday you'll find someone who'll see that beautiful person inside you, Eileen."

Case walked up and took Eliza's hand. "Why don't you give her this? It worked for both of us."

Eliza glanced down at the crystal charm in her hand, then up at Case, her heart overflowing with gratitude. The charm *had* worked: she had found her true love.

Eliza turned to her friend, opened her palm, and placed the crystal in it. "A very wise man told me that this crystal would help me find the one I was seeking." Eliza folded Eileen's fingers over it. "Keep it close to your heart and it'll work for you, too."

"Thank you," Eileen said, blinking back tears.

Eliza hugged her friend again, then glanced at her aunt and Case, who were both smiling at her. "Is anyone hungry?"

"Oh, good heavens, yes!" Auntie Vi exclaimed. "I haven't had a meal since I don't know when."

"I wouldn't mind a cup of tea," Eileen piped in meekly.

"Case?" Eliza glanced at him hopefully.

"What about your ribs? We should call a doctor."

"My ribs are sore, but they'll heal. It's my stomach that's bothering me now."

"I suggest we go back to our rooms to clean up first," he said.

"You look fine," Violet assured him. "No one will ever notice that big black smudge on your forehead."

Grimacing, Case took out his handkerchief and scrubbed his skin. He'd hoped to have a word alone with Eliza, but that looked doubtful now. "There's a restaurant just across the lobby."

Eliza smiled gratefully and linked her arm through Case's. Her aunt did the same with

Eileen, then the four proceeded across the marble floor.

"In fact, I do know when I last ate," Violet continued, as Eileen nodded encouragingly. "It was two evenings ago—or was it three? I'm so hungry I can barely think. All I had were stale peanuts that I found in my handbag."

Case pulled Eliza over to the side, letting Violet and Eileen continue on. "Eliza, this won't wait. I have to tell you now," he said, gazing into her eyes. "You once asked me what I'd do after I caught Caroni, and I told you I planned to continue doing my job."

"I remember," she answered cautiously. "Have you changed your mind?"

"No, those plans haven't changed. But they have expanded."

Her forehead wrinkled. "I don't understand."

Case ran his palm down the side of her face, gazing at her with a full heart. "I want you in my life, Eliza. Forever. I love you."

Eliza was filled with a rush of joy so pure and sweet that she wanted to sing. He loved her!

But had he proposed?

She opened her mouth to ask him, but Case held up his hand. "Wait. Before you tell me that you want to be an opera singer and live in New York, I just want to say that I understand, and I won't hinder you. I just don't want to lose you."

"Case," she began.

"I know life won't be easy with me being a Pinkerton, and I know I'm pretty set in my ways, but I'll always be fair and honest, and I do love you with all my heart. That should be worth something."

"May I speak now?"

Case steeled himself for her rejection. "Go ahead."

"Are you by any chance asking me to marry you?"

For an instant Case was too stunned to reply. He hadn't thought about it in exactly those terms, but yes, he did want her to marry him. "I suppose I am."

She gazed up at him with eyes that radiated her happiness. "I was hoping you were. I love you, too, Case, with all my heart."

Case held his breath, waiting for her answer.

Eliza blew an errant curl off of her face and tugged him toward the restaurant. "Let's go eat."

Case stared at her in befuddlement. For as long as he lived, Eliza would never cease to surprise him. "Does that mean you'll give me an answer after we eat?"

"No, after you've given me a genuine proposal." She stopped in the doorway and glanced around the restaurant. "Oh, there are Auntie Vi and Eileen at that back table."

A *genuine* proposal?

"Eliza!" he said, reining her in.

"Yes?"

"What do you mean by genuine?"

"An authentic proposal, not an implied one."

"It's not as if I've done this before."

"But surely you've read a story or seen a play where the suitor gets down on bended knee, removes his hat, takes his lady's hands in his, and gazes up at her adoringly. It's extremely romantic."

"And that's what you mean by a genuine proposal?"

"Yes."

Suddenly, in front of the entire restaurant, Case dropped down on one knee, took her hands in his, and gazed up at her. "Like this?"

"Case," she whispered, glancing sheepishly at the gaping diners. "Get up. Everyone is staring."

"Isn't this romantic enough?"

"It's very romantic, but—"

"Will you marry me, Eliza?"

Her eyes widened and her mouth opened, but no sound came out. She finally nodded, her eyes tearing. Case stood up, took her gently in his arms and kissed her soundly to wild applause from everyone in the restaurant.

Hand in hand, with Eliza smiling radiantly, they walked to the back, where Violet and Eileen were waiting to hug them.

A moment later, a beaming waiter came rushing over. "Congratulations, sir, and best wishes, miss."

"Thank you very kindly," Eliza replied, settling in the chair Case had pulled out for her.

"We'd like to offer you a complimentary bottle of champagne to celebrate your engagement," the waiter added.

Eliza glanced at Case in amazement. "Do you remember that this is how we started?" She turned to the waiter. "We'd love some champagne. Thank you so much."

When the cork had been popped and the wine poured, all four lifted their glasses in toast.

"To new beginnings," Violet offered, nodding to each one of the them in turn, "with my love and blessings."

"To all of you," Eileen said, putting a hand over her stomach, "for helping my baby and me."

"To my future bride," Case said, his warm gaze meeting Eliza's.

Eliza could only gaze back, her heart so full that words failed her. Then, after her aunt had cleared her throat for the second time, Eliza said in a voice husky with emotion, "To my future husband for sharing his heart with me. To my dear aunt for her love and concern. To my best friend for having faith in me. And to trust, the most important ingredient in love."

Chapter 27

E liza sat beside Case, her hand tucked securely in his, gazing contentedly through the window as the train chugged steadily eastward. Behind them Violet and Eileen sat chatting quietly. They'd left early that morning, two days after Caroni's capture.

"Eliza," Violet said, reaching between the seats to tap her niece's shoulder, "have you and Case decided when you want to get married?"

Eliza glanced at him questioningly, but Case only shrugged. "No, Auntie, not yet," she replied.

"As soon as we get back, you must look at a calendar. Do you have any idea how much there will be to do? Why, there are flowers to choose, and a wedding gown to have made, and brides-maids to select, and food to order, and a hall to secure, and—oh, dear, what am I leaving out?"

"The rings?" Case offered.

"Oh, my, yes, the rings!" Violet took out her fan and cooled her face. "Goodness me, I hope I'm up to it."

"Maybe we should elope," Case said quietly.

Eliza's eyes twinkled mischievously as she smiled at him. "That certainly would solve a lot of problems, wouldn't it? But then Auntie Vi would feel left out, and so would Eileen, and I just can't hurt their feelings."

The whistle blew as they chugged into Des Moines, then the train began to slow.

"Let's get off here and have something to eat," Case suggested.

"No hot dogs for me," Violet groaned. "I still have indigestion from the hot dogs I ate on the way to Omaha."

The noisy engine belched and hissed as the locomotive came to a stop. Case jumped up, took Eliza's hand, and tugged her down the aisle.

"Um—Case?"

"We have to hurry, Eliza. They don't give us much time."

"But, Case?"

"Just a moment, and we'll be outside."

They fell in line behind the other passengers

stepping down onto the wooden platform. Case took her arm and guided her toward the depot.

"Wait for us!" Violet called as she and Eileen huffed after them.

"Case, where are we going?" Eliza asked, holding on to her hat as he steered her through the crowded station.

"You'll see."

They walked out the front doors onto wide, cement steps that led down to the street, and were immediately hailed by the Reverend Josiah Masters; his wife, Mary; and young Henry, all dressed in their Sunday best. The reverend even had his Bible with him.

Was it Sunday? Eliza wondered. She'd lost track of the days.

She hugged them warmly, then introduced her aunt and her best friend. "It's so good to see you again!" she told the Masterses. She studied Henry with a smile. "Have you grown?"

"No, ma'am," he said, ducking his head shyly.

Eliza glanced at their beaming faces, then gazed at Case skeptically. "This isn't a coincidence, is it?"

"How would you like to have all the benefits of an elopement without leaving your aunt and best friend out of it?"

Eliza gaped at him. "How did you—when did you—?"

"I wired the Masterses yesterday."

"But I wasn't expecting to marry you so—hastily."

"Marry in haste, repent at leisure," Violet chirped.

"Don't you also have a saying that there's no time like the present?" he chided her.

Violet put her hands on her chubby hips. "Now how did you know I say that?"

Grinning, Case dropped down to one knee. "Will you marry me right now, in the present, Miss Eliza Lowe?"

"But you don't have a ring," Violet cried, fluttering her handkerchief.

Case reached into his pocket and brought out a gold band. "Will this do?"

Eliza looked from the ring to Case's handsome, sincere face. "Oh, yes, it will do perfectly," she told him. "But there's one thing I should mention first. I tried to tell you earlier, but you hurried me off the train." She lifted her skirt a bit, and peeking out from beneath were two bare feet.

Violet gasped, Eileen muffled a laugh behind her hand, and Case just shook his head.

"I don't know about you, Reverend," Case said, "but I can't think of more appropriate attire for a hasty ceremony." He bent his head to whisper in Eliza's ear, "Plus I've hired a sleeper car for us. So after the ceremony, we can go back and repent—all night—at our leisure."

"Oh, that sounds delightful," Eliza said with a dreamy sigh.

"Reverend?" Case said, and took Eliza's hand in his.

He never intended to let it go.

Dear Reader,

Are you ready for the historical romance that *New York Times* best-selling author Lisa Kleypas calls "the most enthralling reading experience I've had in years"? Then don't miss Adele Ashworth's SOMEONE IRRESISTIBLE, the first Avon Treasure from this Rita Award-winning writer. It's London—the place to be in 1851. Mimi Marsh has adored the brilliant and dashing Nathan Price in secret for years . . . but now their passion is about to burst forth.

Karen Kendall's contemporary romance debut, SOMETHING ABOUT CECILY, marked her as an author to watch. Now she's back with TO CATCH A KISS. It's just as delicious, as sensuous, as delightful as her debut. Tony Sinclair gives the phrase "To Protect and Serve" a whole different meaning when he's hired to bodyguard Jazz Taylor. She's in no mood to be followed around, but soon gets very used to having Tony's very delectable form in her life.

If you want a bold, dramatic love story set in England, don't miss Taylor Chase's HEART OF NIGHT. Lady Claire Darren is a woman who'd do anything for love . . . including entice Sir Adrian Thorne into her arms. He says he wants nothing to do with her—and then he kisses her . . .

Maureen McKade's love stories are just plain unforgettable, and HIS UNEXPECTED WIFE is her best yet. When high-spirited Annie Trevelyan leaves the mountains of Colorado to seek fame and fortune, her meddling father sends sexy Colin McBride hot on her trail. Soon, Colin has marriage on his mind.

One final note, if you're seeking a book that will make you laugh and cry from one of the genre's most beloved authors, don't miss ANOTHER SUMMER by Georgia Bockoven. *New York Times* best-selling author Catherine Coulter says, "Bockoven is magic! Don't miss ANOTHER SUMMER."

Until next month, enjoy!

Lucia Macro

Lucia Macro
Executive Editor

Avon Romances—
the best in exceptional authors and unforgettable novels!